'A work of fiction that is both
Edinburgh but also a story abo
result is a compelling, painful, h:

'A powerful, evocative read with ......
Kidd breathes life into the women whose names have faded from memory, examining their values and our own under the microscope.'

WI Life **magazine**

'This is the story of Britain's most infamous anatomy murderers and Scotland's worst ever serial killers, as you have never read it before.'

Edinburgh Reporter, **John Hislop**

'A gripping tale of murder and mayhem.'

Historical Novel Society Journal

'Mairi Kidd's fresh retelling re-envisions the past harrowing events from a female perspective and lends a voice to the once unvoiced.'

Scottish Field

'Beguiling and atmospheric, this is as much an engrossing character study as a bold reimagining of the infamous anatomy murders.'

Heat **magazine, Lisa Howells**

'Mairi Kidd has a real knack for bringing Scotland's dark history to life and giving an authentic voice to those it has forgotten.'

The Scots Magazine, **Dawn Geddes**

'Gruesomely gripping, this story will stay with you for a long time . . . *The Specimens* is a powerful and dark tale that readers will enjoy, for its familiarity – and yet still be shocked by the audacity and horror of the historical truth.'

Sue Lawrence

'A fresh, feminine take on the horrors of Burke and Hare and their complicit Edinburgh anatomists.'

Sally Magnusson

'Vivid and discomfiting . . . Mairi Kidd holds a lantern up to the brutality of women's lives in Burke, Hare and Knox's Edinburgh. She draws a fine thread between women's bodily experiences now and then, and her voice is so authentic I felt as if I was there.'

Lucy Ribchester

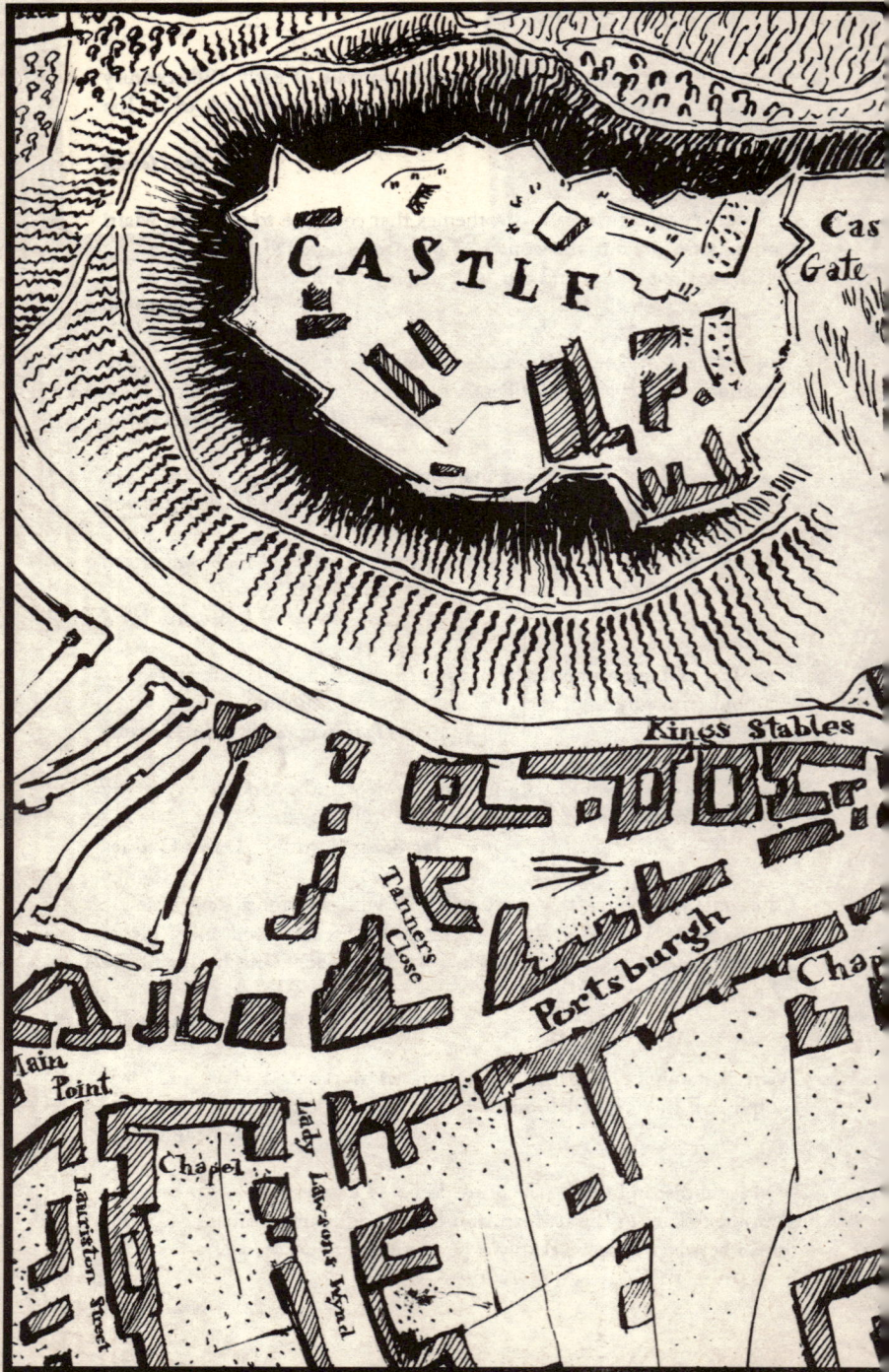

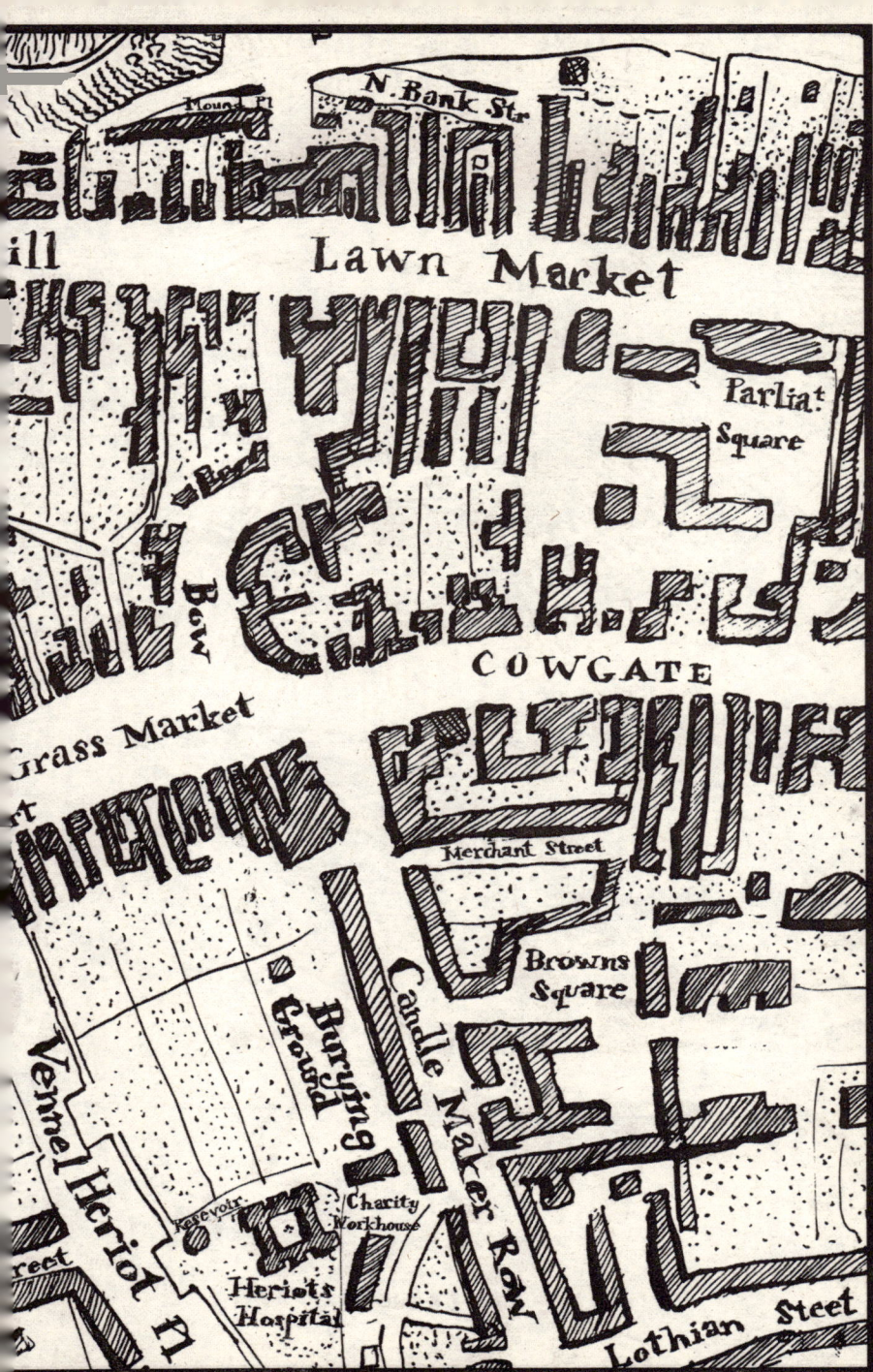

N. Bank Str

Mound Pl

Lawn Market

ill

Parliat Square

Bow

COWGATE

Grass Market

Merchant Street

Browns Square

Vennel Heriot n

Burying Ground

Candle Maker Row

Resevoir

Charity Workhouse

Heriots Hospital

Lothian Steet

Lillypot

Trinity Mains

Laverock Bank

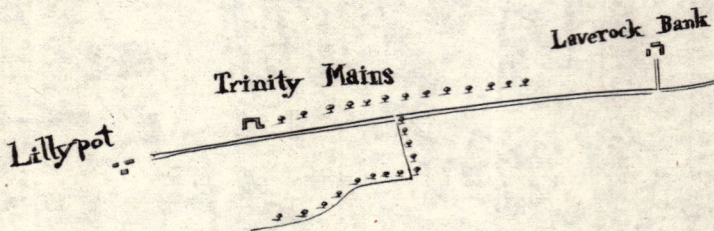

Bangholm Bower

Bangholm Mains

Mr GRANGER'S FEU

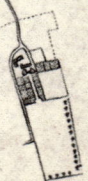

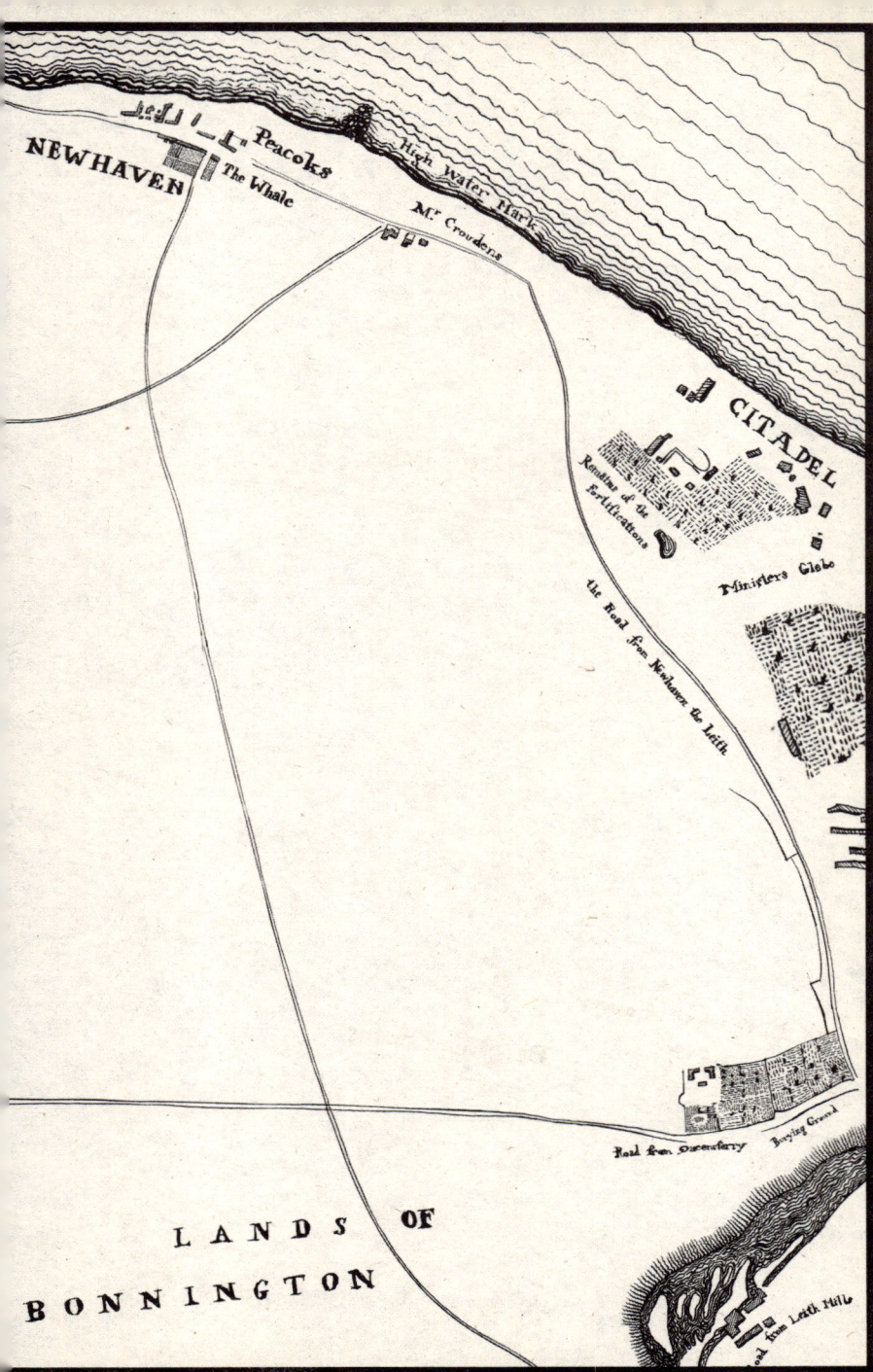

NEWHAVEN

Peacoks

The Whale

High water Mark

Mr Croudens

CITADEL

Remains of the
Fortifications

the Road from Newhaven to Leith

Ministers Globe

Road from Queensferry

Burying Ground

LANDS OF

BONNINGTON

Road from Leith Mills

The
Specimens

The
Specimens

MAIRI KIDD

Black&White

Black&White

First published in the UK in 2024
This edition first published in 2025 by Black & White Publishing
An imprint of Bonnier Books UK
5th Floor, HYLO, 105 Bunhill Row,
London, EC1Y 8LZ

A CIP catalogue record for this book is available from the British Library.

ISBN: 978 1 78530 753 9

1 3 5 7 9 10 8 6 4 2

Typeset by IDSUK (Data Connection) Ltd
Printed and bound in Great Britain by Clays Ltd, Elcograf S.p.A.

MIX
Paper | Supporting
responsible forestry
FSC www.fsc.org   FSC® C018072

The authorised representative in the EEA is Bonnier Books
UK (Ireland) Limited.
Registered office address: Floor 3, Block 3, Miesian Plaza,
Dublin 2, D02 Y754, Ireland
compliance@bonnierbooks.ie
www.blackandwhitepublishing.com

*To Lucy, with love
and in memory of Martin
and Phyllis*

'We remember ... going to another tenement and entering house by house only to find men and women rolling on the floor of a desolate dwelling in indiscriminate drunkenness ... the heart-piercing looks and cries of their infant children assailed us with irresistible appeals for bread to allay the cutting pangs of hunger.'
– Rev. William Tasker, Missionary, reports on conditions in the West Port, 1845, Thomas Chalmers archive, New College Library, Edinburgh

'Before the engravings were finished, a third subject occurred very opportunely ...'
– William Hunter on the procurement of a deceased woman in the 9th month of pregnancy, The anatomy of the human gravid uterus exhibited in figures, 1774

Prologue
Edinburgh, 1819

Puerperal Fever

THE MOURNERS MOVED IN DARK KNOTS towards the kirkyard where the mortal remains of Jemima Lindsay were to be laid to rest at noon. The elderly came first. Loath to place the unnecessary strain of rushing on tired hearts and creaking limbs, they had reckoned to be twenty minutes early, or a half-hour, and then had forgotten ever making that calculation and added half an hour again. There were five uncles and aunts, four old bodies, who might be neighbours, then a weeping wife with her sister, who once might have been Jemima's nurse. A procession of bulky elderly women came next, oxtered up the steep path by younger men who looked to be their sons. Most were sombre – a nasty business, this, a fine young lass dead of childbed fever, her bairnie gone with her to the grave – but the old wives were undaunted; they raised their heads and peered with frank curiosity at the motley crew on patrol outside the walls.

The call for guards to protect the newly dead from grave-robbers had roused some of the rougher inhabitants of the town out of their indolence, attracted by the news that they could be paid to sit up all night drinking whisky, when previously they had been doing so for free. There was of course the additional hope of being in on the killing of a few of the so-called 'resurrection men', and to that end this gang was armed with an assortment of weapons actual, improvised, and uniformly disreputable. One had a sword, so ancient William Wallace would have looked on it askance, another held a spear of sorts, made from a railing with a sharpened end, and a third a wooden club bristling with rusty nails. The bearer of the club followed the first mourners into the graveyard, but a sharp word from an old wife caused him to blush and hide the club as best he could behind his legs.

The grave was dug ready, a raw and gaping wound in the spring green grass, the turfs laid neatly to one side. None among the early birds wished to contemplate that sight any longer than was necessary, and so they took advantage of the fine day to stroll among the tombs and monuments, reading inscriptions or paying respects. A guard followed one group half-heartedly for a few moments for the look of the thing, then lost interest and sat on an elevated slab where he proceeded to pick his teeth with his dagger.

They had all reassembled in time to meet the piteous procession as it arrived. No expense had been spared for Jemima; the steep fee for burial in a kirkyard had been paid, an undertaker engaged, and the coffin was draped in the best velvet mortcloth the parish could supply. The young widower seemed borne along by the press of mourners, as though he would fall to the ground if they did not hold him up. He had thought to be a father, the poor lad, the head of a family. Instead, he would return home tonight to an empty cradle and a cold bed. As they made their slow way up the path, Jemima's tiny, birdlike mother kept up a keening lament that was a knife in the breast of every woman present who had brought a daughter safe to adulthood. *There but for the grace of God go I.*

There were few rites, of course, the Kirk did not permit it, and so soon enough the coffin was lowered into the grave to the sobbing of the mother and the mute staring of the man. They were ushered from the place then, and onwards to the feast where the minister would finally show his face and take a fat fee, no doubt, for blessing the meat. The old women who had arrived in procession had now formed a threesome, arms linked, seeming to step a little lighter now that the sad business was over. They spoke in that odd way that old women did, half the words on the in-breath, as though the thing they would say was too much to be spoken aloud. *Buried in the coffin with her then, the babe, the poor wee soul* ...

At last they were gone, and the gravedigger and his lad could set to and finish the second part of their job, filling the grave and then, when the soil was returned, laying the turf above all. They worked methodically, pausing once to eat and drink from a sack they had to hand. When all was done they packed their tools in the sack, the gravedigger shouldered it, and they made their way out of the gate. The lad stared in fascination at the guards and reached out a finger to test the blade of a sword, but the gravedigger cuffed his ear and pushed him on. The chief guard laughed and got to his feet, stretching and scratching before beginning the task of chaining the gates. He entrusted the key to a sentry, posted three more men to watch the walls, and strolled off to take his own rest until nightfall.

By Jemima's grave, an industrious blackbird investigated the crumbs of earth left behind from the digging, but, finding nothing, flew off to seek better foraging elsewhere. Then the dead were left in peace under the warmth of the sun.

The chief of the guard returned, rested and well fed, to resume his command at dusk. Day sentries were relieved and rougher replacements took up their posts, two to a wall now for the hours of darkness. The chief unlocked the gates and checked the graveyard himself. Finding nothing amiss, he also took the opportunity of relieving himself behind the stone of a long-departed tradesman. Then he locked the gates again and sat on a stool to clean and load his pistol.

Darkness fell.

Inside the graveyard, the door of a grand mausoleum swung open silently and three men crept out with spades, picks, crowbars, and a bundle of wood wrapped in black cloth. A dark lantern blinked for a second, no more, on faces daubed with shoe-black. An observant sentry might have thought them familiar, for these were the well-dressed young men who had helped their 'mothers' struggle up the path that morning. No mean struggle had it been, either, if one considered that a woman could conceal a significant weight of ordnance within the volume of her skirts when secured tightly enough to her body.

The men worked quickly, silently, with the barest flashes of the lantern to orientate themselves and then no light but the moon. One began to lash wood together to form a ladder of sorts, working by touch, pausing every now and then to creep to the wall and listen. The other two began to dig at the head end of Jemima's grave. They worked as efficiently as the gravedigger and his lad had done, and in little more than an hour they had dug down behind the coffin so that the end was exposed. Then the picks were handed down and they waited, alert.

Suddenly, outside the gates, an almighty commotion started up, as though an entire cart of cooking pots had overturned in the street. Taking their cue, the graverobbers raised their picks and their crowbars and prised off the head end of the coffin. Outside, a woman's voice called in panic and feet pounded as the guards ran to her assistance, or more likely to claim their share of any loot on offer. The lantern opened, for a flash, illuminating the ungodly sight of the shrouded remains of Jemima Lindsay being dragged from her coffin by the head. Her shoulders came through easy enough but then she seemed to stick, half in and half out, and one of the diggers had a struggle to free her. He heaved her this way and that and, at last, he managed it, throwing her upwards before beginning his own clamber out of the grave. Above ground, his mate rolled the body in black cloth to hide the white of the shroud. The other digger rummaged with an arm into the coffin, removed it, then used his pick as a hook to fish out the body of Jemima's baby son. This shrouded scrap was unceremoniously thrown to a man above ground and buttoned into his jacket, and then all was a rush, the second digger was hauled out, the kit packed up, the sacks and the body hauled over to the wall where the ladder was waiting. The watchman climbed up first, checked the street and leaped down. Jemima came over next, slung across the shoulder of one of the diggers and handed down. Then the sacks came, and the second digger. He dangled back and hauled up the ladder with his pick.

'Stop right there.'

It was one of the guards, left behind to watch this side of the wall while his fellows investigated the disturbance on the road. He was a large, hulking man with a scar down one side of his face. He raised an ancient pistol and aimed it at the first digger, who carried Jemima. Then he held out a hand in a 'give' gesture.

'Everything in order round there, Robbie?' another guard shouted.

The digger handed over a bag of coin and Robbie weighed it in his hand.

'Aye,' he shouted back, 'except for a stray dog looking for a fuck.' He tucked the coin purse into his jacket and lowered the pistol.

The digger grinned and swung his burden onto a tinsmith's cart that was passing slowly by, laden with pots and pans and pails. The others handed up their sacks and the dead baby, then they melted away into the shadows as the Travellers picked up their pace through the streets of the Old Town.

By the time Jemima's widower woke to the horror of the day, his late wife and son had been purchased by an assistant in the anatomy school of John Barclay. The clerk had paid the eye-watering sum of twenty-five pounds, a greater fortune than many in this city would handle in their lifetimes. His Master considered it money well spent. A woman who had recently given birth and her infant were not a combination easily obtained, and of considerable scientific interest. Why did some women develop childbed fever, why did the afterbirth shred or refuse to come away?

There was an answer to be had, Barclay had a mind to discover it, and there were plenty who would pay to watch him at his work.

The Specimens

Leith, various villages near Falkirk, Edinburgh
1820–1829

1
Anaphylaxis

HELEN HAD LOST COUNT of the blows and kicks, agonies blooming red all over her body, when the punch came that cracked her skull and shook something loose deep inside her ear. The noise of the room was gone, James's grunts and curses, and instead all was ringing, dizzy, sick.

His hands were on her neck then, and Helen knew she was going to die, for there was no breath but there was vomit coming up, with nowhere to go, she would surely choke twice over.

Then suddenly the pressure was gone. She turned on her side and vomited, agonisingly spitting out mouthfuls of a sticky pudding her body had made of the morning's oatmeal mixed with blood. When that was done she spat out stream upon stream of snot, her lips mumbling around something hard and sharp – a tooth, part of a tooth – and then another.

'A tooth for every child,' her mother's voice said in her head, in tune with the ringing, 'that's what the bearing costs you.' The new child Helen was carrying could not have survived James's punches, she knew that, long experience told her that. She retched again, and Mother's voice was gone; the howl of broken ribs joined the singing in her ears instead.

Hours later, or perhaps it was only minutes, when it occurred to Helen to wonder what had become of James, she found she had to use her legs to turn herself and look, as she could not lift her broken body with one of her arms hanging useless by her side. Her left eye would not open at all, it was crusted shut. The right would open just a slit, and it took a moment before she could make sense of what she was seeing.

James was slumped against the table leg, his face swollen beyond recognition, almost, his eyes red and popping and his mouth like the pout on a fish, the lips swollen and purple and gaping. His tongue stuck out between, a strange purply grey, and his chest heaved but it seemed he could get no air. He lifted his meaty arm and thumped his own chest once, twice, three times, leaving a ghost of his fist on the cloth of his shirt in Helen's blood. But he had not cleared the obstruction, if obstruction it was, and then his whole face seemed to be turning purple, his lips as dark as sloes, the tongue black.

'Hhhh—' he wheezed, meaning 'Helen', perhaps, or 'Help', but he could manage no more, and as Helen stared, his eyes lost their focus and his head slumped to one side.

Helen watched for a moment, then two, then five. When she was very sure he would not be coming for her again, she laid her head on the ground and passed out.

Helen's one working eye had closed on candlelight; she opened it next to see the thin grey light of dawn. She was panicked at first, muddled, her body not her own, stiff and broken and everywhere clotted with blood and pain. A wild fear took her then, and she skittered backwards against the wall, looking around for James, who must be waiting in the morning light to finish her once and for all. Her heart only stilled when she saw him, slumped on the floor by the table,

12

his eyes strange and clouded, staring at nothing. Dead and gone to Hell.

Slowly, inch by agonising inch, Helen dragged herself towards her husband's corpse and the door beyond. As she passed him, some childish fear compelled her to reach out and check that he was truly gone. His skin was cold, and in the shadow below his jaw, among the stubble, Helen's fingers touched the hard pin of something that did not belong. She fumbled until she had a grasp on the thing and could pull it out. She held it up to the meagre light cast by the oilcloth window and tried to focus with her slitted eye. A bee sting, that was all.

Helen's fingers curled round the sting as she began again to pull herself towards the door. She needed help, she knew that, her wounds were bad and she had begun to feel a different pain, a gnawing, dragging pain low down in her belly, as the child began to come away. Effie would know what to do. She might curse her, tell her she was a fool for staying; hadn't Effie told her enough times to leave the drunken, vicious sot and go home to her father in the country? But Effie would always see Helen right.

She lost the bee sting as she struggled to open the door, but by then Helen was beyond caring. She lost her grasp on the catch and tumbled across the threshold to lie at last in a daze of pain, in the mess and dirt of the street outside. Her skirts were heavy and wet beneath her, whether with piss or blood she had no way of telling. The rain fell on her, cold and driving, as she waited for the folk of Leith to stir.

After hours, or what seemed like hours, a door opened and the cry went up. A lad hammered on Effie's door and Effie lumbered out in as much of a run as she could manage, winding a shawl about her head as she went. She knelt, painfully, and held her hand at Helen's lips, muttering a prayer as she felt for breath.

'She's breathing!' Effie shouted, and then she was bawling for a sheet and men to lift Helen into it – 'Gentle, lads, gentle!' – so she could be borne into Effie's flat. Effie's grown daughter Maggie was shooed half-asleep from her bed and Helen was laid in it while Effie pressed a ha'penny into a young lad's hand and told him to fetch Agnes Duncan. Then she swung the kettle over the fire and ordered Maggie to the well for more water and her boy Geordie round the stair for such rags as the neighbours could spare.

Helen listened to the bustle through the muffling and buzzing in her ears. She was tired, almost sleeping, and it seemed as though she had left her body and was watching from somewhere else. But that relief didn't last, an awful pain deep in her belly was drawing her back down. She tried to curl herself around the pain but something sharp stabbed in in her side and she cried out. Effie's hands were on her then, soothing her, helping her back up onto the pillow until the peak passed and she was limp again. Effie fetched a rag and warm water from the kettle and began to clean Helen's face. The closed eye gradually came unstuck; it seemed it had only been sealed shut with blood. Helen could see Effie's lined old face, concentrating on her work.

Effie caught her eye and pursed her lips. 'He's made a mess of you this time, lass, and that's for sure,' she said. 'You can't go back. Not ever again.'

'He's dead,' Helen slurred.

'What?'

'He's dead.'

Effie laid down her basin.

'Nay, lass,' she said. 'You haven't killed him?'

14

'No,' Helen said. 'He just … died. I think it was a bee.'

'Right, aye,' Effie said absently, clearly thinking Helen had gone daft. Then she called for Maggie to sit with Helen while she went next door. Helen dozed for a bit, then woke again, in pain, and saw that Effie was back, and Agnes Duncan was with her.

Effie seemed lost in thought as Agnes bent over Helen and began to examine her.

'I'll go to Andrew Fisher,' Effie said. 'He's an elder in the Kirk. He'll know what to do. The bastard's dead alright, I've never seen the like of it. His face all swollen and blue, like he'd been hanged.'

'Hanging'd be too good for him,' said Agnes. Then she raised Helen's skirts and slid a finger inside her, and Helen howled in protest.

'Bide here for now,' she said to Effie. 'The dead are in no hurry, and I have need of you.'

Then Agnes washed her hands, speaking crisply and kindly to Helen as she did so.

'I'm sorry, lass, but your travails arna over yet. I'd spare you it if I could, but I cannot. Your waters have broken and the pains you feel are birth pangs. You're doing fine, but there's a fair way to go. You've done it before, you know what to do, and we'll help you as best we can.'

'But surely … Won't it just … come away by itself?' Effie asked. 'I lost three back in the day, before they quickened.'

'She's six months gone, at least,' said Agnes. 'There's nothing for it but for her to birth this poor wee craitur, broken ribs or no. Do you have whisky in the house? And a clean shift? I need to set her arm back in first, and she'll puke when I do it.'

When all was over, the agony of the arm and the long struggle of the labour and the birthing, Helen lay in a daze of pain and drink and watched Agnes and Effie as they covered the thing that lay in Effie's basin with a cloth.

'What will you do with it?' she asked, forming the words as best she could.

'Bury it in the yard,' Agnes said. 'Is that what you want? I'll say a prayer, if you like.'

Helen closed her eyes. 'James always fed them to the dogs, when I lost them. He said to do other was a waste.'

Agnes stared then swallowed, hard. She and Effie exchanged a look.

'Aye, well,' Effie said. 'He's deid.'

Helen spent more than a month at Effie's, in the end, sleeping in Maggie's truckle bed while Maggie bunked in with her mother in the box-bed in the wall. Agnes came daily, for the first week, to bandage her ribs and see to the milk till it dried up, and dose her with herbs against fever. She came less after that, twice a week perhaps, and one day she brought with her a kitten pinned into her blouse, a runt another wife had thrown into the street from the second storey of a tenement. She asked Helen to keep it in the bed with her. She could feed it milk from the jug, Agnes said, watered down a wee bit, and that way they both might have the comfort of one another.

Effie snorted at that, but she fetched the milk herself until Helen was well enough to be on her feet. The wee tabby cat survived, and then it thrived, and Father Black said they should call it Jezebel after the queen in the Bible, for she had been thrown out of a window too, only that Jezebel's landing had a sorrier end.

Father Black came often, to sit with Helen, and to help as best he could to settle the matters of their lodging room and monies owing to her from James MacDougal's employers at the sawmill. Not that there was a lot he could do – folk of James

MacDougal's faith were sorely abused, and even a priest had little standing – but he spoke for Helen, as did Effie's minister, since Helen had been raised a Presbyterian. In the end a small amount was settled on her in respect of wages owing, the furnishings of their room and her husband's tools. James himself had been laid to rest two days after his death, in the local burying ground. The mortsafe went into the grave with him, a great cage that contained the coffin so that none should dig it up and open it once it was in the ground. Two friends of James's had paid for it, it seemed, rough types who owed him a gambling debt. The safe would soon be dug up again, Father Black told Helen, James would be of no use to the graverobbers' customers now, but Helen had no need to worry about any of it.

'Indeed!' Effie snorted.

Father Black did his best not to hear. No, he said, there was nothing to do at all, all was in hand and the two men well pleased to receive half of James's store of whisky in thanks. The rest had gone to Agnes, with some coin, food, and small crocks, and she too had been well pleased with her payment.

At last Helen was well, or as well as she might expect to be. Her ear had never healed properly, so she had to incline her head towards a speaker to hear them over the strange ringing sound in her ears. She had been weak, after so long abed, but as soon as Helen could stand, she asked for a broom for the floor or a pot to scour; she had been a burden to Effie long enough. Effie was kind, said if she had had the room, Helen might have stayed as long as she liked, but Helen knew she did not have the room. Maggie was grumbling and bleary-eyed from Effie's snoring, and she needed her own bed back. And so, Helen gave Effie as much of her money as the older woman would accept and tied the few things she still owned into a bundle. She thought about leaving Jezebel – she was a fierce mouser – but in the end the cat leapt up beside her on the cart that was to take her towards her father's village by Falkirk, and so it seemed the choice was not Helen's to make.

The carter took Helen along the road south of Polmont and let her off before Falkirk, at the crossroads by Parkhill Woods. From there she walked to Redding with Jezebel following, darting here and there into the grass after insects and beasties, then returning to wind around her mistress's legs as though she was determined to trip her up.

Helen saw Peter Gaff before he saw her, sitting on the stoop outside his house mending a pair of boots. He looked up, shading his eyes against the sun, and peered at her for a moment as one might a stranger. Then recognition came, and he got to his feet and drew her to him. Suddenly shy, Helen stooped her head. She knew she still looked a state; her face was clean enough and much of the swelling gone down, but the ghosts of the bruises still showed and her lip was not quite healed. Her father put her from him and looked at the ground.

'We never knew,' he said. 'When you married him, we had no idea he was a brute.'

'How would you?' Helen asked. 'You never raised a hand to my mother.'

'No,' said Peter, 'nor anyone else either.'

He shook his head and sighed.

'Come away in,' he said. 'I'll see what I can find to eat and drink. The others will be back and looking for their dinner soon anyway.'

But Helen hung back for a moment.

'Do they know?' she asked. 'That their father's dead?'

'Aye,' he said. 'All the bairnies know. But Helen . . .' He broke off and shook his head again.

'What?'

'Your lasses . . . They know you're their mam, and they know James was their da. But . . . they know because I've told them. They *know* it to be true, they don't *feel* it. This is their home, they forget I'm their granda, no their da.'

Helen's eyes smarted. 'They don't remember living with me and James?'

He shook his head once more. 'They were too wee, when it happened.'

Helen closed her eyes for a second, hearing once again the cry as Maisie tumbled into the fire. It was so clear in her mind that she thought her father might hear it, too, but he just stooped through the door and into the shady room inside. After a second, Helen followed.

The children began to wander in, in ones and twos, as Peter laid out cheese and bannocks and small ale and milk. He sent them to complete their chores and to wash and then they all crowded round the table together to eat, the wee ones keeking under their lashes at the stranger in their midst, reddening if they caught her eye. Helen sat with her brother John and sister Grace on the bench – they were sixteen and eighteen now, Grace home for her day off from service and John apprenticed to a joiner and going there every morning and home at night. Peter sat on a stool with Helen's wee daughter Annie on his knee and said the Grace, thanking God for the food and their health to enjoy it. Helen looked round the room, bare and small but trig and clean with its limewashed walls and scrubbed table, and thought of her mother. Mam had been gone four years now, although still Helen expected to see her take her place beside Father and begin to hand round the bannocks. Helen's older girl Maisie stood with Margaret and Elspeth and Andrew on the other side of the table. In the low light, the scar on her face seemed gone, almost, although Helen's fingers itched still to reach out and feel the rough shine of it. Instead, she focused on her bannock, breaking a piece off and choking it down with a sip of ale.

Jezebel was an instant favourite of the younger children, and when they had eaten and attended to their chores, Maisie and Margaret spent much of the evening pulling around a piece of string for her to chase. When they went to bed with the other girls, Jezebel went with them, although Helen knew she would abandon them in the middle of the night to attend to her mousing. Hopefully they would wake to a row of little corpses on the floor, instead of in their bedclothes.

Helen slept with Grace and their sister Lizzie that night, and she liked it. She saw now how much she had missed having company, James MacDougal always out drinking and Helen's bairnies sent away so she had always slept alone.

In the morning, she helped dress the children and wash their faces, and when they had gone off to work or lessons, she picked up a basket of mending and took it outside into the warm day. Her father joined her with his tools and wood, and they passed a quiet forenoon together, Peter carving soles for his shoes and boots and Helen darning and mending shirts and stockings, trousers with threadbare seats, and fourth-hand jackets falling apart at the seams.

At last, Peter stretched and yawned and said he would put some stew on the fire for their dinner. Helen finished patching a worn-out elbow, bit off her thread and followed him inside.

'There's work at the harvest over by,' he said, as they ate. 'I'm heading over myself, next week, make a bit of money to add to the cobbling. Do you want me to tell them you'll come too?'

Helen swallowed.

'I thought maybe I could stay here a while longer,' she said. 'I could care for the bairnies while you're gone.'

Her father looked at his bowl.

'I canna keep you, Helen,' he said. 'I can barely feed my own bairns, even with the money John and Grace bring home, and then I have yours as well. And ... well ... looking after bairns is no ...' He tailed off and shoved a spoonful of stew into his mouth.

No for me, Helen thought. Even though it was long, long syne, that terrible day Maisie went into the fire, and not like any of the bairns were on leading reins now.

'Besides,' Peter said, through a mouthful of bread, 'the harvest will be great crack for you, Helen. You can camp with the other women, save yourself the tramp back; you always liked that, liked company and a drink.'

'Aye,' said Helen, and it was true, she did like company and a drink. But it was hard when a women had to choose between that and her own bairns. She had no need of whisky in the morning anymore, after all, had only ever taken it to dull the ache of James's latest beating – he'd cracked her tooth, that time when Maisie fell, and part of it had remained in her gum and half-crazed her.

'I'll set you out there,' Peter said, 'and leave you with the women. Lizzie'll mind the bairns here, she's a steady lass.'

'Very well,' said Helen, though she wasn't pleased.

Peter was as good as his word, letting the wife who was heading up the women's and children's gangs know that Helen was coming with him, and walking her out there himself before he went off with his scythe to join the reapers. She was set to work alongside three women she didn't know, all from further afield than herself.

Rachel was a great strong red-head, taller than most men, and as fond of a drink as Helen herself. Betsey was a cottar's wife, small and dark and well used to hard work. She was happy to be away from home and her husband for a few weeks; according to her he was a feckless article, more like to gamble away their money than use it to feed their bairns. Betsey's wages would go in her own pocket, she swore, and he wouldn't have any chance to fritter it all away. Then there was Jean, a widow woman who had no home to call her own and instead went from place to place seeking work. She was a kindly soul, and Helen liked her best of all. The four of them worked together, and they slept together in a rough tent, and one of the others would always go with you when you went to piss; you couldn't be too careful with so many men around.

It was a good month, for all Helen began it in ill-humour. The work was hard and in the first days she felt the weakness of her body, her damaged shoulder aching so she had to pause and stretch her arm above her head, and her ribs still sore. She was hard-pressed to get herself moving in the morning, so seized up she seemed. As the days wore on, though, she felt herself grow stronger, her shoulder eased and the bending became easier and she was able to keep up with the others and even outstrip Jean. The weather held, and they made good progress, following the reapers up through the rigs, binding the sheaves and gathering them into stooks to dry. They began at dawn and stopped when the sun was at its highest for the midday meal, oatcakes and bannocks and cheese and meat the farmer's wife brought out with a great team of helpers, with good ale to drink or whey for those that liked it better. Then the gangs set to again until dusk, and when at last it was too dark to continue, they sat together round their bonfires, drinking and talking, exchanging snuff and tobacco for their pipes. Many of the workers were Travellers and other tramping folk, but at least half of them just locals pressed into service, and with hours so long they chose to camp in the fields most nights and enjoy the drink and song and company.

There was a large band of Irish, from all over the north of that island, and among them were a wheen of fine singers and storytellers who were in great demand around the fires. Rachel paired off with one of them, an older man named Seán, and seemed well pleased with her lot. The others were much enamoured of another man, one William, a stocky creature with thick ginger hair and a pleasant, open face. He had a snub nose, too, almost like a child's, but his body was solid and strong. He was well spoken and Betsey said she'd heard he was a nobleman's son, but Rachel said that was nonsense; proud of the knowledge she had from Seán, she was, lording it over them. The family had had money, she said; Seán had heard his father was a lawyer or a doctor, something like that, but there had been an almighty falling out and now William Burke was down on his luck and no better than any of them, for all his handsome face and dainty speech.

'He'd keep a woman warm at night,' Jean said longingly, one night when he was singing by the fire.

William looked over at that and Helen coloured, thinking he had heard, but he didn't look at Jean; instead he looked at Helen and smiled, bowing his head as though it was to her he sang and not to the twenty or more folk around the fire. It was a pleasant sensation, for all she was sure it was nothing more than that easy charm all the Irishmen seemed to have when they were in their cups of an evening. She couldn't understand the words of the song, it was in their own language, but it sounded bonnie enough, what she could hear of it, and she ducked her head down to listen over that bell that was her constant companion, ringing in her ears.

It had been a long time since Helen had thought of a man with anything other than dread, or of herself as a woman that a man might look at, except maybe with pity, or disgust, as she cringed past on the street, head bowed to hide the bruisings and swellings of her face. She knew her figure was decent, she wasn't tall and strong like Rachel but she had a neat enough shape, although her chest was flat. Her hair was a reddish brown, darker than Rachel's bright ginger, and straighter, and there was no grey in it yet. None of the harvest women had a looking glass, but Jean had a wee knife, polished to a shine, and Helen did her best to see herself in it, although it cut her up into slivers – dark eyes, turning down at the corners, and heavy brows with a great deep crease between them, a long nose, and lips that were neither thin nor full. She was lucky James had taken the teeth from the back of her mouth only, and it didn't show if she was careful not to smile too widely. Her cheeks were tanned, her nose as well, but they all had that, working outside in all weathers. As far as she could tell, she was no beauty, but she had nothing to be ashamed of, for all the ill-treatment her face had taken in its time.

The next night, she waited until there was a lull and then she sang, quiet at first but then swelling out as her nerves fell away, her favourite of the songs she'd learned from her mother, 'Auld Robin Grey'. It was the story of a young lass who loved a lad called Jamie, but he had no wealth and so had gone to sea, vowing to make his fortune before he returned to marry her. But then her parents were ruined and the lass forced to marry an old man, and kind though he was to her, her heart was broken when Jamie returned and found her lost to him.

Helen had a decent voice still – the choking James had given her seemed to have done no permanent harm – and she received a warm round of clapping and cheering when she was done. Someone pressed a stone bottle into her hands and she clutched it in shaking hands and took a swig from it – whisky, it was, and good and strong. She found herself tired out then, and she said to Jean that she would go to her bed. Jean got up to go with her, although Helen could see she would have preferred to stay.

As they made their way to the tent, they brushed against a man's body in the dark. He raised a lantern he carried and smiled at them, and Helen saw it was William Burke.

'Nelly,' he said, and for a stupid moment Helen didn't realise it was her he meant. 'You're not leaving, are you? I was hoping for another song.'

'I am,' Helen said. 'I'm tired.'

'No,' he said, 'there's not so many nights left now,' and he drew her back to the fire, bringing her to sit beside him and passing her a bottle. Jean drew back, returning to her own place by the fire.

'You're a fine wee *céirseach*, Nelly,' William said. 'That's what we call a blackbird in Ireland.' He laughed. 'You'd be a Missus Blackbird,' he said, 'with your bonnie brown hair. A sweet voice you have, and something in the way you hold your head reminds me of a blackbird too.'

Helen blushed. 'I don't hear well on this side,' she said. 'It was a blow to my head. It took away my hearing.'

'Who did that to you?' William asked.

'My husband,' Helen said. 'He ... well, he's dead now and it doesn't matter.'

William seemed shocked. 'Oh, Nelly,' he said. He put a hand on her back and she felt it burn her, almost, like a brand. '*Mo chéirseach bheag.*'

Helen didn't return to her tent that night, or any of the other nights of that harvest season. Instead she slept with William in a bow-tent he had constructed of branches, on a bed of leaves and good woollen blankets. The first night he held her, that was all, and she lay awake the whole night through. He kissed her in the morning, when the first notes of birdsong woke the camp, and they were late to the morning muster.

A few days later, on the Sabbath, Helen woke at first light to find the weather turned cold of a sudden, and a dead bee lying on the leaves before her eyes. She picked it up and turned it over, looking for the sting in its behind. Then she turned over, careful not to disturb William, who had been deep in drink the previous night and was sound asleep. She pressed the bee sting into his skin and held her breath. Nothing happened. Relieved, Helen closed her eyes and drifted off to sleep, thinking of a blackbird's nest, cosy and snug. She did not want the harvest to end.

2
Hymen

Susan's fingers felt clammy as she lifted the lid of the box that contained her wedding gown. It was folded in tissue and gently she unwrapped it, lifting it out by the bodice and holding it to the light, checking the colour was as she expected, the palest shale of tea. Mrs Babbington took it from her and exclaimed over the fineness of the stitching and the sheen of the silk. Together, they hung it from the top of the press to help the creases drop out of the long skirt and Mrs Babbington fluffed up the great puffs of the sleeves. Then Susan turned her attention to the other boxes. The first contained underpinnings made of the finest lawn, trimmed with rosy ribbons of silk, stockings, and a garter. Those made her feel strange, and hot, the fabric so thin as to be almost transparent, hard to imagine Robert looking on her in such a thing. The last box contained her slippers, made of the lightest satin, lined with cotton and trimmed with grosgrain ribbon and rings of pearls. No use for walking, of course, but then she had only to step into the carriage and out again at the kirk.

All was well made, restrained, entirely appropriate to an orphan girl who had once been the paid companion to the sisters of her betrothed. Mary and Jessie had insisted on that, fingering the fabrics and leafing through the pattern books with a practised eye, refusing anything extravagant or showy, steering Susan towards plain good quality and subtle colourings. They dressed more richly, as was their right, but perhaps they needed to; their standing might have been higher than Susan's but neither had half her looks, Mary with a face like a mealy pudding and Jessie as scrawny as an old hen. It had never occurred to Susan that her beauty might be an affront to them; they were rich, after all, and with enough money any woman may be married well. Indeed, they never treated her any differently, Mary fawning as she had always done, the big lump, and Jessie smirking, although they were quick to strike a deal with the dressmaker for a lower price – perhaps the shoes did not need so many pearls, after all.

Robert's mother had been dead a few months by then, that was why it had fallen to his sisters to support Susan in this way, since she had no one of her own. It was Jessie who had found her lodging with Mrs Babbington; she said it would not be seemly for Susan to be married out of Newington Place with Robert sleeping in the next room. Mary made a great show of agreeing with her – she was always the echo of her sister, slow and dull where Jessie was sharp and hard. She would never say anything nasty of her own account, but neither would she stand up to Jessie. Susan was a little offended at their fuss, she had never had any intention of staying once Robert had proposed. Father had seen her schooled as well as any lady and she knew she had nothing to be ashamed of in her looks or her manners. Robert's mother would never have stooped to bring her into the Knox family home had it been any other way.

It pained Susan that Father had not lived to see her married. She knew he'd be pleased with her, engaged to a young man with brilliant prospects, one who'd travelled to the Cape and Paris, and who looked set to become one of the foremost anatomists of the day. But she did not think their backgrounds so very different, when all was said and done. Father was a merchant, not so very low, and Robert only the son of a school-master. She did not understand – then – that those may be the very worst kind of families, the ones who desperately seek to improve their station in society. She did not see how they were sensitive to any slight, sought to stamp out any reminder of origins of the average sort. Robert was the family's great hope; how could Susan have thought they were happy for him to take a *servant girl* as his wife?

Susan would have plenty of time to reflect on that later, but when Robert proposed, it had never occurred to her to doubt his motivations. He loved her, she was sure of that, and she also thought he knew himself lucky to get her. He had had the smallpox when he was a child, and it had pitted his skin and blinded his left eye, so that a full moon of milky white shone where in the other eye the iris was blue. A gentler man might have overcome the obstacle, attracted romantic interest even, by reason of his scarring, but Robert was not that man. His wit was as acerbic as his countenance was frightening. Jessie tattled that he was a bully at school, and often in trouble in the Cape, and slow, plodding Mary agreed, as she always did, but Susan had ignored that, thinking it jealousy speaking. And all the while they were sniggering behind their hands, waiting for the day she would be gone and Jessie would have the run of the house and the account books and no need to worry about husbands ever again, only clothes and sweetmeats and gossip.

Susan and Robert's banns were read not, as Susan had imagined they would be, in the lovely new Hope Park Chapel where the Knox family worshipped, or indeed anywhere else on the south side of the city where their acquaintance lived. Robert said, instead, that he had arranged for the banns to be read outside the city, in the old kirk in South Leith, as Robert was registered as living at a cottage he had outside the city at a place called Lillypot, and Susan had been born in the parish of Leith. They would be married there too, he said.

At first, Susan had been disappointed, but Robert said they could not do more, not when they should still properly be in mourning for his mother. And in any case, Robert said the old Leith kirk was a fine building and the minister a remarkable man, another High School boy like Robert himself, although many years his junior. That had cheered Susan, at the time, as she had been worried at the thought of being required to marry in mourning attire.

On the morning of the wedding, Susan woke at dawn and could sleep no more. Mrs Babbington brought her tea and toast at seven, although she could eat nothing, her stomach was fluttering so that she worried she might be sick. Mrs Babbington helped her dress, curling her hair and styling it most prettily, then rubbing a little of her own rouge into Susan's cheeks.

'I've never seen a bride so pale!' she said, and she rubbed Susan's hands and then gave her a tot of brandy from a flask. It burned in Susan's stomach as they walked down the stairs together. Inside the door, Mrs Babbington kissed her and wished her every happiness. She seemed a trifle misty-eyed, telling Susan that she remembered her own wedding day with fondness, and missed her husband still for all he had been dead near on twenty years.

Then Mrs Babbington opened the door and Susan stepped outside into the morning sun where Robert was climbing out of the carriage to supervise the loading of her trunk. Susan stood on the step, dazed, wondering whether she might fall, but then Robert finished instructing the coachman and his hand was firm on her back, helping her into the carriage and climbing in beside her, opposite Mary and Jessie in new dresses and bonnets. Susan felt she was floating free of her body, somehow, so she looked at them and seemed hardly to know them, Mary in an ugly brown frock and jacket that brought out the shadows under her eyes and the paleness of her skin, so she looked almost dead, and Jessie in a black and red striped coat and hat with a great plume of feathers, looking more like a pecking hen than ever, with her scrawny neck and beady eyes.

The sisters chattered away as they drove through Newington, past the university and across the North Bridge towards Leith. Susan said little, feeling still a stranger in her body, and Jessie laughed at her nerves and they chattered among themselves some more, Jessie with pert comments and Mary murmuring agreement, and somehow Susan didn't notice that they had already passed the kirk at Leith until they were already at the Shore. Robert helped her out of the carriage then, before handing down Mary and Jessie, and ushered them into an inn. He told them it was an important place, where the Scots kings long ago had stored their arms, and then where a hospital for plague victims had been established, although Susan couldn't see why any of that mattered when they should be at the kirk. Then they were seated at table and wine was brought and Robert began on a story of the odd things he had eaten in France with his friend Thomas Hodgkin, raw steak mixed with egg and caperberries, snails in butter with garlic, and the fried legs of frogs. Mary and Jessie laughed and gasped and professed themselves appalled.

When at last she could get a word in, Susan asked when they were to go to the kirk.

Robert smiled and took a drink of wine. 'There's no need of it,' he said. 'Under Scots law any couple may marry by saying they are married and setting up home together.'

Susan had no idea what to say to that, but it seemed she was not required to say anything. Jessie struck up to say yes, brother Robert was entirely correct, that was all that was required and given that both their families were in mourning, surely it would be the best and most appropriate thing in any case. Mary agreed, and then Jessie produced a ring which Robert put on Susan's hand, saying it had been their mother's, and then Mary and Jessie clapped and smiled, Jessie kissed Susan and called her 'sister', and Mary rose clumsily from her seat, offering her soft, damp cheek for Susan's kiss. Robert ordered brandy for a toast and said Susan was 'like the sun in its meridian, spreading a lustre throughout the world'. He explained this was originally said of the old king George, for all he was mad, which seemed to Susan less than romantic, but it provided an opening for Jessie to begin to reminisce about the new king's visit to Edinburgh.

'Do you mind on it, Susan? Did your father take you? So round in his kilt. And his stockings – pink stockings, of all the sights!'

And it seemed all was done and the others quite content with affairs.

The food came, and Susan still could not eat, but the rest feasted most heartily. Then Jessie took Susan upstairs to a room where her trunk was waiting and helped her out of the wedding gown, unlacing her corset so Susan stood there in nothing but the thin shift of lawn. She struggled with a sudden desire to cover herself with her hands.

Jessie sat Susan down and began to unpin the pretty curls Mrs Babbington had fixed on her head. Susan winced as she pulled out the pins. 'You know what happens between husband and wife?' Jessie asked, as she raked in Susan's bag for a brush and began to brush out the length of her hair.

Susan nodded. She was not entirely sure, in truth, but she could not bear to have Jessie's gleaming eyes on her any longer; sitting on that hard chair in the shift that covered nothing, the woman seemed to be taking pleasure in her rough ministrations, and Susan wanted her gone. When she was alone, although it was barely noon, Susan climbed into the bed, where she lay shivering in a daze of confusion and fear, listening to the sounds of the inn and trying not to think of Father lest she begin to cry. At last, she heard Robert's step in the hall outside and the door opened. He carried a bottle of brandy and two glasses which he placed on the dresser.

'Poor Susan,' he said, and he smiled. 'This isn't quite what you expected, is it?'

Susan didn't speak; if she had, she knew she would have begun to cry.

'Here,' Robert said, and poured her a tot of brandy.

Susan took it and drank, the second shot of brandy today, and indeed only the second of her whole life.

Robert gave her another, and another, and she drank again. Her lips felt numb and she was light-headed, as though she had spun around and around and made herself dizzy.

Robert was watching her, and there was something in his expression she could not make out. He stood and began to take off his own things, sitting down on the bed again when he was dressed only in his shirt. He reached out a hand and touched Susan where the thin shift clearly showed the rosy tip of her breast. He pinched her there, hard, and then again, and asked her if she liked it. Susan didn't, but she mumbled that she didn't know. Then he pulled the shift down and began to kiss her, roughly, all the while pinching her breast so she felt an odd ache low in her stomach. Then he said the next would hurt, and it did, she felt something tear and it hurt her enough that she tried to fight him, but he seemed to like that, he held her down and redoubled his assault until she had to bite her lip so as not to cry.

Susan slept then, unaccustomed to the brandy, and did not wake until morning. Robert kissed her when she woke, and said it would not hurt so much the next time, and he would leave her to dress alone. There was blood on the new shift, and Susan bundled it into the trunk, knowing she would never wear it again. She thought about sending the wedding dress back to Newington Place, but then she realised she might need a good dress on their journey, and Jessie and Mary had been so careful to order her one that might be worn again! She cursed them then, in her mind, the bitches, picturing them lording it over the fine house in Newington while Susan slept in an inn – Mary lying abed waiting for toast and jam, no doubt, while Jessie clawed through her mother's baubles for the best pieces to match that morning's dress.

Susan put on a plain cotton dress and her boots and went to join Robert at breakfast.

After breakfast they set out in the carriage, on their wedding journey that was no wedding journey truly seen. Robert was solicitous of Susan's comfort, making sure she was wrapped warm enough and had a comfortable cushion. He told her about the place they were going to, a region of wild hills and lochs where Walter Scott had written 'The Lady of the Lake'. Scott seemed a great hero of Robert's, being another High School boy like himself, and one who also had suffered an illness as a child that had provided an additional obstacle to advancement. This was the first time Susan had heard Robert refer to his own disfigurement; Scott's, it seemed, was a disease that had left him lame. Robert was greatly interested in this disease, he said a surgeon called Underwood had written of it years ago, but he had retired young and his writings had been neglected since. Robert himself wished to study it further, but struggled for access to specimens for dissection with the characteristic marks of the disease – wasted lower extremities and strange twistings of the limbs. Then Robert remembered that Underwood had delivered the Princess Charlotte, who had died so sadly in childbirth three years back, and began to explain how he believed that catastrophe might have been avoided.

The road had become rough, and the carriage was rocky, and Susan found the line of conversation oppressive. Perhaps Robert realised this, because he changed tack and talked of the places they might see, and Scott's novels, which everyone in Robert's circles knew to be by Scott for all they were published anonymously. Susan had not known that and felt herself stupid. She had devoured *The Heart of Midlothian*, believing it to be by a woman, writing under the obviously made-up name of a schoolmaster in a made-up town in the Borders. She was almost sorry to find it was Scott, she had loved Jeanie Dean and thought only a woman like herself could have conjured up such a lass.

They stopped the first night at Linlithgow, where they saw the Great Palace before the carriage left again in the morning. The next day they travelled to a burgh called Airth on the banks of the Forth, where they saw a fine castle and a bonnie old kirk in poor repair. Susan felt she might burst into flames should she step within its walls, but anyway, Robert preferred to roam in the graveyard making jokes about the mortsafes and the graverobbers, and so she was spared that fate. By the third night, they had reached the great city of Stirling, and on the fourth they reached the crooked old inn at Brig o'Turk, where they would spend the coming weeks. Wherever they stayed, Susan and Robert were lodged as Dr and Mrs Knox and it seemed it was known they were on their wedding journey, for there were many congratulations and compliments for Susan as the bride. She burned with shame at these, but it seemed this was the way even for brides who were really married, and no one thought anything amiss besides Susan herself.

It seemed to Susan in those weeks that she no longer stood on solid ground. They exchanged the swaying of the carriage for the pitching of little boats and long tramps across wet earth, and everywhere they went, it seemed that something was designed to remind her of the lie on which her new life was built. At Balquhidder they saw the stone slab where Rob Roy MacGregor slept with his wife on his right hand, and Susan thought her lucky, that long-ago woman, for all she was married to an outlaw, she was married before witnesses, not carted off to an inn and defiled. At Aberfoyle they saw a tree that was said to be a minister of the place, transformed by the fairies as punishment for a book he wrote that revealed the secrets the little folk held dear. Susan felt her own secret burn within her, she had never planned to live as now she did, a fallen woman by her own lights, and whose lights mattered, if not her own? In a remote place, far from anywhere, they tramped across the moors to see some stones of great antiquity, some in a circle, one a great monolith, and others with curious hollows carved in them in ancient times. A place to punish transgressions, perhaps, streak sinners out and kill them with knives of stone. Susan wondered if she should lie down there, herself, and add to their blood with her own.

Robert maintained this was a fancy of Susan's, he said they were married perfectly legally once they were declared as such in the eyes of all the world. He seemed determined to be patient, in those days, only falling into a temper once, when a guide maintained that water drunk from the hollows of some stone or other could cure a range of ailments, from the falling sickness to the measle. Robert said the measle was caused by infection in the blood and could not be cured by water, a man called Home had proven that almost a century past, and soon they would understand the falling sickness, too. He stamped off then, walking quickly, and Susan was left to struggle along behind.

When they had been in the place some three weeks, it transpired that Robert had some medical work to do at a place called Glengyle. He told Susan to pack her best dresses, for the people they were to visit were gentry, the Laird of the place and his Lady. The Laird had some ailment dating from his time in the militia and they were to spend five nights there while Robert did his best to effect a cure. Susan was glad then that she had brought the wedding dress, shook it out to check for spots and marks, and packed it ready for the journey.

They sailed across Loch Katrine in an eight-oared galley, through the waters in which Scott had set 'The Lady of the Lake', arriving at the old house at Glengyle in the middle of the day to be greeted by Lady Jane. Susan burned with shame at the thought that she should be complicit in deceiving this good woman, who understood she was receiving a married couple on their wedding journey, and it was with great relief that she saw they were to sleep in separate rooms, just as the Laird and the Lady were used to do themselves.

'I well remember my own marriage,' the Lady Jane confided in Susan as she took her up the stair. 'It is a trying time, is it not? To go from being much alone, or with other women, to being all the time in the company of a man? I thought you might like a brief respite.'

Tears sprung into Susan's eyes and Jane gave her hand a brief squeeze.

'Have you a mother living?' she asked.

'No,' said Susan. 'She died birthing a child when I was a little girl. And my father the summer before last.'

'Well,' said Jane, 'I never had a daughter, only three sons, and so I will not scruple to dote on you for as long as you are here.'

They dined that night on venison and the Laird and Robert sat up together late talking of their travels, for John MacGregor had been many years in England and – his wife aside – rarely had a chance to speak with another who had travelled beyond these parts. Susan retired alone to her room and slept more soundly than she had done in all the nights since her marriage.

She and Jane walked all around the place over the coming days, visiting the small burial enclosure to the west of the house where Jane pointed out the memorial to Gregor Black Knee who had fought in the Risings of 1715 and 1745 and been raised by Rob Roy, who himself had been born in the house here in the mid years of the last century, the old house, that was, that had stood on the same ground. There were carvings around the walls with the initials of those long-departed MacGregors, and Jane recited their stories to Susan as they walked.

'You are an Englishwoman, are you not?' Susan asked shyly. 'How come you to find yourself so at home here?'

'It took some time,' Jane said, 'and I was lonely for a time, especially when my first son was born, and I seemed always tied to the house. But my husband is a kind man, and the place is beautiful, and it is my birthright, for I am a MacGregor too, for all I grew up far from here. The story of our people is not a happy one, as perhaps you know. We fell foul of powerful men and it was a great task to rebuild our fortunes even to the degree we have achieved today.'

There was no more talk of MacGregors then, as Jane turned instead to the management of a marriage, calmly and matter-of-factly outlining for Susan the ways in which she and her husband managed things between them when it came to the marriage bed. She tied a white ribbon on the doorhandle when he was welcome to spend the night in her chamber, she said, and a red ribbon when he was absolutely prohibited. She explained the best times each month for a woman to get with child, and how Susan might recognise these and plan her nights. 'The sooner you succeed, the sooner you may be left in peace,' she said. 'For a while.'

As this counsel proceeded, Susan felt her ears and cheeks grow redder and redder and suddenly she blurted out the whole sorry business, how she and Robert were not really married at all, only by some irregular means Robert insisted was real but Susan had no proper witnesses, no banns, no paper to prove it had ever happened.

Jane looked grave.

'Let's into the house,' she said. 'I have sherry wine. I think we need it, before we talk any more of this.'

Susan cried a little with relief then, and Jane bustled around fetching wine and biscuits and insisted she ate and drank and calmed herself before they spoke further. Then she sat with Susan and stared into her own glass.

'I cannot think he means to cast you aside,' she said. 'He brought you here, after all, did he not, into our home? He introduced you as his wife and I cannot think he would have done so unless he truly believed it. But you are young, my dear, and he is . . . how shall I say it? He is not an easy man, I think. Rather too critical. Do you recall that tale he told us at dinner, of his falling out with the surgeon Charles Bell when he was a young man at Waterloo? It did not strike me as wise for a man who was at the start of his career to cross swords with any superior, let alone a man of Bell's power.'

'I am a little afraid of him,' Susan admitted. 'I never know what he is thinking. He seems determined to be kind, but he dismisses all my concerns as though they were nothing.'

'I think a child is what you need,' said Jane. 'All men desire children, do they not? Surely he will regularise the marriage when there is a child? But perhaps I am thinking too gloomily. He is going to take you home, is he not? He can hardly take you home, introduce you as his wife, and then cast you aside! It would be a scandal, and I think he cares for his standing in the city. He seems to wish to be the greatest anatomist of all.'

'He already thinks he is,' Susan said. 'He resents the fact that others don't always agree.'

The last two days at Glengyle were easier for Susan, now her secret was known, and she saw Jane watching Robert when he was with her, enquiring about his plans for his anatomy school and his life in Edinburgh. Robert said his main ambition was to persuade the College of Surgeons to establish a museum of anatomy in the city, and he believed he had good reason to think he would succeed.

Jane looked at Susan then, and Susan could see what she was thinking – Robert cared for his reputation, he had no interest in a scandal.

When they left Glengyle, Jane made Susan promise to write. 'I travel little,' she said, 'but one day, perhaps, I might visit Edinburgh, if Himself keeps well enough.'

Robert seemed well pleased with the cure he had effected, and the Laird's payment, which Susan guessed would go some way to covering the expenses of their trip. They spent a last week at Brig o'Turk, easier with one another, and then it was time to pack their trunks again for the journey home. Robert said they would go first to his cottage north of the city at Trinity, Susan would like it there.

'I would prefer to go to Newington Place,' she said. 'I'm tired of travelling, I would wish to be settled as soon as I can be.'

But Robert was insistent, saying he was jealous of her company still, wanted her to himself a few days longer. He spoke then at length of the cottage, which he called Lillypot, how he wished for them to spend most of their time there.

Susan laughed at that and said how could it be, did Robert not need to be in the city to keep his practice growing?

'It's a short enough ride in a carriage,' said Robert, 'but a world apart, a green and pleasant place free from the foul humours of the city. When the children come they will be safer there, I don't intend to father a string of corpses, as so many others seem content to do.' Then he shook his head, as if to dispel the ghost of his words, and smiled at her. 'It's not as though you have any fondness for Mary or Jessie, now, is it?' he said. 'I know you dislike them and I can't say I blame you. They did enjoy playing fine ladies when they had you to wait upon them. I should think you'll be glad to be free of them and mistress of your own house. I can't say I have much liking for their society myself; I shall enjoy being at Lillypot instead.'

Susan said nothing, thinking this fancy would pass once Robert returned to his work in earnest. The cottage did indeed turn out to be a pleasant place, not really a cottage at all but a squat stone-built house of a middling size, lime-washed and solid, set back from the road in a small grove of trees. It was a few miles east of Leith, out along a rough road in the lands of Trinity where the Masters and Mariners of Trinity House raised monies for the assistance of destitute sailors and their families through the operation of a farm and the occasional sale of a plot of land to the wealthy for the building of a summerhouse. Robert said it was private enough to leave a house locked up for months together.

Inside, Lillypot was simply but tastefully furnished, the rooms painted in pale colours of distemper like sugared almonds, with furniture of light wood and pale upholstery to match. Susan was surprised to find the place had a staff of its own, a housekeeper, a cook, a gardener, and a maid of all work. The housekeeper was a Mrs Scott, a plump, comfortable-looking woman, and she welcomed Susan most cordially, showing her to an elegant room she said was Susan's own, and bringing water to wash off the dust of the road. When Susan was washed and changed, she ventured out to find Robert, but Mrs Scott told her he was gone.

'Gone?' Susan said, stupid with shock. 'Gone where?'

'Back to Newington Place, I suppose,' said Mrs Scott. 'I'm sure much business has piled up during his absence.'

'I want to go too,' said Susan. 'Bring me my cloak and my shoes.'

'Now?' said Mrs Scott. 'Och, that won't be possible, Ma'am. We're very quiet here, there's no transport except our own, and Doctor Knox has taken our carriage. But you must be tired, Ma'am, why don't I serve the dinner now, and then you can take your rest?'

Susan fought a rising panic in her throat. 'Did he say when he'd be back?' she asked. 'Doctor Knox?'

'I'm sure it's no my place to ask,' said Mrs Scott. 'But are you quite well, Ma'am? You look that pale. Shall I fetch you a draught?'

'No,' said Susan. 'I'll ... I'll just go to my room.'

'I'll bring up a tray with your dinner then,' said Mrs Scott. 'We cannae have you wasting away.'

Susan had no appetite, but she didn't wish to offend Mrs Scott, and so she ate what she could manage and then put the rest outside the door. She heard Mrs Scott take it away, and then the familiar noises of any house in the evening, the sounds of clearing in the kitchen, fires being set for the following day. Last of all, she heard Mrs Scott lock the door and climb the stairs to her own room at the end of the hall.

In the morning, Susan found Mrs Scott in the kitchen supervising the cook, whom Mrs Scott introduced as Mrs Foster. 'Mrs Foster doesn't live in,' she says. 'She comes over from a farm a mile or so hence.'

'Perhaps Mrs Foster can see me to Leith when she is done,' said Susan, smiling at the cook. 'I can find a carriage there, I think, to take me into town.'

'Och, Leith is miles from here, Ma'am,' said Mrs Scott. 'And Mrs Foster lives quite the other way. But if you have any letters, Mrs Foster will pass them to her brother who will take them with him when he next goes to town.'

Susan wrote to Jane and passed the letter to Mrs Scott with coins to pay for the postage. Mrs Scott handed the coins back, she said Doctor Knox paid for all the household expenses here. Susan considered writing to Robert, to ask him to come, but shame would not let her.

Days passed, and then a week, and then a month, and Robert did not come.

Susan now understood this was a prison of sorts, her marriage a sentence that had begun in that inn at Leith and would last until she died. It was all genteelly done, of course, nothing so coarse as locks or keys, threats of ill treatment or even outright refusal to let her leave. Mrs Scott was all smiles, and John the gardener and Elsie the housemaid were kind, but they were Susan's jailers nevertheless. If Susan said she would go for a walk, Mrs Scott would find a reason she was needed in the house. Elsie took her cloak for mending, and it never returned. John took her stout boots outside for cleaning, and Mrs Scott replaced them with pale satin slippers with kid leather soles, quite unsuited to the ground outside. Letters went out in Mrs Foster's pocket, but none ever returned.

Mrs Scott had sight of all her bodily functions, which Susan knew she reported to Robert, for when at last he came, he knew her courses had stopped and she was with child. He professed himself delighted, ignoring all Susan's weeping and protestations. He went to fetch Mrs Scott, who said Doctor Knox thought Susan had become overwrought; would she not take a seat while Mrs Scott fetched her something restorative? Mrs Scott was a great believer in restorative draughts in small glasses. Susan sometimes lost whole days to these sticky measures, waking the next morning with a pounding heart and a dry mouth, and no memory she could muster of going to bed.

Susan sat in the chair waiting for her draught, wondering whether she might have married a butcher, or a candlemaker, or a baker after all. She might have served in the shop then, gossiped with neighbours, ventured out into the streets with her basket to choose fish for the dinner. On Sundays she could stroll to the kirk with her husband, arm-in-arm.

In the morning, Robert was gone.

3

Blast Trauma

A MUFFLED BLAST ROCKED THE GROUND beneath Helen's feet as she skirted the edge of Hallglen Farm, lugging her sack of laundry on her back. A mile or so away, the canal navigators were making their way through near on half a mile of solid rock under Prospect Hill, and all because the landowner at Callendar didn't want to see the canal from the windows of his great house. He wrote to all his rich friends across the country, and they took up his case, for all he was nothing but a jumped-up coppersmith from Aberdeen. Now he was dead but still the canal must be hidden from view, no matter how many lives of Highlanders or Irish that might cost, to spare the feelings of his brats. Helen's father said they were dirt, the Forbes', just coves squatting on the lands of the rightful Earl, who had lost it all a century ago after leading his men into battle at Sheriffmuir.

The blasting was always going to take an age and so, spotting an opportunity – or perhaps a worse fate if he didn't act – the farmer at Hallglen had let the navvies erect huts and other shelters on his lower rigs. Some of these were snug enough, and built to stand a season or two, but many looked like to collapse at the first gust of wind, little more than rotted straw held together with a stick or two of wood and a length of twine. Some men had their families with them, but others were bunked in together, three or four six-foot men snoring and farting in a shelter not big enough to serve as a pigsty.

The roughest of the men had no want for Helen's services, but there were plenty who sought to keep their linens in as good order as they could, and Helen made the trip twice each week to pick up their dirty sarks and shifts and return them clean. She charged well enough, the navvies were well paid, and there was the chance to pick up cobbling jobs too, carrying the boots home for mending and bringing them back in a day or two with the linens.

The walk out from home was pleasant, this early in the summer, but the return was harder, the weight of the washing made worse by the fact it was so very noisome. Helen was glad indeed when the one-room cottage she shared with William came into sight.

Despite all her fears, William had not left his Nelly at the end of that harvest season in Redding in the year of James MacDougal's death. Instead, he had asked her to travel on with him, as his wife, when he went to sign up as a navvy on the Union Canal. The work would be hard, he said, but his back was strong, the money good and the food plentiful. Of course Helen agreed, she would have agreed to go to the moon and live on green cheese so long as William would be with her.

In fact, the canal-digging life turned out not to be for William. The navvies were great, strapping men who dug muck by the ton come rain, hail or shine, slogging their way through clay and rock and mud, armed only with picks and shovels. The work of field and harvest was nothing by comparison, and William's health did not stand up to the hard labour in the rain and slime and cold. His high spirits left him, and Helen saw she would have to find a way to persuade him he could leave the camp without losing face and come with her back to Redding to recover.

'We don't need much to get by,' she said. 'We could go on the tramp, hawking goods, maybe; you have a silver tongue, William, you'll charm the pennies out of those farm wives. And my father will always help us find work at the harvest or the tatties or the berries.'

It was nighttime, and Helen was helping William change a mustard plaster on his chest by the poor glow of a rushlight. William said nothing, and it seemed to Helen that he didn't want to meet her eye.

'Oh, Nelly,' he said at last, 'I have more than myself to keep.'

Helen frowned, not understanding.

William blushed red. 'I have a wife,' he said.

'I know,' said Helen. 'Me.'

'No, Nelly,' William said. 'Another wife. In Ireland. And two children. I send them money from my wages.'

Helen stared at him for a moment, and he grew redder still. Then she blew out the rushlight and lay down beside him in the dark, hearing her heart beat fast.

'Margaret,' she said. 'Is that her name? I've heard you say it in your prayers.'

'Aye,' William said. 'Margaret Coleman.'

Helen felt hollow, as she had in the days after Maisie had gone in the fire. 'Will you go back to her?' she asked. 'And your children?'

'No, Nelly, no!' William exclaimed, and he took hold of her, smearing a mess of mustard on her shift. 'We went our separate ways years back.'

'Why?' Helen was not reassured, not yet.

William let out a deep sigh, triggering a fit of coughing. When at last he got his breath back, he wheezed out an account of a fall-out with his wife's father over a piece of land that was in her dowry.

'She took her father's side,' William said. 'We married too hasty, when I left the militia, and after that she came to be disappointed in me. They thought I had more than I did. I'm well spoken, you see, but that's because I spent some time as manservant to a minister of religion. You know me, Nelly, I always have an eye to the main chance and I paid attention to the preacher and learned to speak fine and mind my manners. So ould man Coleman thought my father had money, and when he understood he did not, he tried to refuse me Margaret's portion.'

'Surely that would hurt his daughter as much as you,' Helen said.

'He said he'd keep her himself,' said William. 'He preferred to keep his wee parcel of land all together, you see. It makes more money that way.'

'So what happened?' Helen asked.

'I left,' said William. 'I had to get away, a man cannot live in his father-in-law's house under such conditions without losing his respect for himself. I wrote to Margaret to ask her to come, but she said no.'

Helen was struggling to sort it out in her mind. This Margaret Coleman had had everything – a piece of land meant for her, a strong and decent man for a husband, and bairnies – but she had chosen to turn her back on it all and remain in her father's house. Meanwhile, Helen had never had any tocher whatsoever, her man was a brute who beat her, her bairnies were all dead or taken away, and even though she had need of it, there was no place for her with her father. The only piece of luck she had ever had was meeting William.

Well, she thought then, *if she is so careless as to lose such a man, why should I scruple to take him for my own?* She felt anger warm in her chest and she raised her chin.

'You would have kept her if she came,' she said, 'and she chose not to, but instead she is with her father, and they have the bride portion that was owed to you. Why should that not keep her? How can you send money home when you don't have it?'

William looked thoughtful.

'Perhaps you're right, Nelly,' he said. 'I've always reckoned myself an honourable man, but it may be that I have been played for the fool.'

Mollified, Helen began again on her project to persuade him away from the navvy life, and William seemed relieved now to agree.

They did go on the tramp, for a bit, after that, buying clothes and other necessaries in the town of Falkirk, used but serviceable, and selling them round the farms and navvy camps. But then Helen's father, taking liking to William, said he would apprentice him as a cobbler and then he would have a more certain trade. They took a one-room cottage at Maddiston, a few miles from Peter's own, and for all it was a small and sooty and a tumble-down sort of place all together with a great lump in the wall where the chimney had slumped in, it was well situated by a spring and Helen saw that she could take in laundry too, work she liked well enough though many others hated it.

William went most days to Peter Gaff's to learn the cobbler's trade and Peter professed himself well pleased with him; he was a quick learner, he said, with quick, strong hands. Peter was able to take in a wheen more work, and there was plenty demand, what with the navvies getting so close now and all their families and followers, although enough of them went barefoot most of the year. There was enough to pay William an apprentice's wage, although Helen's brother John was put out, there had been no apprenticeship for him when he was of age, for all he had wanted it. John couldn't stay sore at William long, though, William was too good a companion, and the two men took to drinking and carousing on the occasional evening. Peter Gaff wouldn't have approved of course, he was a fell religious man, but Helen and William lived at enough of a distance that he need know nothing of it. William was a good reader and writer, and soon Peter was asking him to read from the Bible and say the Grace, for William had a fine way with words and remembered well his time with the minister in Ireland. After a while, William seemed to take a liking to the business, and Peter gave him his own Bible. Secretly, he congratulated himself on saving the soul of a heathen, Helen thought, although she didn't say as much to William, she had learned he had a high opinion of himself and she didn't want to drive a wedge between him and her father.

William's Bible was not there, that afternoon when Helen returned from Hallglen with her washing, which likely meant he had taken it to Father's, perhaps meaning to go out among the men to share a psalm or a lesson when the day's cobbling was done. There were plenty that liked that well enough, missing their home places and home kirks, and William was popular amongst them for his fine voice and ready smile. He wrote letters for them, too, taking a coin or two for payment; many of those boys would never see their mothers and fathers again, William's price was nothing when you thought how it kept those heartstrings connected, all the way across the sea to Carlingford or Carrickfergus. Not that all of the navvies were Irish, by any means – a great many were Highlanders or local men, although William said the Irish got the worst deal of it by far, most likely to be cheated by the foremen and blamed for any trouble that blew up within twenty miles. Helen knew that was true; listening to some of the village women you'd think the Irish were responsible for all the woes of the world, even as their own men took the briefest of pauses from beating them senseless or drinking themselves stupid to take their own chance at the wages and beef and beer the navvies got. They were as quick with their fists as any other, and careless with it, so that many came home with limbs missing, or stood charges for violence on a body.

Helen began to sort through the washing, taking care to empty each sack into its own pile so as not to muddle the garments on return to their owners. Then she fetched water from the spring, stirred the fire to life and filled the great pot that hung from the chimney by its chain. She dragged the washtub into position – this was just a barrel William and father had cut down for her and set into a sort of stand, with a cork she could take out to empty it – and fetched lye soap and her paddle while the water heated. She swung the pot out, tilted it on the chain, careful not to scald herself with any splashes, and set to. By the end of the day she had the lot washed, wrung out and hung up to dry, some on frames in the house and some on the lines outside.

William had still not returned and so Helen heated herself some stew and had just settled down to eat it when there came a knock at the door. It was a young lad, his eyes huge in his face and his breath coming short with the speed at which he must have been running.

'Mistress Burke?' he stammered out.

'Who's asking?' said Helen.

'Will you come to the camp at Hallglen?' he asked. 'There's been a terrible accident. Three men are dead. Mrs Lynch is asking for your help.'

'Is it her man?' Helen asked, throwing a few items into a sack and pulling her shawl about her.

'No,' the boy said, 'it's her lad.'

He set off like a hare with the hounds at his heels, and Helen was red-faced and panting before they'd gone half a mile. By the time they arrived at the camp, she thought her heart might burst. There were people milling around everywhere, a strange mix of anger and fear in the air, and yes, excitement too; plenty folk enjoyed any drama going, the gorier an accident the better. Helen paused for a moment to catch her breath, her hands on her knees, and when she straightened and stepped forward, she walked smack into a man.

'I'm sorry,' she stuttered, stepping back, but the man waved her apology away.

'You can run into me any time, my darlin,' he said.

Helen didn't know how to respond to this levity in the midst of disaster, but at last she decided a quick smile would do. She knew the man, an Irishman like William, but there the resemblance ended. Where William was broad and fair and smiling, this creature was sleek and sly and quick to temper. He was well known among the teams, his anger always simmering just below the surface until something might come along and cause offence. His weaselly face bore the ghosts of many past quarrels, with a badly healed scar on his brow and another skittering down the margin of his eye; he was lucky not to have lost it by the look of things.

Helen had never liked this man and tried to steer clear, but it seemed she had judged her response correctly, he made an exaggerated bow and waved her towards the Lynches' shelter. Once she stepped inside, the navvy was forgotten.

Edward Lynch had been broken as if he were a doll thrown on the floor by a child in a pet. His limbs lay at odd angles, the skin bloody and torn and one hand quite gone. The angle of his head was not natural, and everywhere were burns and cuts, dark and clotted with blood and dirt and gravel. Someone had begged trestles from somewhere, and he lay on the board they'd used to carry him down, his mother standing over him, keening. When Helen spoke her name, she threw herself into her arms.

Helen soothed the woman as best she could and then she spoke firmly to her. 'Cloths, and straw, and water,' she said. Then she raised her voice and spoke to the others. 'Leave us be for now,' she told them. 'We will see to him.'

The mourners filed out and the poor mother shuffled back with cloths and water and straw. Helen put her in a seat and poured her a cup of whisky. Then she set to and began to clean the lad, straightening his poor limbs as best she could, although they had begun to grow stiff. She rolled him this way and that to get the shroud under him, wrapping him with the missing hand under his good one. By the time she was done, he looked more peaceful than she could have hoped.

Just as she finished her task and began to clear up the straw for the fire, the sacking over the door was pulled back and William came in. The poor mother raised her head and began her sobbing anew at the sight of another friendly face.

William sat on a tree stump they were using as a stool and patted the woman's hand. 'A day of lamenting,' he said. 'A great day of lamenting indeed.' He brought his Bible out from a satchel, opened it, and began to read.

'For if we believe that Jesus died and rose again, even so them also which sleep in Jesus will God bring with him. For this we say unto you by the word of the Lord, that we which are alive and remain unto the coming of the Lord shall not prevent them which are asleep. For the Lord himself shall descend from heaven

with a shout, with the voice of the archangel, and with the trump of God: and the dead in Christ shall rise first: Then we which are alive and remain shall be caught up together with them in the clouds, to meet the Lord in the air: and so shall we ever be with the Lord.'

The woman stood then and crossed to look on her lad, quiet now and drawn into herself. William took Helen's arm and they moved towards the entrance of the hut.

'We'll give you a moment alone, Nora,' he said, 'and then we'll send in the others.'

The woman nodded, and Helen and William stepped out through the low opening. A man with tear tracks in the dirt of his face stepped up and clapped William on the back, handing over a purse of coin before stepping back and bowing his head. William nodded and took Helen's arm to leave.

It was a sombre walk home. Neither Helen nor William had much to say. It was cold in the house, the fire gone out, but they fell into bed and clung together until they were warm.

'Poor lad,' Helen said. 'I never saw the like of it. What happened?'

'An accident with the blasting,' William said. 'Three of them were in there when a charge went off early. He wasn't the worst of them, if the foreman was to be believed. He said he threw up when he saw what was left of the frontmost man, and he's a coarse devil himself, it would take much to shock him.'

Helen shuddered.

'Still, we gave them comfort, Nelly,' William said. 'We're a good team, are we not? I think we should start making plans for our future. I'm near finished learning the cobbling, we could go to my brother in Edinburgh and make our fortune.' He kissed her neck and moulded himself around her back. Within a moment he was snoring.

The next day Helen dallied about the house. There was no point taking the laundry to the camp, no one would be seeking it today. Instead, she decided to walk to her father's and see the bairns.

When she arrived, she saw she'd been beaten to it by a neighbouring wife, a biddy she couldn't stand. The woman was breathless with excitement, leaning over William as she shared the juicy tidbit she'd had from the camp that morning.

'Clean gone,' she said. 'Not the young lad, his family were keeping watch, but the others had no one, or the watchers were gone in drink, you know the Irish—' She blushed, realising her blunder, but in a moment she got past it, the news was too good not to share. 'Aye,' she said triumphantly, 'the bodies were gone! The resurrection men had had them, what do you think of that?'

Peter Gaff blew out his breath so his cheeks puffed up. 'The longer I live,' he said, 'the less I understand my fellow man.'

4

Primigravida

AS THE OLD YEAR DREW TO A CLOSE and the new one began, it seemed to Susan that life began to draw in around them at Lillypot, trapping them there so they were all imprisoned together.

In the first days of the year it rained and rained, so that the road churned up and Mrs Foster struggled across the fields with her skirts tied around her waist and sacking bound around her legs. As January wore on, it froze, and then at the start of February the snow set in, so Mrs Foster could not come at all for three weeks together. For some days even John could not get out for supplies, and Mrs Scott not only had to turn cook, but had only the preserved stuff in the pantry at her disposal.

It made little difference to Susan what Mrs Scott cooked, as she could not eat anything anyway. She had been wretched for weeks, vomiting until her head swam and the floor seemed to pitch and sway below her feet like the deck of a ship. The muscles in her belly hurt from the retching and it felt as though the very nerves of her stomach were aflame.

Mrs Scott fussed over her like a mother hen, clucking worriedly as all of Susan but her belly grew thinner and paler and dark rings bloomed beneath her eyes. She brewed infusions of mint or ginger to settle her stomach, baked dry biscuits for her to nibble, had Mrs Foster cook her small bland meals and clear broths and chamomile jellies, in hope she might be able to keep them down. It was to little avail. The sickness persisted despite all their efforts, until Susan woke one day to find it a little less, and the next day less still, and a week or so later she found she could eat, and drink, and make her way from the sofa to an armchair without worrying that she would lose her footing altogether and crash to the floor.

After that it seemed that all was growing and growing, Susan's body swelling faster than she ever thought possible, so Mrs Scott had to let out the seams on all her gowns and connive clever ways with net and lace to trim her bodices so her bosom might be decently covered. Fine red lines appeared on her flanks and her breasts and her back ached, while strange flutterings in her belly gave way to more definite jabs and proddings that Susan found odd and unsettling at first, only growing used to them as the weeks went on.

In the second week of April, there was a fluster as a cart pulled up outside the house. Having tied up his horse at the gate, the carter tramped to the door and called for Mrs Scott. She read the note he handed her and called for John to help the man unload. Then she and Elsie began to push the furniture in the dining room back against the walls and roll back the carpet while the men carried in great heavy chests and crates, piling them up in the middle of the floor.

'Careful, John,' Mrs Scott admonished as the two men set down a crate with a thud. 'Those are the Doctor's things in there. Dinnae break them!'

When all the crates were stacked to Mrs Scott's satisfaction, two trunks and a carpet bag appeared. Mrs Scott produced a purse from somewhere about her person and paid the carter while John carried the trunks up the stairs and into the room beside Susan's. Mrs Scott dispatched Elsie to lay Robert's things on the bed and ascertain what might need ironed before it was hung in the press. Elsie hefted the carpet bag and scuttled up the stairs.

'I'll send John out for a chicken,' Mrs Scott said to Susan. 'Doctor Knox likes a chicken for his dinner. I'll have the butcher come by next week and we can place a proper order for the next few months.'

'Months?' Susan said.

Mrs Scott looked at as though she was soft in the head.

'Doctor Knox will be here until well on in the autumn,' she said. 'Surely you knew that? There's no teaching in summer. It's too hot, for . . . och, you know.'

But Susan didn't know, and eventually Mrs Scott took pity on her.

'The bodies dinnae keep in the warm,' she said. 'That's what they do, isn't it? Cut up dead bodies so they can learn the doctoring.'

'Yes,' Susan said. 'Quite.' In truth, she had never thought much about what anatomists did. She had always pictured Robert working with a pen and paper, making notes or annotating diagrams. Of course, she knew he must also wield a scalpel but she couldn't quite imagine the scene, and she had no real wish to; his hands touched her own flesh, after all.

In the end Robert did not arrive that night but the next, and he was in fine fettle, throwing off his jacket and loosening the stock at his throat even as he came through the door. He kissed Susan soundly and looked her up and down, patting her belly delightedly and saying he had missed her but was happy to find her so well and so comely, he knew he had been right that this was the place for her with its sweet air and clean water. He wished he could always be at Lillypot himself, he said, he never could relax in the city, always yearning for the time when he could lock the door of his rooms and come here to his real home.

Mrs Foster produced a good dinner and Robert and Susan ate together in the kitchen, very informally, since the dining room was full of crates. Those contained books and other materials for Robert's great project, he told Susan, the work he must do to persuade the College of Surgeons to build a proper museum for the collection of his friend and partner John Barclay. Robert had in fact left the last few weeks of teaching to an assistant, the better to focus on instructions for how the museum should be designed to ensure it properly housed the collection and supported the teaching of anatomy. The lecture season had already been a great success, he said, with more students attending his and Barclay's classes than any other in the city and a fine profit in the bank. Now he had other work to do, but plenty of time to do it, and hadn't they managed things well so that he could be here at Lillypot with Susan until her lying-in was past?

Susan smiled a little queasily; she was very uncertain of the precise details of lying-in. One or two attempts at extricating information from Mrs Scott had led her no further than understanding that, before the thing that happened *happened*, she should braid her hair because otherwise it might become so knotted they would have to cut it off. That being largely useless information, she had questioned Elsie a bit while she set the fire of an evening. Despite having siblings, Elsie didn't know a lot more than Susan herself, except for the general observations that there would 'be Hell to pay' and that babies 'got out the way they got in', but Elsie could not be quite sure how that was. Susan now knew how they got in – she did her best to communicate this to Elsie – but she couldn't see how the parts involved in that business could possibly provide a route out for a full-grown infant. Robert would know, presumably, and at some point Susan would have to find a way to swallow her horror enough to ask him.

Robert refilled his wine glass, sat back in his chair and looked quizzically at Susan, who realised she had not been listening for the last few moments.

'Have I spoken too much of work?' Robert asked. 'If I have, then I'm sorry. It is in my nature, I think, to focus too much on it and too little on pleasure. Perhaps I should take a holiday before I begin my writing. Would you like a trip to the sea?'

Susan forgot all her worries then, in the thought of a trip away from Lillypot, and she readily agreed. Robert promised to make arrangements for them to set out three days hence. Mrs Scott could have a holiday, he said, and John and Elsie, and return to see their people.

The place Robert chose was close, to the northwest of the city, in a wee village called Cramond. There was an inn where they lodged, with a great sandy beach a few minutes' stroll away, and an island a little distance from the shore. Robert said it was possible to walk across the sand to the island, when the tide was out.

They arrived in time for dinner and went early to bed, Susan worn out by the carriage journey and Robert happy with a jug of wine and a good lantern for reading by. The next day, after they had breakfasted, they walked to the sea. It was a bright day, and warm, but Robert said the water would be frigid, it would not warm up until late in the summer. It would be too cold to bathe, he said, but then some spirit of wildness took hold of him and he stripped off his clothes to his underpants and ran into the sea.

Susan stood and watched, laughing, as he made his way out into the deeper water and at last dived in. Then, suddenly, she couldn't bear not to be in the water herself. She kicked off her shoes and stockings, stripped off her coat and frock, kilted her shift up to her waist and waded in up to her knees.

The first touch of the water was hot and cold, like a brand, but in a few moments Susan's feet seemed to grow used to it. She was always too warm, anyway, these last months, and the cold water soothed her feet and ankles, silly stems struggling under the weight of her swelling body. She began to plough through the water, wishing she could go in further, let the water take the weight of her and soothe the grinding ache that was always there in her hips and back. She waded a little deeper, to the thighs, but then a wave surprised her, wetting her shift and taking her breath away with its cold touch on her belly. She made her way out just a little, dug her feet into the sand, leaned back and breathed as deeply as she could.

Robert did not last much longer, coming out of the water at a run, gasping and shaking. They bundled themselves into their clothes as best they could, hands clumsy with cold and skin sticky with wet and salt, and then they made their way to the inn as fast as Susan could walk. Robert called for hot water and a tub, and when it arrived they fell about laughing, the tub was nothing more than a barrel cut in half. They took turns standing in it to sponge each other down, breathless with mirth and tickling and embarrassment, and then they went to bed, more at ease with one another than they had ever been before.

The rest of the trip passed in much the same way. Robert walked to the island and back at low tide while Susan looked in rockpools and sunned herself on the sands. They walked to see a mill driven by a man-made fall on the river and picnicked on the banks. On the last day the weather broke and Robert

61

said he would teach Susan to play chess in the inn, but she managed to prevail upon him to play cards instead, teaching him Piquet and then, when he professed himself exhausted by the counting, beating him roundly at Vingt-et-un. She had so much money off him in the end that he promised her his mother's jewellery box if only she wouldn't ruin him by demanding payment. He said it in jest but then he seemed to grow thoughtful; Susan should have a share of his mother's jewels, he said, was there anything she would especially like? Susan said she would like the locket his mother sometimes wore, made of clear rock crystal, she had always said it was lucky. Robert said he would send for it when they got home, but he didn't believe in luck, just science, and he hoped Susan wouldn't turn out to be a subscriber to quackery.

When the holiday was over and they were installed again at Lillypot, Susan half-expected that the easy atmosphere between them would vanish, but it seemed Robert did feel at ease there, where there was no formality and his temper barely showed. The second day back, he began the work of unpacking his cases, stacking books and papers in piles and placing odd bones in grids on the table. Susan asked if she could help, she wrote a fair hand, and he agreed and gave her pages and pages of words to copy out in separate lists ordered according to a set of symbols he marked against them. He said she should stop if she was tired, and indeed she found she could not sit more than an hour or two together before she had to move about a while and then find a new position to sit in that let her be comfortable again.

At night Robert and Susan sat together, Robert in his shirt sleeves with his collar open and Susan in a shift and dressing gown, and they played cards or he read to her, pausing now and then to help ease the aches and stiffness in her back and feet with the pressure of his hands.

Susan felt she would split apart if she grew much more. Mrs Scott said as much, one evening, as Susan and Robert sat together in the parlour. She had come to show Susan her work in letting out her dresses yet again, the second time in two weeks.

'Is there any way you could have mistaken your dates?' she asked, with a fretful glance at Susan's belly.

Robert took offence at that, speaking sharply to Mrs Scott, who quickly withdrew, but when she was gone he frowned at Susan.

'Come over here to the sofa,' he said, and he helped her lower herself onto the cushions. Then his hands were on her belly, through her shift, and she saw him frown in concentration as he pressed and prodded here and there. He got up and left the room, returning with a sheet of parchment he rolled into a cone. He pressed one end to her belly and bent an ear to the other, moving it here and there, holding his hand at Susan's wrist all the while.

'What is it?' Susan asked, feeling her heart flutter in panic. 'Robert? Is something wrong?'

'No,' said Robert. 'At least ... No. But I think you have two in there, my love.'

'Two?' Susan couldn't quite make sense of it.

'Two,' Robert said. 'Twins. Here—' He wove Susan's fingers through his own and pressed her hands over her belly, on opposite sides, one high and one low. 'One head is here,' he said, 'and another here.'

Susan tried to feel, but her fingers told her nothing.

'Could you hear them?' she asked. 'With the paper?'

Robert's laugh broke the tension. 'I thought perhaps I might hear their hearts beat,' he said. 'But I couldn't.'

Susan had an idea. 'Are there pictures?' she asked. 'In your books? That show what a woman with child looks like, inside?'

Robert thought for a moment. 'Yes,' he said. 'Smellie. Not Hunter.' The last he said with a shake of his head, and then he left the room. Susan kept rubbing her fingers across her belly but still she struggled to make any sense of the shapes below her skin.

A few minutes later, Robert was back with a slim volume.

'It's old,' said Susan.

'Yes,' said Robert. 'But it's still the best we have.'

He sat down beside Susan and leafed through the pages. Finding what he sought, he turned the book so that she could see.

'The ninth table,' Susan read. Opposite was an image of an infant, lying head down and facing away, inside a shape like an egg balanced on the narrow end.

'That's a babe at term,' Robert said. 'Its head is down, do you see? Ready to be born.' He traced the egg shape around the infant with his finger. 'This is its mother's womb.'

Susan touched the drawing where a branching image like a tree sat above the feet of the infant. 'What's that?' she asked.

'The afterbirth,' Robert said. 'The proper name is *placenta*. It's the link between the babe and its mother. One side is attached to the womb – here, see – and the babe is attached by its navel cord, here. That gives the means for the mother's body to nourish the babe. There is a sac, you see, around all, and the waters are inside it.'

'What are these?' Susan asked, pointing at dark shapes below the babe that looked like the wings of a moth.

'The mother's hip bones, and her pelvis,' Robert said.

'And this?' Susan pointed at an odd shape, a little like a mouth, directly under the child's head.

'The neck of the womb and the birth passage,' Robert said. 'When the child is ready to be born, the womb contracts – that is the reason for the birth pains – and the neck of the womb opens wide so the child can enter the birth passage.'

'What happens then?' Susan asked.

Robert looked at her thoughtfully and then turned the pages of the book.

'This shows what happens,' he said. He showed her a picture of the child seen from the side, its head tilted back, and briefly he explained its journey downwards through the birth canal. Then he turned to another drawing of a woman's privy parts and pointed out how they were swollen, with the crown of the infant's head visible as it made its way into the world.

Susan felt a little faint.

'I'm sorry if I have shocked you,' Robert said. 'I didn't know you didn't know this.'

'No one told me,' said Susan.

'No,' said Robert. 'I suppose no one did. It's all perfectly natural. We were all born this way.'

Susan didn't say what perhaps they both were thinking; her own mother had not survived the birth of her younger brother, and he had followed her to her grave.

'Is there a woman with two?' Susan asked. 'In the book?'

Robert looked at a contents list and turned the pages again. Here the image was of two babes, one head down and one head up.

'Some twins have two afterbirths,' he said. 'Some share only one. Those are the ones we call identical. I don't think there is a way of knowing before they are born.'

Susan touched the image with a finger. 'May I have the book to read?' she asked.

Robert closed it sharply. 'I do not think it wise,' he said. 'It is a treatise for midwives to hone their skills, and so it dwells on difficult cases. I do not want you doing likewise.' He went out of the room, returning without the book.

On his return, Robert sat down at the desk and began to trim a fresh quill.

'Twins are often born early,' he said. 'And I will ask Mrs Scott to make enquiries about a wet nurse to help you.' He smiled at Susan, but she thought there was something strained in the smile.

'Lots of mothers have two,' Susan said. 'Don't they?'

'Yes,' said Robert. 'Lots.' He picked up his pen and began to write. Susan left him there and climbed the stairs to bed, weary to the bone.

It transpired that Robert's letter was to a man he knew, a Frenchman who called himself an *accoucheur*. This man was to attend Susan in her confinement. He wrote to Robert to advise they should engage a clean and competent midwife, and they should tell the woman that the reckoning was like to be two or three weeks before it might normally be expected. They should send for him only when Susan's Time was upon her. There would be ample time for him to reach them and he would rest in the house until his assistance was needed, which he boasted he could perfectly judge from the cries of the labouring mother. For the last weeks, he advised that Susan rest at home, wearing only soft stays and bedgowns, and take her exercise only in the grounds of the house. He advised on diet and prescriptions for any costiveness, and he sent great lengthy instructions for the preparation of the birthing chamber and the gathering of necessities for mother and babes.

Susan's cheeks burned at the thought of a man taking any involvement in matters. She thought Mrs Scott shocked at the idea, too, but that was balanced by her obvious delight in having a programme of activity to manage. Everyone else in the house was busy, it seemed, Robert with his museum project, and the servants with their work and their preparations; only Susan seemed to feel the time so very long. Her legs hurt, her ribs hurt, her skin felt tender and stretched, she couldn't sleep or even sit comfortably without rising every few moments as a new ache or cramp assailed her. At times it seemed her innards had been entirely taken over. Mrs Scott said it was as well she was in her bedgown, she was so very large.

At the start of July the midwife arrived and was installed in the stifling attic with Elsie. She was a comfortable woman and Susan felt calmed by her presence. She helped Mrs Scott to ready the birthing room and wash and press the linens she had procured. She set Susan herself to folding these and putting them away, and she found her many other tasks to use the regular fits of nervous energy with which she found herself possessed. It seemed that Robert withdrew from Susan with her arrival, only appearing out of his study in the dining room now and then, apparently interested to have the opportunity to question and quiz the midwife about her experience, the signs by which she should recognise this or that phenomenon, cases she had managed previously. He seemed well enough satisfied, and the midwife herself said she was perfectly happy to refer to an accoucheur if she found herself at all difficulted; she had done so before and all cases had ended happily. She seemed determined to repeat to Susan that she had delivered many women of two and even three babes; one had delivered no fewer than three sets of twins, in fact, and another mother prone to twins had by that means increased her family by four children within fifteen months. Had they other children? Susan asked. The midwife said that most did, in her experience twins were more common in later births, but she had heard of first-time mothers delivering twins perfectly safely, of course she had.

At long last Susan rose one day to find her daily discomforts replaced with stronger pains in her belly and thighs, which became stronger and more frequent as the day wore on so that she groaned and struggled to move her body into any position in which she might find relief. The midwife helped her walk around the chamber until the pains became too strong, and then she helped her kneel before the bed.

Susan had forgotten all about the accoucheur, but it seemed that Robert must have sent for him as he planned, as long hours later, towards the next morning, she felt a change in the pressure in her loins and cried out in pain and panic, and a moment or two later the man entered the room with Robert behind him and a great leather bag in his hands. He had the midwife help him lift Susan onto the bed and onto her back. Susan howled at the increase in pain and pressure and the midwife protested that she could manage a while yet, but the man cut her short, demanding a clean bedsheet to spare Susan the sight of his work. From then Susan could no longer hold the thread of their discussions, focused only on the awful pressure that seemed ready to tear her asunder as her body strained and fought to expel its burden. She heard her own voice cry out, overwhelmed by pain, and then there was one more pain, one more great effort, a dreadful burning sensation as something in her split apart, and she heard the thin, reedy cry of an infant. The accoucheur handed the child to the midwife, who tied off its birth cord and cut it with scissors. Then she handed it to Robert, before she turned to aid the accoucheur with the delivery of the second twin.

The man's hands were above the sheet on Susan's belly now, feeling here and there. He said something to Robert that might as well have been in Hebrew for all Susan could under-stand it, and then he took a bottle from his bag and poured a dose of something into a glass. The midwife held it to Susan's lips and Susan did her best to swallow, choking as another great pain rolled across her belly and flanks. The midwife put something between her teeth and then she was being pulled to the end of the bed so the midwife could climb up behind her, holding her steady with her hands behind her knees. With one hand, the accoucheur began to press on her belly, and then there was an awful intrusion, his hand slid through her poor abused privy parts, hurting her so badly she howled through the thing between her teeth, and then his hand was in the very body of her, rummaging and fumbling. Another pain came and the man grunted while Susan gave a mangled howl, and then he was pressing and pulling all at once, outside and in, until something moved downwards and outwards and Susan felt her privy parts stretch and fill again. There was a hot gush of fluid, but the pressure didn't go. The accoucheur was still tugging and pulling and she was being ripped asunder again – she would surely die now, no one could survive this agony. And indeed it seemed she *was* dying; her vision was fuzzy and her lips were numb, and she closed her eyes on blessed darkness.

When Susan woke, she was in bed, in her own bed, and the midwife sat in a chair beside her.

'Am I dead?' Susan asked stupidly. Her voice was cracked and broken.

'Heavens, no,' said the midwife. 'You had a very severe time, but it is over now and you will be well again when you have had your rest.'

'Where are the babes?' Susan asked.

'Tomorrow,' the midwife said, 'sleep now.'

In the morning Susan woke to a baby's cry and struggled to rise, crying out in pain as she put her weight on her nether parts. The midwife caught her by the shoulders and helped her back down, telling her it was normal, she had torn a little and bruised much, and the accoucheur had placed some stitches there. It would be sore for some weeks, and hot at first, but it would heal.

Then the midwife brought her the first twin, a little boy. She looked for the second, but the midwife shook her head.

'Now you must be brave,' she said. 'The other was in a difficult position, and it was a dreadful effort for him to be born. The accoucheur got him out as quickly as he could, and Doctor Knox did all he could for him, but nothing they tried could get him breathing.'

Susan stared.

'It happens,' the midwife said. 'Even with one. But it's harder on twins if they share the afterbirth.'

Susan felt the tears come then, and the woman hugged her and soothed her. Then the baby began to cry and the midwife helped her put him to the breast.

'I'm sorry,' Susan said.

'What for, lass?' the midwife asked. 'It was a hard one, a first birth and twins. Your man the Doctor was that afraid for you.'

'I won't be able to have more children, will I?' Susan asked. The memory of the accoucheur's hand in her belly made her gag, almost; she was convinced she must have been damaged beyond repair.

'No reason why not,' the midwife said. 'It'll go easier, another time, you'll see. It's bound to.'

Susan finished feeding the baby, and the midwife took him and put him in his cradle.

'Where is . . . his brother now?' Susan asked.

'Doctor Knox took him,' the midwife said. 'He's gone back to the city. He sat with you all night, and he only left when he knew you were safe. He'll leave you to recover for a while, he says. It's the best way. I'm here, and I'll take good care of you.'

5

Nausea

THE DAWN LIGHT WAS A MEALY GREY and Helen yawned and stumbled over her own feet as she made her way to the Lawnmarket. First she went by the West Bow, but the crowd was so dense that she could not reach above half way. She retraced her steps through the Grassmarket instead, climbing up the steep wynds and out through Blair's Close, squeezing her way back through the crowd and up to the Castlehill. From there she had a clear view of the scaffold where Andrew Fullarton would meet his Maker at nine o' clock that morning.

Some of the sightseers had been gathered since the night before; William had seen them as he made his way home from a prayer meeting. The public houses were closing and they came spilling out, singing and dancing and cheering, he'd said, set to continue the revelry as long as they could, before the citizens of the upper stories of the Lawnmarket began emptying their chamber pots out on their heads. They would all have had a bottle or two tucked in their pockets and shawls to fend off the cold, no doubt, as they dozed away the few hours till dawn in a doorway, or curled against the barriers put up ahead to contain the crowds.

Their persistence had paid off, numbers had swelled enormously since the dawn and the overnighters had the best view by far. There hadn't been a hanging in Edinburgh for more than a year, just reprieve after reprieve, and folk were fair daft to see a man suffer his fate. This was a brute, they said, to be hanged for Highway Robbery, having assaulted a poor cowherd on his way home from Lauder fair in the Borders to St Leonard's in the south of town. Fullarton was with two others, and they wounded the cowherd most grievously, making off with his money, the stock from his neck, and his umbrella. Fullarton took his sentence stoutly enough, folk said, but his wife fell about in hysterics as the judge told him to lay aside any hope.

Helen had arrived at her place some time before six, and had entertainment enough that she did not feel the first hour of waiting long. There were churchmen of every persuasion preaching, some folk singing psalms and others rowdy choruses, and the occasional scuffle breaking out as scuffles will in any great crowd. The mood was good, though, in the main, with plenty of women and children among the gathering to keep it so.

After the bell of St Giles struck seven, the windows in the upper stories of the houses on either side of the Lawnmarket and Castlehill began to open and the gentry appeared in their finery, having paid handsomely for the right to watch the business from the comfort of a chair. Some of them threw coins into the crowd and laughed to see the scramble that resulted. One woman had a most peculiar instrument, a pair of small, shiny metal things like tumblers, fixed together in the middle, which she held in front of her eyes, the better, Helen thought, to see. Her coat and hat were very fine, but showy, and Helen wondered if she was a lady, or just a very successful hoor.

The last hour dragged on, the boredom only relieved around the half hour when a girl fainted and was passed hand-over-hand above the heads of the crowd, all the way from below Riddle's Court back to the Castlehill. There was great laughter and swaying in the mob then, but the girl was passed carefully enough and set down near Helen, where there was more space. She seemed well enough, and even upset that she had lost her place. Her faint had likely been due to her hangover rather than any finer feelings, and indeed she soon ploughed forward again and Helen lost sight of her in the crowd.

The day brightened a bit after that and then the bell struck eight. There was a great cheer and the condemned man appeared on the scaffold, his hands already bound. A hush came over the crowd then, as someone spoke, but it seemed it was prayers or other religious observances that were to happen next, and the hisses and cat-calls and jeers began again, and a few near the front threw rotten cabbages and other muck onto the scaffold.

When the prayers were finished, Fullarton himself came to the barrier at the front of the scaffold and began to address the crowd. Helen couldn't hear him, she was too far away, but his words were repeated back and back again, like a wind rippling through the barley crop. It was fell religious stuff, how he had kept bad company and broken the Sabbath and committed drunkenness, that was why he had committed his crime, he said, and then he said he beseeched them all, every last man, woman and child among them, to learn from his bad example and never do likewise. Then he was seen to make his farewells to those around him before he mounted the drop, where the hangman began to make his preparations. Someone in the crowd shouted, 'Bonnets off!' and it was picked up and shouted again and again, and everywhere heads were bared, and bald pates and uncovered hair gleamed in the weak sun.

All the time Fullarton's legs were being tied, the hood placed over his head and the noose laid and tightened around his neck, it seemed that the man was praying most fervently. At last he gave the signal, and he dropped. A cry came from the crowd, but there was not a twitch from the body thereafter, and it seemed Fullarton had died without a struggle. Some were disappointed, it seemed; the mood changed in an instant and the jeers began again, aimed at the hangman this time, for depriving them of the spectacle they had expected.

Helen was no longer enjoying herself. There had been no show, no bravado at all in the man. No villain at all really, just a lad foolish enough to think a few shillings and a cowherd's umbrella worth the risk of a meeting with the hangman. He had had youth and health and good looks, and a wife who loved him, and now he had a stretched neck and was nothing at all. Wearily, Helen turned and began to make her way through the crowd and back towards Blair's Close. Just ahead, the workmen digging the new road around the Castle Rock hefted up their picks and shovels and began again. A hawker lad with a tray of pamphlets yelled as she passed, 'ANDREW FULLARTON'S Last Dying Confession!' and Helen yelped and pressed a hand to her bad ear, it still hurt sometimes if a noise was too loud or too close.

When she reached the Grassmarket, it was alive with the din and stink of trade, every vendor of eatables and drinkables in the city seemed to be betting that the hanging would have left folk with an appetite and a thirst. The smells of roast meat and fried pastry and pickled whelks fought with the spices of cakes and puddings, turning Helen's stomach, and she hurried on until she heard her name called from an ale stall.

'Were you at the hanging, Nelly?' Helen was *Nelly* to everyone here, it was almost as though she had left her old self behind when they left Redding and came to Edinburgh. William had quickly become a well-kent face, between his cobbling and his Bible-reading, but Helen recognised this man as one who'd come to the house for drinking, not for prayers.

'I was,' she said. 'It was a sorry matter, though.'

'I heard it was a glum business,' the man said. 'Too godly, maybe, for dancing, was he?' He laughed heartily at his own joke and gestured to Helen with his ladle.

'Thank you,' she said. 'And I need spunks, too, if you have any.'

The man handed over the ale cup and the matches, and took payment only for the latter. The ale was good, and she felt her stomach settle.

'It's fair unsettled you,' the ale-man said, watching her. 'I took you for a woman with a strong stomach, Nelly. There's not a little Burke on the way, is there?'

'No,' Helen said, finishing her ale and handing it back. 'Just tired is all, and that's fair refreshed me. I thank you.'

When she had taken leave of the man and walked on, Helen found his words still running round her head. It had not occurred to her before now, but the last time she had fallen with child was before James MacDougal's last terrible beating of her. She hadn't looked to, and William said he was not sorry either that they had never conceived; they had spent so many years on the move and a child would have made a hard life harder. Perhaps James had shaken loose more than her eardrum, she thought, but maybe it made no difference, since everyone thought she was such a poor mother that her babes must be taken from her, just because of one accident that could have happened to anyone.

Back at their lodgings, there was no sign of William. Helen thought about crawling back into bed for an hour or two's kip, but then she decided she would be as well to set out again and take advantage of the crowds along with the other traders. Not the used clothes today, she thought – no one would be looking for those after a hanging – a souvenir would be what they were after, to remember the occasion by. She fetched a peddling tray they had, and began to lay out on it the small items that William made with off-cuts of leather from the cobbling, tobacco pouches and coin purses and needle cases and book markers for Bibles, and a small set of cases for calling cards that had a pattern stamped along each side and sold for a premium, calling cards being the business of those with more money than most of Helen's customers. Helen wished she had thought to ask William to stamp the date on the items, that way she could have asked a penny or two more for a thing folk could get out to show others when they told them they had witnessed the end of Andrew Fullarton.

Helen stuffed a handful of coins in her pocket for change, hefted the tray and set out again for the Grassmarket. The bulk of the crowd had abandoned the Lawnmarket now and made their way down in search of food and drink, and the stalls and carts were doing a roaring trade. Keeping a weather eye out for thieves, Helen made her way through the crowd, calling out her wares. Before long she had sold several of her pouches, all her purses – she always put a ha'penny in for luck, increasing the price by a penny to compensate – and even one of the calling card cases. That one had gone to a finely-dressed woman wearing patches on her face in the shape of hearts who said her gentlemen would be excited by an item from the hanging, some of them liked to feel a ligature around their own necks. Helen charged a fine price and was delighted by the transaction, even if she preferred not to think of the gentlemen. She hoped she would never have to make her living by any such trade.

A few more sales of the smaller pieces and Helen felt herself flagging. A printer lad appeared in her path, hawking an account of the hanging; the printers had outdone themselves getting that off the presses when it had only happened that morning, and the crowd fair flocked to get hold of a copy. Helen's own purse was heavy against her thigh and she decided she had done enough for the day. She made her way to a pie stall and bought a fine pie for herself and William, steak and kidney, with a baked potato each from another trader that would eke the meal out for two days at least. Then she bought a piggy of ale and one of whisky and made her way home with her tray of bounty.

Helen's good humour was dented a little when she pushed open the door and found William seated at the table with another man, and both in their cups.

'Nelly!' William exclaimed with a great grin on his face like a baby with a full napkin. 'Come and meet my friend. You'll never guess his name, it's only ... *William*!' He broke out laughing at that, delighted to have met a namesake, despite there being hundreds, if not thousands of them in the city. If Helen went in conniptions every time she met another Helen, she thought, she'd be carted off to the Lunatic Asylum in no time at all.

The other William got to his feet and made a drunken attempt at a bow, which set William off laughing again.

'William Hare, Mistress,' the man said. 'At your service.'

He needn't have bothered with his pantomime; Helen knew fine who he was. He was the navvy from the canal with the scarred face and the hot temper, the one she had collided with on that awful night when the Lynch lad was ripped to pieces in the tunnel explosion. She gave him a tight little smile and set to unpacking her tray, laying the food on the table and putting the unsold stock to one side for sorting. She hoped the man did not intend to stay to eat; that way there would be nothing left for tomorrow, and Helen's plans for a day spent in her nightgown would be for naught.

She needn't have worried, however, the men were too far gone in drink to want her pie, though they were glad enough to make a start on her whisky when their own was done. Helen poured herself a big tumbler of her own to last the evening, and then she settled down to work her way through a plate of pie and a tattie while they continued their ramblings and rantings. William was telling again the story of his father-in-law in Ireland and how he had lost all that was rightfully his, and the other William was swearing and cursing the way things were in Ireland, so bad that any man with an ounce of sense had no choice but to leave, as he saw it. He had found a great place here in Edinburgh, he said, with a woman called Margaret Laird who was Irish too, they had known each other growing up, although she was married to a Scotsman now and settled here. They had a lodging house in the West Port, he said, five beds in one room and a double in another, and Margaret gave good prices to any Irish folk who wished to stay with them. In fact, he said, why didn't Burke and Nelly think about coming there to stay?

William seemed quite taken by that idea but Helen said she liked the place they had well enough, it had all they needed and could keep themselves to themselves. William said it was mighty expensive to live in their own lodging, though, it might be cheaper to have a room in a larger place, if the company was good. William Hare suggested they go and see this Laird woman, right then and there, to see what they made of her and the place. Helen said no, she was tired and for her bed, but she readily agreed to William going, she was only too pleased to be shot of them and have some peace. And so they buttoned themselves into their jackets and set out, leaving Helen to finish her pie in blessed silence.

Helen was settling down to finish the last of the whisky in the piggy when there came a chap at the door. Sighing, she got up to open it, expecting to see William, back again and ready to drag her out, but instead she was met with a filthy face and a grin from which several important teeth were missing.

'Is Mister Burke there?' the apparition asked. 'I've got leather for him.'

'No, Effy,' Helen said, and then she took pity on the woman. 'In you come, you can show me.'

Evidently afraid that the invitation might be rescinded, Effy bolted inside, depositing a collection of filthy articles inside the door – two sacks, a riddle, a short-handled rake and a trowel. These were the tools of her trade, gathering ashes to sell on as fertiliser, and raking through the rubbish in the ash-carts in hope of finding scraps of things to sell. She visited William regularly with small pieces of leather, scavenged from the tips outside the tanners' shops. William bought these for a few pennies, using them to make repairs for his poorest customers.

Effy sat herself at the table and Helen sat down opposite, offering her a cup of ale.

'Have you any whisky?' Effy asked, looking pointedly at the measure in Helen's cup.

Helen sighed and poured her a good-sized dram and Effy took a slug and swallowed, closing her eyes in delight. It was hard to tell the age of her, she might have been anything from thirty to fifty or even older.

'You must meet most folk in these parts,' Helen said.

'Aye,' Effy agreed. 'A goodly number, onywey.'

'Margaret Laird,' Helen said. 'Do you know her? She has a lodging house in Tanner's Close.'

Effy frowned. 'Laird ...' she said, and shook her head. 'I dinnae think so. The only lodging house in Tanner's Close is Logue's place.' She took another swig of her whisky and wiped her mouth, leaving a smear in the dirt across her face. 'Maybe his wife is called Margaret ... Aye, I think she is. She always cries hersel *Mistress Logue*, ken.'

'That's it,' Nelly said, remembering William Hare's stories about the woman's husband. 'Margaret Logue is her married name. Her own name was Laird.'

Effy sucked at her gums.

'She's a targer, that one,' she said. 'Hard-faced, wi a wee thin mooth so she aye looks in a temper. Did you ken she worked as a navvy on the canal at Falkirk?'

Helen snorted. 'Never,' she said.

'Did so,' Effy said. 'Happed hersel in a pair of breeks and signed up as a man.'

Nelly remembered well how badly William had stood up to the work, and she knew fine no woman could have shifted the weight of muck those men moved. Maybe she'd been one of the women that lived among them, though, that seemed more likely. If she had, she mightn't have wanted it known, and Helen couldn't blame her for that.

'What sort of house is it she keeps?' she asked Effy, although as she said the words, she realised Effy was unlikely ever to have been welcomed inside.

'Fine enough, I'm sure,' Effy said. 'Logue's a guid man, he lets me kip in the stable when it's cauld out. The woman takes in bairns as well as lodgers.'

'Takes them in?' Helen said. 'What for?'

'Ken, if their mothers cannae keep them,' Effy said. 'She watches them for a few weeks or helps find new folk for them.'

'Why?' Helen asked. She had never heard of anyone taking in a bairnie that wasn't kin.

Effy snorted. 'For coin,' she said. 'Why else does anybody do anything?'

That was true enough, Helen thought. Edinburgh wasn't like Redding, life was hard enough there but it was harder still here, this far from the land, and folk had to make their way as best they could. Like herself and William, with his cobbling and her trading. She no longer did laying-outs, there were too many folk here who did that already, women who would deliver a baby, nurse the sick or wash a corpse. Maybe she would like to live at the Logue house, she thought, if there were bairnies there. It might salve the sorrow at not having her own – although, somewhere in her heart, Helen hoped that Maisie and wee Annie might still come to live with her, one day, when they were old enough and the business with the fire forgotten at last.

There was still no sign of William when the whisky was finished, and Effy shooed out into the night with tuppence to buy herself a dinner. Helen often spent the first part of the night by herself, and now she wondered if she might like to be in a house with other folk she knew. She might get on with this Margaret; she had gone about the navvies' camp too, after all. The only thing that worried her was Hare, she was afraid of him. He was poorly named, no gentle beast at all, but more like a fox with his leering grin and sharp teeth. But then again, she would be with William, and what harm would he ever let come to his Nelly when he was near?

6

Secundigravida

I N THE EARLY DAYS OF YOUNG ROBERT, Susan found she did not hate Lillypot so much as before. She had time for nothing but the baby, and her needs were shaped by his own, so she slept when he slept, roused to feed him when he roused, and took the air only when she took him out into it. Lillypot was as good a nest as any for a new mother and her chick, and indeed even better than most, for meals appeared on trays and baths were filled and laundry vanished, so she was free to give her whole self over to the task of doting on her child.

They had planned for a wet nurse, since they had expected to have two babies to feed, but the midwife said she thought it would do Susan good to feed the child herself. It was exhausting – often it seemed he was barely off the breast before he was crying again with hunger – but Susan was glad of it, he was hers and she his, and no one else had any place in the business. Slowly, she came to know his cries and his needs and his wants. When he was tiny, she learned she could stroke his hand, and he would grasp her own, and if she stroked his foot, his great toes curled under and the others fanned out like a tiny flower. If a door closed or Susan dropped a book, he would close his hands in tight fists as though he would fight. In his sleep he sometimes jerked and twitched, and if Susan appeared too quickly before him when he was awake, he would throw his arms and legs out wide in shock, and then curl in on himself, as though for protection. He was in all ways fascinating, and Susan drank him in.

The midwife stayed for the first weeks, and Susan was glad of her, she often felt weepy and fretful, and unsure of herself, having never had the care of an infant before and having no mother or other woman relative to guide her. At first the midwife dealt with most of the napkins, and the bathing, showing Susan how to hold the child, how to dry him, how to deal with the rashes and swaddle him, how to dose him for colic and soothe his little pains. She gave her orders to Mrs Scott and Elsie, and Susan thought she quite enjoyed it, ruling the roost in a house where there was plenty of help available, and any food or drink or service she might desire to be had at a word.

In fairness to Mrs Scott, she seemed not to mind, she was as besotted by young Robert as anyone and Susan thought she looked for any excuse to attend to them herself, instead of sending Elsie as she might usually have done. Elsie, in her turn, jostled to be first to bring up a tray or fetch the washing pail, keen for a look at the baby or even a rare chance to hold him while Susan used the pot or took her own bath.

The day the midwife left, Susan wept, but the woman patted her cheek and said not to take on so, she would manage very well, she was a fine mother and no child could have a better. That made Susan weep even more, but the midwife smiled and said loudly to remember she was not alone, Mrs Scott was as good a helpmeet as any mother could have, and Elsie too; they loved their mistress as well as she loved young Robert, and as she cared for the baby, they would care for her in turn. Mrs Scott preened like a mother hen at that, and Elsie blushed in pleasure, and Susan smiled through her tears; the midwife was a wily woman and knew how people might be lulled into thinking her words were less instructions than praise for the fine intentions they had had all along.

The night before, the midwife had spoken quietly with Susan, saying it was not her concern to advise her mothers about their affairs, but she thought Susan should know that feeding an infant herself helps a woman space her family out, she was less likely to get with child right away. Too many children in too few years was hard on a woman, she said, and those who got with twins once were prone to do so again, so Susan might well think of giving her body a good rest between times and continuing to feed young Robert as long as she was able. Susan thanked her and squirrelled the information away in her mind.

As it happened, the method proved not foolproof, and before the year was out Susan knew herself to be with child again. She was not as sick as before, but she was sick enough, and her milk dried up so she could no longer feed young Robert. He was eating solid food by then, of course – Elsie had taken great pleasure in spooning pap into his mouth as soon as he would take it – but Susan missed that time together, it had been easy then to forget she was a prisoner here.

They had all promised Susan it would be easier the second time, as surely there would be one babe only, but Susan could not discern much difference, except for the slightly less disabling sickness. Her belly seemed to swell even sooner than before, so by the time she was five months gone she felt as big as she had been at six the year before.

The steps in the dance of their lives were familiar now. The year had turned, and spring had come, and with it came Robert, removed to Lillypot for the warmer months with his great packing cases and boxes. The house seemed to rise up and shake itself, like a bird wakening in its nest, Mrs Scott and Elsie taking rugs and curtains and linens outside to beat on the line, lifting jars down from shelves to clean underneath them, and dusting and polishing everywhere so the furniture and the skirtings and the doorhandles gleamed. Then the house settled itself again in a new position, to accommodate Robert's work into the rhythm of their days.

As the months had worn on, with Susan growing and growing, she had again begun to think that she was carrying twins. She knew her dates very certainly, as Robert had gone more than eight weeks without visiting them in the winter, and although Mrs Scott said nothing, Susan thought she had noticed, too, for she said there was little she could do to let out Susan's gowns again, they were worn through with all the stitching and ripping out. Even Robert noticed the state of her wardrobe – on his second night at home he said Susan was looking very dowdy, what was Mrs Scott thinking of, not offering to order new gowns as her Mistress required? Mrs Scott looked quite put-out at that, but she pursed her lips and said of course, the Master was quite right; she would send John to fetch samples of fabric and designs and when the Mistress had chosen what she wanted, Mrs Scott would see to it that it was ordered.

Susan had thought little of clothes since her marriage, and she was surprised by the delight she felt when Mrs Scott presented her with the sample books with their snippets of fabric and trim and the thick sheaf of fashion plates the draper could replicate. In the end she chose two dresses for now, made in the same high-waisted pattern with a fall-front bodice, with a button-up section under so no corset was required. She chose a peacock-blue taffeta and a tawny cotton with a floral sprig, deciding the bodice of the fancier one should have diagonal embroidery and the plainer one not, and both should have removable long sleeves so that she might wear them long if the day was cold. She ordered six shifts for wearing under, and she wanted three frocks for after, too, but Mrs Scott fretted over measurements for the latter, and so in the end they agreed that those should wait. Instead she ordered new nightgowns, and a shawl, a comb for her hair, and three new lace caps.

Three weeks later the drapers' boy came, and Mrs Scott helped Susan unpack the boxes and hang the dresses so the folds dropped out. Susan dressed for dinner in the taffeta frock, with one of the new lace caps and Robert's mother's locket, and Robert said she looked very well. She stole a glance at herself in the mirror in the parlour as she passed and almost started to see that she did indeed look as handsome as she had ever done – it had become a fear of hers, for months now, that a much older woman would look out of the glass at her if she stopped there, and she had taken to avoiding it in dread.

In the end Mrs Scott must have said something to Robert about Susan's suspicion of twins, for over the next days he asked her some questions about the sensations in her body. He spent a while with his books, and then he asked if he might measure her. He had her lie back and used a string to measure the height of her belly, and then he said it was indeed larger than the books said it should be, and so he pressed and prodded and said he thought perhaps it might be twins again. No matter, he said, in any case he had arranged for an accoucheur and the man was to come to them next month, and stay as long as he was needed.

Susan wasn't sure if this reassured her or frightened her, after the last time, but she had little time to worry about it as, just then, young Robert seemed to become possessed of a demon. For months he had slept through the night, but now he set up great howls and wails at all hours, and the whole household was tired and crabby from lack of sleep. Robert put up with three nights of it before he removed back to the city, leaving Susan and the servants to muddle through as best they could. Susan was glad to see the back of him, the whole business was miserable enough without Robert glaring at her as though she was somehow to blame.

Young Robert was in the grip of this demon for three long weeks, and then it seemed it departed as quickly as it had come. The whole household slept through a night, and then another, and young Robert smiled and laughed again from dawn to dusk. They had a few days of this bliss before Robert returned, bringing with him the accoucheur, a Frenchman, and a young, red-headed man the accoucheur introduced as his assistant. They were not lodged at Lillypot, to Mrs Scott's relief, for there was no space for them there. Instead they slept in the coach-man's rooms in a house nearby, although they both spent large parts of each day with Robert in his study being shown – Susan assumed – his museum plans.

The assistant was a curious young man, deeply shy, and with very little English, and a deep blush spread from his neck over his face to his ears any time Susan so much as looked his way. Mrs Scott was very distracted keeping all these men fed – they took their meals at Lillypot before going home in the evening – and Susan heartily wished the business over and all of them gone.

When they had been there a week, Mrs Scott appeared with a dose for Susan after dinner and said Doctor Knox was keen she get some rest, there were great circles under her eyes and she was pale. The dose would help, she said. Susan said she didn't want it, but Mrs Scott insisted. She seemed in a strange humour, not cross exactly but not happy either. In order to keep the peace, Susan took the dose. It seemed strong, and she felt her eyes and legs heavy as she climbed the stairs to her room. She struggled to unfasten her dress and when she lifted the pillow to find her nightdress, it wasn't there, and in its place was a strange gown she'd never seen before. She was too tired to do anything about it, so she pulled the odd linen thing on and collapsed into bed.

If she dreamed, she had no memory of it, but in the middle of the night Susan half-roused to find herself lying on her side, so she saw Mrs Scott perched on a chair by the side of the bed. The housekeeper's usual look of determined good nature was nowhere to be seen, and instead her mouth was grim and a spot of red burned bright on each cheek, as if she was angered somehow. Susan opened her mouth to ask what was wrong, but just then she felt herself lifted by the haunches and her gown raised, and she heard low voices and felt odd sensations as she was moved this way and that. She began to lift her head, but Mrs Scott saw her move and said something she couldn't make out, and then the spout of an invalid cup was between her lips with more of the sticky dose, and the darkness took her again.

In the morning, Susan woke to a pounding head and a dry mouth and an odd sense of unease. She was in her normal nightgown, and there was no sign of the other, so she wondered if she had dreamed it all. She was nearly sure, though, that Mrs Scott had been in her room in the night, she didn't think she had dreamed that. She got up, slowly, feeling her body strange and alien, and crossed to the dresser to pick up the bell and ring for the housekeeper. Before she reached it, though, she heard a hissed exchange outside the door – Mrs Scott and

Robert, and by the sound of her voice, Mrs Scott was very unhappy.

'I'll have nothing to with such a thing again,' she was saying.

Robert said something Susan didn't quite catch, but there was something about children dying, and Robert preventing it if he could . . . Did Mrs Scott not remember the footling that was lost?

Mrs Scott's answer was too low for Susan to hear, and then her footsteps descended the stair. After a moment, Robert's followed. Susan stood with her back to the door and tried to make sense of it, but then she found she did not want to after all, she wanted just to get through these weeks and deliver her babies and then Robert would leave her to her life here. She was determined, though, that she would not swallow any more of Mrs Scott's doses, she would hold them in her mouth until she could spit them out in the pot or the coalscuttle or a planter.

That afternoon, Mrs Scott sent Elsie to sit with Susan and sew. Elsie brought a tray with shortbread and some sort of infusion the accoucheur had instructed Susan to drink. It was bitter, but Elsie added honey, and that made it better. At night time she came with more of the same, and again in the morning, and twice through the next day. She said Mrs Scott had asked the accoucheur what it was, and he said it was made of the leaves of raspberries, and something else awful-sounding but Mrs Scott couldn't remember what it was in order to tell Elsie after, she didn't recognise the name. She said the accoucheur wanted to bring Susan's time on, before the babes grew too big.

The tea alone didn't achieve much, and that night Robert came to Susan in the parlour and said that the accoucheur meant to try something else, something new that could help Susan. He said it might hurt, but she should be brave, it would be for the best in the end. Susan must have looked at him in horror, because he asked crossly if she did not trust him, and Susan was fairly caught then, because of course the answer was *no*, but what woman could say that to her husband? Instead she asked if there was not to be a midwife; she had asked Mrs Scott the same question time and again but she said she did not know.

No, Robert said, Mrs Scott would support Susan when her time came, and the accoucheur would manage the business from beginning to end. He told Susan to go up and put on her nightgown and lie down, and to send word by Mrs Scott when she was ready for the accoucheur. Mrs Scott took her up, seemingly keen to avoid her eye, and Susan wondered how content she really was to act midwife as well as housekeeper and jailer, the poor woman must wonder what she had done when she had taken the job at Lillypot.

Mrs Scott helped her strip and put on her nightgown and then she lay on her side on the bed and waited while Mrs Scott went to fetch the men. She stared at the candle-flame, feeling her heart flutter in her chest with anxiety. Then they came in, and the accoucheur instructed Mrs Scott to hold up a sheet while he worked so Susan would not be discomfited.

Susan could not imagine how she might be more discomfited at this point.

Mrs Scott held the sheet, and the accoucheur asked her to lie on her back. He pressed here and there on her belly for a time, and then he said she would feel an intrusion, and she did, something cold and foreign parting her privy places. The accoucheur spoke to Robert in a low voice, and then to his assistant, telling him to raise a lamp. A moment later, he spoke to Susan, telling her all was well, her time was almost upon her and it would help for him to separate the bag of waters from the neck of her womb. He said she might feel some discomfort as he worked. She relaxed in relief as he pulled the foreign thing out, but then she felt her muscles clench anew as he pushed something else inside her instead, it seemed rougher and hurt her more. His fingers, she realised, oiled somehow. It was awful and then it was worse, Robert and the assistant watching as the accoucheur kept forcing his way inside until she felt as though he had breached some seal inside her, and he rummaged and pulled and it hurt, for half a minute or more it seemed, so that she heard her own voice raised in pain. Then he withdrew his hand and said to Robert the goal was achieved. Robert said to Susan that she had done well, and the accoucheur said she might have a show with some blood – did she know what that was? – and soon, he hoped, the birth pains would begin.

They left her alone after that, and Susan tried to calm her breathing and her tears. Mrs Scott tucked her in and asked if she could bring her anything, but Susan couldn't imagine looking anyone in the eye after that, and so she said she was fine, she merely wanted to sleep. It was true, she did want to sleep, but she found she could not; she had to get up to use the pot, finding the signs the accoucheur had described, and then towards morning, she began to feel great cramps across her belly, much stronger than the early pains she had felt before. She bore these alone as long as she could, but at last she knew she must summon help, and she rang the bell. Mrs Scott appeared, with curling papers fluttering around her face, and she led Susan to her own room which was made ready for a lying-in; Mrs Scott, it transpired, had been sleeping in the attic with Elsie for the last two weeks. The accoucheur came then, and he deaved Susan with his attentions, making her lie when she would rather walk, and prodding at her between pangs in a manner that made the next come quicker, so she had no respite from the pain at all. Almost immediately he got her flat on her back and stretched a sheet across her so she could not see, although she knew that Robert and the assistant were there, and she hated it.

Around midday, the accoucheur began issuing instructions to Mrs Scott, who got behind Susan to support her while she delivered the first of her twins. The baby cried immediately, and Robert showed her to Susan – a little girl. After a few moments, the pains began again, and the accoucheur said that all seemed to be well, and a few minutes later, the second twin was born. Again, Susan heard the baby's cry right away, and tears came into her eyes with relief. This one was a boy, they were not identical twins, not like the first pair, and all was well.

The accoucheur saw to Susan's hurts, and then he instructed Mrs Scott on how to wash her, bind her belly and pad her privy parts. Once that was done, Mrs Scott helped her back to her own bed, and Elsie came with the babies and Susan put them to the breast. Mrs Scott had a great list from the accoucheur of how she should manage the feeding of them, but Susan laughed at the sight of her trying to read from it; by now Mrs Scott was more frazzled than anyone could ever have imagined.

'Tell Robert to send for Mrs Wilkinson who was here before,' she said, 'or another good midwife. He cannot expect you to nurse me, on top of your other tasks. Tell him I will not support it.'

Mrs Scott looked immensely relieved, and scurried off with her message to Robert. It seemed he had agreed, for Susan slept a while, and when she woke, Elsie told her John had gone to fetch the midwife.

It was a curious time, the first weeks of the twins, more tiring than Susan could ever have imagined. It seemed there was never a moment's peace – if one was asleep the other was awake – and if both slept for even a moment together, young Robert wanted his mama and she had to rouse herself and attend to him. She stayed upstairs for three whole weeks together, and she barely noticed the time passing.

When at last she came down, Susan discovered Robert's things gone, and in their place a great package in the dining room.

'What on earth can it be?' she asked Mrs Scott.

'A present from Doctor Knox,' Mrs Scott said. 'To congratulate you on the birth of the twins. It's a dolls' house, Ma'am. The Doctor thought you would enjoy it.'

Susan didn't know what to say. It seemed a bad joke, a house within a house, in case she ever forgot that she was imprisoned here well and truly, no longer even a matter of locks and keys but of babies, nurslings, trapping her here forever.

She turned on her heel and went back to her children.

7

Periorbital Haematoma

HELEN'S FIRST, DAFT, THOUGHT on meeting Margaret Logue was that the woman had a conker in the socket where her left eye should be. Looking twice, she saw that it was a shiner, but swollen so badly that it had come up shiny and round, and bruised a purple so dark it looked almost brown. The other eye was normal, almost, except for a line of bruising underneath it, a darker ghost of the lines that appear when a body goes without sleep for too long.

Helen's heart went out to the woman then, for she knew well what it was to be beaten so. She smiled, and bobbed her head, and then she raised her hand and touched it to her own cheek with a grimace, to show she pitied her.

Margaret Logue stared at her blankly, then nodded briskly.

'William says you need a place to stay,' she said. 'He's been a good friend to me, and he vouches for you, too.'

'We do,' Helen said, after a second's pause to sort out her Williams. The woman meant William Hare.

'We have rooms here,' Margaret Logue said. 'I can't drop the price, my man won't let me. Unless ...' She looked at Helen appraisingly. 'Are you good with babbies?'

'Aye,' Helen said, although she felt her cheeks colour. It was true enough, she thought, the only trouble she had ever had was Maisie's accident, and now she knew to be on the lookout when bairnies went too close to the fire.

'I take them in,' Margaret said. 'When their mothers can't care for them. They pay me, so they do. Some pay me to keep them from week to week, some pay me to keep them forever. I'm well suited to it, and it's a fine trade, I turn a fine profit at it, so I do. But the wee demons never seem to lay off their crying and fussing, it drives me to distraction.'

Helen hadn't heard of this trade before and doubted that Margaret really was well suited to it, if crying bothered her, but she thought it wise to say nothing.

Margaret clicked her tongue and went on. 'You could help me with them,' she said. 'That way we could take a few more in. Some of them are only here till I find a better place for them, and between the two of us we could manage double easy enough. I could drop your rent, if that suited. A shilling off a week.'

Helen nodded, although she had no idea if this was a fair bargain or not. She wished William hadn't gone off into the kitchen to drink with Hare.

'That's settled then,' said Margaret. 'We'll drink on it.' She made to usher Helen out of the room, but then she stopped. 'Can you read?' she asked. 'I could use a reader to help with the adverts. For places for the babbies.'

'I can,' said Helen, 'though I'm a poor writer. But William writes a fine hand.'

Margaret smiled and held the door open for Helen to make her way to the kitchen where the fire was lit and William and William Hare were sitting with Logue, all already halfway in their cups. They finished a bottle, and then a second, and by then it seemed it was agreed that William and Helen would move to Tanner's Close in a month's time.

In the intervening weeks, Helen went over a time or two to help Margaret with the babies in her care. There were three on the first day, a tiny newborn girl Helen fed with milk from a spoon, and twins of around half a year. Then there were four, the first three joined by a bonnie, tousie-haired lad who seemed set on taking his first steps, hauling himself around by the chairs and table-legs and grinning proudly at Helen all the while. Margaret tutted at that, though, and tied him to a seat by a tape at his wrist so that he fretted and fussed and rubbed his chubby wee arm raw. Helen helped clean them and feed them and dose them with a syrup Margaret said she swore by, it soothed all sorts of colics and coughs, and bought her a moment's peace from the whining. Sure enough, even the big lad conked out a few minutes after he had his dose, though Margaret still left the poor wee scone tied to the chair.

The next time Helen went, there were only two again; Margaret said the baby girl had taken a fever and died of it, and the sturdy yearling had been adopted by an elderly couple from out by Haddington. They had never had children of their own and they were fair delighted to take such a strong, curly headed lad home. For Margaret's part, she said, she was delighted to be shot of him, he was a right menace and had driven her near distracted.

'Where's his own mammy?' Helen asked, thinking Margaret really had no notion of bairnies, the child had been a charmer.

Margaret laughed. 'Out making her living, as must we all,' she said. 'But she'll be back to dump another on me before the year is out, you mark my words.'

'Have you ever had any of your own?' Helen asked.

'No,' said Margaret. 'I saw to it that I never did and I pray I never will. William says you're barren. Have you never had any?'

'I have,' said Helen. 'I have two daughters living. With my father. In the country.'

'Well then,' said Margaret, 'you'll understand these hoors better than me, Helen. You've left your babbies too.'

She straightened the lace cap she wore over her curly hair and walked out of the room, leaving Helen to blink at the sting of her words.

That night, Helen tried to say to William that she didn't want to go to Tanner's Close after all.

'What? Why not?' he asked. They had both been drinking, Helen had needed a glass or two before she had the courage to say anything.

'I can't say, exactly,' she said. 'It's Margaret and those bairnies. I don't . . . I get a funny feeling off her.'

'Ach, Nelly, you and your "feelings",' William said, without rancour. 'If we listened to your gut, we'd never do anything. We'd still be out in the country eating dandelion roots and pignuts.'

'One of them died,' Helen said. 'A wee lassie. Just a scrap of a thing.'

'Well now, that is very sad,' William said, 'and I'll remember her in my prayers tonight. But babbies die, Nelly, it happens all the time. Sure, didn't you lose enough of them yourself, in your time?'

Helen sighed. It was true enough, what he said, bairnies did die. But still she couldn't shake the feeling that Margaret Logue gave her, as though she was a snake and Helen a fat, stupid hen with a gaggle of chicks behind her, and even if Helen somehow managed to shepherd the wee ones away, there was Hare, the fox, waiting in their path with his sly smile and sharp teeth.

Suddenly, she became aware that William was watching her.

'What on earth ails you, Nelly?' he asked. 'You just did the strangest thing, like you were a hen hiding something beside you. You brought your elbows up like this' – he mimed wings, held back defensively – 'and then you looked around as though there was a big tomcat there!' He roared with laughter. 'Oh Nelly,' he said, 'don't go daft on me now. I'd not want to send you off to Bedlam to join the poor lunatics there!' He began to clown about, rolling his eyes and howling like a dog, and in the end, Helen had to laugh and cuff him about the ear, whereupon he pulled her onto his knee and began to kiss her soundly.

Helen had meant to bring up the subject of not moving the next morning, but in the event she had no chance. Sometime before the dawn, there came a knock at the door and William hauled himself from his bed with great groans and swearings to answer. Helen's head was pounding and she buried her good ear in the pillow in hope of sleeping on a while longer, but then William was back, shaking her awake.

'It's Hare,' he said. 'Logue died in the night. Margaret's asking me to go over there and say a prayer.'

'What? What happened?' Helen raked on the floor for a shawl and pulled it round her, peering at the door, but it seemed William Hare had disappeared as fast as he had come.

William shook his head as he fastened the stock around his neck.

'I have no notion,' he said. 'I'll come back as soon as I can.' He kissed Helen on the forehead and rushed off into the dark. Helen lay back down in the bed and tried to sleep.

It seemed it was an apoplexy, William told her, when he returned later in the morning; Logue's face had been all twisted, with bulging eyes and the tongue hanging out. Helen shuddered. She had spent the morning skulking about the cold room half-heartedly mending a jacket, she was in no mood to hawk her wares around the street with her head pounding and the sour taste of last night's gin in her mouth. She asked how Margaret was bearing up, and William shrugged.

'I can't say she seemed over sorry,' he said. 'There was little love lost between them, I don't think.' He smiled at Helen. 'You would miss me if I were gone, would you not, Nelly?'

'I suppose I would,' said Helen. 'But then you don't raise your hand to me like he did to her. I've never seen a shiner the like of thon one she had the first day I saw her.' A thought crossed her mind. 'What about the bairnies? Were they there?'

'Just one wee lass,' William said, 'a real wee dote, so she was, but Margaret says her mother will be back for her before Logue is buried.'

'She'll not be wanting us now,' Helen said, trying to keep the relief from her voice. 'I wonder where she'll go.'

But William shook his head. 'She's not going anywhere,' he said. 'Everything Logue had is hers now. And she'll want us more than ever. It won't be easy for a woman on her own.'

'She'll not be alone, though,' Helen said.

William cocked his head. 'What do you mean?'

'Well . . .' Helen thought it was obvious. 'Her and William Hare . . . I mean, there's a fondness between them, is there no?'

William's brow creased in thought, and then he chuckled. 'I suppose there is, when you put it like that, Nelly. Maybe Hare has fallen on his feet after all. Sly dog.'

'Are you sure it was a natural death?' Helen said. The question took her by surprise, she hadn't really known she was thinking such a thought before it was out her mouth.

William didn't seem shocked at all, though, almost as though he had wondered the same thing himself. 'I think so,' he said. 'I've seen him take a turn before, so I have. He came round that time, but he had the same look on his face for a moment, and I thought he was a goner.' His sunny face turned dark for a moment, but then he seemed to shrug the thought off, like a dog shaking water off its coat.

'Come on, Nelly,' he said, 'let's walk out for a bite to eat. They'll bury Logue on Thursday, and we needn't think more on them till then.'

Logue's burial was a stingy affair, no mortcloths or other niceties, and afterwards Margaret had such mourners as there were back to the lodging house for a mean feed of oysters and penny pies. William said some bonnie words and sang a hymn, and then the drinking started, and with stomachs barely lined, it wasn't long before the grousing and argy-bargy followed. Helen and William sat to one side, out of the main throng, but if Helen had hoped they'd go unnoticed, she was disappointed. As the drinking reached its height, Hare sidled over and sat down beside them, a glint in his eye that promised no good.

'A sad day,' said Helen, for the want of anything better coming to mind.

'No, a happy one,' said Hare. 'You can be the first to congratulate me, Helen. Now Logue is out of the way, I can marry Margaret at last. I'm the happiest man you ever did see.'

Even William looked a bit shocked at that. 'Should you not wait a bit?' he asked. 'Out of respect for the man's memory?'

'Respect?' Hare repeated, incredulous. 'The man was a brute. Sure you saw Margaret's face manys a time when he took his fists to her.'

Takes a brute to know a brute, Helen thought, but she knew better than to open her mouth.

'Still and all,' William said. 'You should wait a bit for the look of the thing.'

'Three weeks,' said Hare, 'till the banns are called. Then you'll stand up beside us in the kirk and see us wed. There's no man I'd rather have by my side.'

There wasn't a lot that William could say to that, so they drank to it, although Helen could see it sat ill with William still, to toast a widow's betrothal at her own man's funeral.

Later in the evening, when most folk had left and those still there were half-cut or asleep, Margaret came to sit with them. She was well gone by then, raising her cup with some care to tap it off theirs.

'You gave your man a fine send-off,' William said.

'Better than the bastard deserved,' Margaret replied, taking a draught of whisky. 'Do you know what it cost me to bury him?' She didn't tell them, but she wasn't finished with her grousing. 'It's a scandal,' she said. 'Not even a holy man to say a word over the grave. Should have sold him to the anatomists, so I should.' She snorted and took a long pull of her drink.

William Hare scratched his nose. 'Damn if that's not a good idea, Margaret,' he said. 'Shame you didn't think of it sooner.'

'I didn't lick it off the stones,' Margaret said. Helen had no idea what that meant, but by then there was no chance of finding out, Margaret and William Hare were laughing and William seemed asleep, or near to it.

'We'll have a fine time together when you move here to the close, won't we, Nelly?' said William Hare.

Helen hated him using that name – it was William's name for her, a pet name – but she tried to smile, raising her cup and drinking to this thing she didn't want, but couldn't see a way of escaping, a stupid hen shut up in her coop with a fox.

8

Cytomegalovirus

ROBERT CONTINUED TO COMMANDEER the dining room when he was at Lillypot to progress the specimen index project he planned for the museum, where at last he had been appointed curator. Susan found she must take her meals with him on a tray in the parlour, or upstairs with the children. He breakfasted with her every day, then took a walk. In the middle of the morning, he would return and follow a specific system of preparation. First he must cast off his jacket and roll his shirt-sleeves to the elbow. The ink and the blotter must be just so, and his papers and cards must be arranged in a particular way. Any volumes he intended to consult must be ranged about him on a small stool and a table he kept in his study for this purpose. There was even an order in which he approached these arrangements, as though the small ritual sharpened his mind, as a notary might sharpen his pens. Only when all was ready could he begin.

So much Susan had observed when helping, although increasingly Robert did not wish her help, preferring instead that she should try to keep the children quiet so that he could work undisturbed. He was not a fond father, never given to sitting a babe on his knee or chucking it under the chin – in fact, it seemed he was not fond of infants at all. Perhaps he would come into his own when they were older, Susan thought, although she imagined him rather more as a terrifying tutor and interrogator than a companion and guide.

The need to maintain peace in the house threw Susan and Elsie together much. They took turn about on the night nursing and comforting, and when the children woke early, as they inevitably did, Elsie brought the twins to Susan and took young Robert with her as she swept the hearths and set the fires, setting him small tasks of stacking kindling or fetching brushes and black-lead to keep him occupied. Once her morning chores were complete, Elsie got the children breakfasted while Susan ate with Robert downstairs. Susan came back upstairs then, and the two of them oversaw the dressing, Susan seeing to young Robert who liked to 'dress himself' and took, therefore, at least three times as long as Susan might, while Elsie dressed the twins. This was a favourite task and she sang and tickled their tummies and pretended to bite their feet until they laughed and squirmed and squealed.

Susan supervised their play then, and Elsie attended to her own duties, bringing the midday meal. Robert's was taken to him as he worked and Elsie and Susan sat together and took their own while the children ate, feeding one twin apiece between spoonfuls of soup. Susan had had little experience of children before her own had come, and she was grateful for Elsie's easy knowledge, the 'clip clop' of the 'horsie' as she inveigled a spoon through clamped lips and the neat trade-offs she managed with young Robert, one more forkful of peas before pudding, or an extra story at bedtime in exchange for a clean plate. Try as she might, Susan could remember little of her own earliest years; her memories seemed to start later, and the oldest of them seemed to be less of things she had done than of sensations and sights and objects – her mother's voice, the smell of her father's pipe, the blue button eyes of a rag doll she had loved.

In the afternoon there were naps and, if Robert needed no help, Susan slept too; she was with child again and not too big as yet, so her sleep was good. When they woke they made an excursion outside into the garden for young Robert to run around and poke into plant beds and play with his ball, and the twins to tumble and roll on the grass and pick daisies with their clumsy fingers. Tea was next, and then Elsie took over for bathing and bed while Susan ate with Robert in the parlour downstairs. Elsie brought the children down for their goodnight kisses, and Robert listened to small Robert lisping his prayers. Then Elsie would take them up to bed and Susan and Robert would pass the evening in work or reading.

It was natural, of course, that Susan and Elsie should come to be accustomed to one another as they collaborated on the shared project of the children. Susan liked Elsie, who was quick and clever, and she thought Elsie liked her, in so far as any maid likes her Mistress. They talked easily enough of the children, and a time or two Susan thought about talking to Elsie about her situation, but Mrs Scott was prone to popping her head round the door to check on them once or twice a day, in the guise of bringing soup, or folded laundry, or a dose for colic. Susan knew Elsie had her instructions to keep her distance and button her lip – she had heard Mrs Scott reprimanding her once for forgetting herself and addressing her betters before she was spoken to.

'Mind and dinnae forget your position, Elsie,' she had said, 'there's the Master, and the Mistress, and then there's the likes of you and me. It's no for a serving lass to speak to the Mistress as an equal. The Master could skelp you for that.'

That reassured Susan, in a way, it seemed to show Elsie was not an active participant in her jailing, she was under Mrs Scott's thumb also. She decided she wouldn't press Elsie, for the time being, although now and then she would ask where she had learned to do this thing, or that, or if she remembered having her milk teeth, or what her mother's name had been. These queries seemed safe enough, deriving from their chatter about the children, and Elsie answered perfectly happily, growing ever easier in Susan's company. She had been fond of her mother, it seemed, and perhaps spoiled as the only girl in the family, but then her mother had died. Elsie laughed and said it had been just her in a house full of lads, and she had run wild with them, out rabbiting and playing ball and roaming the streets of the Old Town.

Susan filed all this away in her memory, imagining each fact on its own small card, like Robert's specimen notes. If Elsie could become her friend, then perhaps, one day, she could be prevailed upon to help Susan and the children leave this place.

'I had no brothers or sisters,' she told her. 'Is it hard, to always obey Mrs Scott's orders when you were used to running wild?'

Elsie didn't answer for a moment, but then she laughed and said she was growing used to it; she was grateful for the position, her father couldn't keep her. Then she picked up young Robert and asked if he would like to go rabbiting and running around the heichs and the howes of the great volcano of Arthur's Seat in the Old Town, where his Elsie had grown up? Robert repeated 'rabbit' with great delight, and Susan told him his father must have run about there in his young days, too, he had attended the High School that was only a stone's throw from the great volcano.

If Elsie had sought to change the subject, it had worked, and Susan didn't quiz her again. For a week or two the days passed in the same way as ever, but then came a day when Robert said he had business in town, and Mrs Scott was to go to a funeral, but Susan would have Elsie and John with her in case she had need of anything, and Mrs Foster would come and make their dinner. Off went Robert and Mrs Scott in the carriage after breakfast, the latter dressed in her best, and Susan and Elsie and the children went about the first part of their day as usual. After lunch, which Elsie heated up and brought to them, Susan had barely stretched out on her bed and closed her eyes when there was a great crash and a wail from below.

Downstairs, the door to Robert's study was closed and she could hear an odd noise behind it.

'Elsie?' she called. 'What has happened?'

Elsie didn't answer but she continued to make the strange noise, a sort of high-pitched keening.

'Hush, Elsie,' she said. 'Let me in. Whatever has happened, I can help you to put it right again. I know how Doctor Knox likes his papers and his things.'

There was a pause, and then Elsie pulled the door back. There was an odd smell in the room.

'I just came in to set the fire,' Elsie said. 'But I've broken a big jar. It was on a stool, and I didn't see it. But . . .' She broke off and gestured to the floor, where a great pool of liquid was spreading out, with a greyish thing in it that Susan could make no sense of at first. Then she peered closer at it, and she saw it was a human hand, but with three fingers and a thumb only. She made a noise of her own, almost without realising.

'Why has the Master got a thing like that?' Elsie asked, her voice still in the pitch of her keening.

'He . . . He studies such things,' Susan said. 'All doctors do. That way, they can learn how a body should be, and what might go wrong with it. Now, I think we must see if we can put that . . .' She couldn't say the word. 'We must put it in another jar. Does Mrs Scott have a large pickling jar?'

Elsie looked as though she might be sick, but she hurried out of the room. When she was gone, Susan took out her handkerchief and dropped it over the hand. Then she took the tongs from the fireplace and, as carefully as she could, she picked up the hand and dropped it on a piece of paper on the desk, fighting down nausea as she heard the noise the thing made as it landed.

In a moment, Elsie came back with a large stoneware jar.

'Vinegar too, I think,' Susan said. 'I don't know if that's right, but I know the water is a sort of pickling solution. Can you bring me some?'

When Elsie had gone, Susan once again used the tongs to pick up the hand and did her best to manoeuvre it into the jar. She didn't get it in quite cleanly, and the greyish fingers seemed to curl around the lip as if to grip it, before the whole slid inside. Elsie returned with a great flagon of vinegar and Susan poured it in without looking, all the way to the top.

'There,' she said. 'Nothing to cry over. Now fetch some sacking for the broken glass, and a mop and a bucket, Elsie, with warm water and soap. Let's get this mess cleaned up.'

When that was done, and the paper that the hand had rested on consigned to the fire with Susan's handkerchief, Susan sat Elsie in the parlour while she went to check on the children. When she came back, she poured Elsie a glass of sherry wine.

'I'm no supposed to let you in to the study,' Elsie said. 'No when the Master's out. And Mrs Scott'll have my guts for

108

garters that I was so clumsy and broke the Master's jar.' She shuddered again, clearly thinking of the contents of the jar.

'I won't tell them if you won't,' Susan said, feeling a sense of excitement all of a sudden at the possibilities sharing a secret with Elsie might offer. 'We'll say Robert – I mean Doctor Knox – must have left the door open and one of the twins got in and pulled the jar down. I'll say it was my fault, but you cleaned it all up.'

'But that's a lie!' Elsie said.

'Yes,' said Susan, 'but better a lie than you lose your position.'

Elsie looked at Susan tearfully and nodded.

'Well, now,' said Susan, 'there's nothing to worry about. Drink your sherry, and then you can lock the room and get on with your work as normal. I'll tell Doctor Knox tonight. But before that you must find a time to tell John I let the twins crawl around the house and one of them got into the study and caused all manner of havoc.'

'I will,' said Elsie. 'You can go outside with the children by yourself. I'll come out after and tell him I've been clearing up your mess.'

Susan had to trust that Elsie would manage her part of the bargain while she prepared herself to lie to Robert. They ate their evening meal with the children, and then they bathed them and put them to bed together, before Elsie went down to the kitchen to iron some linens and Susan took herself down to the parlour. By that time she truly was quite discomfited, and a glance in the looking glass showed that her face was pale, and her eyes red. She rubbed them a time or two as though she'd been crying.

At last, Robert came. Susan was attempting to complete a piece of fine work, but as soon as she heard the door, she cast it aside and got to her feet.

She met Elsie in the hallway, coming from the kitchen. Robert was removing his gloves, Mrs Scott following behind. Robert looked quizzically at Susan.

'Are you quite well, Susan?' he asked.

To her surprise, Susan found that she was quite overwhelmed, and burst into tears. Behind her, Elsie began to stammer out their story, that the Mistress had brought the twins down after their midday meal, and the door of the study was somehow open, and one of the twins got inside and pulled a glass jar over. The child was well, but the jar was ruined.

'Elsie cleared up the mess,' Susan sobbed. 'And she put the . . . the thing in the jar in another jar, in vinegar. I told her to do it, Robert, I'm sorry if it was wrong. But I had such a fright.' And she broke down in tears once more.

Robert seemed more concerned than angry, asking whether the child was cut, or swallowed anything in the jar, but Susan said no, she was fine and they had checked her limbs for glass, but there was nothing, only her frock was wet and they had stripped it off her and washed it right away.

'Well then,' said Robert. 'There's no harm done. Come, Susan, you should be in your bed. It was quick-witted of you to think of vinegar; I don't know if it will have saved my specimen, but the principle was accurate, you've remembered well.' He steered her towards the staircase with an arm around her shoulders.

As she climbed the stairs, the tears flowing as freely as if the story were true, Susan thought they had got away with it. But as they reached the turn in the stair, she saw Mrs Scott looking through narrowed eyes at Elsie, and she knew there would be a price to pay.

The next day Susan was unwell, with a sore head and a sore throat. Robert said perhaps she had inhaled some of the fumes from the liquor in the jar, although Marjorie seemed well enough;

he had checked her limbs and there were no cuts, and looked in her eyes, which seemed quite as usual, and indeed she was in fine fettle altogether. Susan said she should go to the children, but Robert said no, she should stay in her bed, Mrs Scott and Elsie would see to the children, and Susan found that she was glad of it, her heavy eyes were closing of their own accord.

Susan slept that whole day, dreaming of hands and feet and nightmare things in jars, and woke only after dark, when Robert was there and said she had a fever and he had brought her a draught. Then he helped her use the pot and she slept again and woke late into the morning, feeling herself again, the heat of fever gone, only weak.

Presently Mrs Scott came into the room and told her it was good to see her awake and looking more herself again. Susan thanked her and asked for the children: would Elsie bring them in to see her?

Mrs Scott said she should rest more and see the children later. That evening, she brought them in herself, although Robert said they should not stay long, their mother had been ill. Young Robert seemed solemn and the twins crotchety, and Susan asked what ailed them, but they only cried and whined until Mrs Scott took them away.

The next day a stocky, red-headed girl Susan had never seen before came in the morning with a ewer of hot water for washing and a cup of tea. Susan struggled into a sitting position and asked who she was. The girl did not react. She put the tea down beside Susan, and sat the ewer in the bowl, and then she bobbed a curtsey and was gone.

Susan drank the tea and then, feeling her heart race with the effort, she got out of bed and washed her face and neck with water from the ewer. Then she pulled on a dressing gown and with careful steps made her way to the children's room.

Mrs Scott was there, presiding over breakfast.

'Good morning, Ma'am!' she said, with apparent pleasure. 'I didna expect to see you out of your bed!'

'Where is Elsie?' Susan asked.

Mrs Scott looked down. 'Elsie has left us,' she said. 'She's gone home to her father.'

'It wasn't her fault,' Susan said. 'It was Marjorie.'

Mrs Scott sighed. 'I know you mean kindly, Ma'am,' she said. 'But you needna dissemble for Elsie. I know fine she'll have been the one to leave that door open, as she went about her cleaning. She's a through-other lass, and her mind is never on her work. I wanted to give her a chance, but I had my doubts. And, think! Much worse might have befallen our wee Marjorie, through her careless ways, and how would we all have felt then, the poor wee bairnie?'

Susan felt the trap shut around her, its springs made from her own lies.

'I think I'll go back to my bed,' she said. 'I feel a little faint.'

Susan did feel faint, and moreover there was an odd roiling in her belly. As she made her way back to the room, the roiling gathered in a sharp bolt of pain that made her fall against a dresser in the hall. She felt a gush of something hot between her legs, and looking down she saw a red stain spreading on her nightgown. Mrs Scott appeared in the children's doorway, alerted by the vase that had fallen from the dresser, and Susan saw her mouth working but she couldn't hear her over the rushing in her ears. Then Mrs Scott was calling for Robert and half-carrying, half-pulling Susan into her bedroom.

'It's too soon,' Susan said, 'far too soon.'

'Hush, now,' Mrs Scott said, 'it may be nothing, you've been upset. All will be well, I'm sure.'

Then Robert came, and cursed, and there was more blood by then, and Susan rolled in on herself to contain the pain. Mrs Scott was staring, and Susan looked at her and knew it was a lie, all would not be well.

They came later that night, twins again although no one would have credited it. There was no cry, they were too small even for that. Susan asked to see them but Robert said better not, and Mrs Scott took them away in a basin, covered with a cloth. Susan asked why it had happened, and Robert said there was something wrong, one twin was much larger than the other, as though it had had all the goodness from Susan that was properly the other's share.

'But why?' Susan asked.

'We don't know,' Robert said. 'That's why we do what we do, studying the dead in hope of helping the living.'

Susan opened her mouth to say, please, no, not my babies, but she found she couldn't, it was as though she was in a story and there was a spell on her tongue. If she spoke, then it would all spill out and she would ask what he did with that first little boy, the twin wrenched from her body, the child she never saw and never held, and if Robert's answer confirmed her fears, then she thought she would truly go distracted.

Instead, she turned her face to the wall and closed her eyes, although the tears came still.

Robert sat there for a while in silence, and then, at length, he blew out the candles and left the room.

When Susan was well again and rose from her bed, she discovered the red-headed maid who had brought her water sitting with the children, as Elsie used to do, while the twins gummed their bits of bannock and young Robert clumsily spread butter on a piece of oatcake. Unlike Elsie, though, she sat there in silence while they chattered and babbled on.

'What's—' Susan began, and then she felt rude. 'Excuse me,' she said. 'I'm Mrs Knox. The Mistress. We've not been introduced.'

The girl didn't respond, not even to turn her head to the door. Susan cleared her throat and tried again.

'Hello?' she said.

Nothing. The mad thought came to Susan that perhaps she had died and not known it – she stood here as a ghost and no one could see her – but then Robert said, 'Sit down, Mama,' and it came to her, instead, that this was her punishment: the new twins were gone, and Elsie was gone, and this woman had been sent in her place and told not even to speak to Susan, or look at her.

Then young Robert said, 'Joanie's ears no work,' and Susan felt relief flood through her, so she became light-headed almost, and sat down hard. The maid started, and Susan put out a hand to soothe her, and the maid smiled shyly and bobbed her head, then pointed to herself and said her name, although her voice was the oddest Susan had ever heard.

Young Robert offered Susan an oatcake and a piece of cheese he had assembled, and she accepted it, finding she was hungry. He prattled on, and Susan found she was glad of the maid's deafness; she need say nothing and so there was no need to gather her wits, just eat her oatcake and smile at her children and do her best to think of nothing at all.

Susan didn't go down to dinner that night, and so Mrs Scott came with a tray. While Susan ate, she busied herself about the room straightening this and putting away that. Susan asked about the maid, and Mrs Scott said she was a good, clean lass, and she couldn't hear a word, but if you stood in front of her and spoke clearly, then she could more or less make out what you said by watching your lips.

'I wonder how she learned to do that,' Susan said. 'She must have had a kind mother, or someone else to take the time.'

'Doctor Knox asked her all about it,' Mrs Scott said. 'She told him she wasn't aye deaf, or at least not so deaf as she is now. She could hear folk speak when she was a wee lass. She can speak, you know, but the sound is strange and so she doesn't like to do it.'

'I wonder why it happened,' Susan said. She was only musing out loud, she didn't expect an answer.

'Doctor Knox had a look in her ears,' Mrs Scott said.

'Of course he did,' Susan said.

Mrs Scott pretended not to hear that, and Susan almost smiled – the housekeeper was deaf too, in a way, but her deafness was of a particular form that came and went as suited her.

'He said he might find a blockage or the like,' Mrs Scott said. 'Since her hearing had been there, and then gone. But he said there was nothing of that ilk. He didna ken what made her so at all.'

Mrs Scott finished her work and took the tray from Susan, who indicated she had had enough.

'Doctor Knox is going back to town tomorrow,' she said. 'So we will be quiet here.'

'Thank you,' Susan said.

'Will you come down, do you think, Ma'am?' Mrs Scott asked. 'I wondered if you might like to open yon great article the Master sent. The dolls' house.'

'Perhaps,' Susan said. 'I'll take my breakfast in bed, if you'll be so good as to bring it, Mrs Scott, and then I'll see.'

9

Dropsy

WILLIAM BURST INTO THE NEW ROOM at Tanner's Close, disturbing Helen at her work. With one arm he cleared a space on the table for the row of bottles he carried. Helen jumped to catch the pile of half-cut-out pattern pieces and pinned garments that fell to the floor, sending her stool clattering over.

'Careful, William!' she protested. 'I've got that all ready to sew, and it'll take me hours to put it back right again if you jumble it up.'

But William paid no heed.

'Ah, come on, Nelly,' he said. 'I work you too hard. Put those shears and tangles away.' At this he swept her threads and scissors into a basket, undoing in an instant all the work she had done to untangle them that very morning.

'What's wrong with you, William?' Helen asked. 'Have you gone clean skite?'

William laughed and went to fetch each of them a mug from the old dresser Helen had set with plates and cups and bowls, so they might eat at the table in their room when they wished to avoid the kitchen and the Hares. He tipped dregs of coffee into the bucket they kept for slops and poured two generous measures from a bottle.

'Your health, Nelly,' he said, handing her a mug. '*Do shláinte*.' He settled himself at the table with his back to the fire, in their rickety old chair.

Helen shook her head, but she knew there was nothing to be done when a mood like this was on him, and so she righted her stool, chinked her mug off his and drank.

The taste of the stuff was unfamiliar but it was good, nothing like the rough whisky and gin he normally brought home. Helen sipped again, enjoying the sweetness of it, the warmth of it moving down her throat. It tasted like a currant bun. 'What is this?' she asked.

William grinned. 'Sherry wine,' he said and began to search in his pockets for the playing cards he carried there.

'How did you afford that?'

William didn't answer, just grinned and patted his nose with one finger. 'A game of Birkie?' he asked.

Sewing be damned; Helen nodded, pushed the basket under the table with her foot and watched William deftly shuffle the cards.

'What are the stakes?' she asked.

'Good woman, there, Nelly!' William said with a grin. 'Let's see, now. If you can take my whole hand off me, I'll give you . . .' He looked in his pocket, and Helen caught a glimpse of paper notes, a good two or three of them. William pulled out a shilling and thumped it down on the table. Helen picked it up and turned it over. It had a picture on it of the old king, the one that made him look for all the world like a bull wearing a crown of leaves.

'Poor Farmer George,' she said. 'They say *he* went clean skite, in the end. Wisnae himself for years.'

William snorted. 'I wouldn't mind going daft if I could live as he did,' he said. He finished his shuffling and dealt the pack between them. 'Right,' he said. 'I'm going to slaughter you, woman!'

'Will you, aye?' said Helen, and turned over her first card.

Later that night, in bed, William seemed agitated, twitching and moaning and murmuring incomprehensible things. Helen had drifted off easy enough, full of sherry as she was, and the dinner William had gone out to buy of pork chops and potatoes, pea soup and currant cakes. They had feasted like the gentry, but William's tossings and turnings disturbed her so often she found she could not sleep again.

'Does something ail you, pet?' she asked, as he sat up and clutched at his head. 'Have you a pain?'

'What? No, no. I'm sorry, Nelly. I'll lie on the floor.' William began to extricate himself from the blankets.

'No, no, there's no need for that,' said Helen. 'Anyway, it's too cold. Turn around and I'll rub your back. That aye soothes you. Was it a bad dream?'

'Aye,' said William. 'Something like that.'

The next day, William seemed still possessed of the nervous energy that had beset him in the night. He went out to fetch breakfast, returning with bannocks and curds and whey, but he had barely sat down to eat before he was on his feet again, saying he should be out and about his business. Helen wanted to ask him about the money in his pocket, but she knew better than to try while he was in this humour, he'd only deny it and then he'd grow angry, and while she knew he wouldn't raise a hand to her, he could cut her well enough with words alone. So she kept her counsel and got out her work, dumping the tangled threads he had swept onto the floor on the table to sort out.

William paused at the door and turned back to her. 'I'm sorry, Nelly,' he said. 'I've an odd humour on me. It was the bad night that did it. You have a good morning now. I'll come back with a bite for you later on.'

Helen nodded and bent her head to her work. She only hoped Margaret Hare would stay clear for just one day. The woman had been like a constant shadow at the corner of Helen's eye since they moved in, seemingly always at their door to ask for a hand reading a letter about a babby, or a loan of some sewing thread, or William to come and help Hare with some task or other. Helen had grown used to it now, for all it deaved her, but at first she had jumped near out her skin any time she opened the door and found Margaret lurking there in wait.

Thankfully it seemed Helen was in luck, for there was no sign of Margaret that day, and when she ventured outside for a breath of air, she heard the sound of voices as she passed the Hares' bedchamber. There had been some drinking last night, judging by the moaning and groaning and grousing. Margaret only had the one bairnie with her these days, and Hare was complaining sorely about its whining and complaining. No doubt there'd be a dose of something down its throat before too long.

Helen passed a pleasant enough time outside, buying a few new hanks of thread from a peddler woman, and she got on fine with the sewing after she got home, managing to finish a pair of breeks for a wee laddie and a man's waistcoat she had cut from a woman's skirt ruined on one side by an ember from a fire, and putting them by in the lower part of the dresser. William didn't come back before evening, but she hadn't expected him to, and anyway she could wait for food, there were a few morsels left over from the night before.

When he did come back, William was clearly the worse for drink and there was no sign of the bite he'd promised. He seemed listless and distracted, and when Helen asked if he'd gone to a prayer meeting, he said no, he'd been with his brother Constantine. Helen rolled her eyes at that, but she told him to sit and she went out herself with a covered dish to fetch a meal. There was a sausage seller by the mouth of the close and she thought the smell of fried onions and potato might cheer William up on this cold night, so she bought two portions and took herself home. When she arrived, though, there was no sign of William. Helen tiptoed along the corridor and stopped outside the kitchen, listening. William was there with both the Hares, and by the sound of it, spirits were high and the drinking had begun in earnest. Helen turned tail and took her sausages back to the room to eat in peace. William could have his cold tomorrow.

In the middle of the night, Helen woke to the sound of muttering in the dark room. She fumbled for matches and lit a candle. William was sitting at the table, with his hand on his Bible, praying. He was very drunk indeed.

'It's the middle of the night, William,' Helen said. 'Will you no come to bed?'

'I can't,' William said. 'I can't sleep.'

'Too much drink,' Helen said.

'Aye,' William said. 'And I've done a thing that weighs heavy on me, Helen.'

Here it was then, Helen thought, at last he had come to it.

'You can tell me,' she said. 'Whatever it is.'

William put his hand in his pocket and took out three notes and a scatter of coins.

'An old lad died in the room upstairs,' he said. 'Donald, his name was. He'd been a soldier.'

'Aye,' said Helen. 'I know. Well, I never heard what his name was but I knew an auld man had died. It was just before we flitted here. I saw them take the coffin out. Is that money his, William? Did you take it? Is that it?'

'No, no,' William said. 'Not that. You see . . .' He seemed to lose his nerve then, but he took a deep breath and started again. 'Do you remember,' he said, 'when Logue died and Margaret joked she should have sold him to the anatomists?'

'No,' Helen said. 'But I can't think she meant it. What a thing to say about her own man!' Even as she spoke, though, Helen realised that she could quite imagine Margaret making a jest like that. And perhaps it wasn't a jest – the besom was probably capable of selling her own husband's corpse if she thought there would be a profit in it.

'Well . . .' William said, and stopped, looking at Helen like he expected her to understand something.

'Well what?' Helen asked. 'Logue's dead and buried, and the auld man too. What of it?'

'We took his body out the coffin,' William said, all in a rush. 'Myself and Hare. We put it under the bed. Then we filled the coffin with bark from the tanners' and nailed it shut again so no one would know. After the parish men had taken the coffin away, we stowed him in a tea chest and we took him to Surgeon's Square. Hare said the fellow we needed was called Monro, but when we asked for directions to find him, a young lad sent us a different place. Two men there looked at the body and then the Doctor came and offered us the money.'

'Oh, William,' Helen said, appalled. 'What a thing to do. The poor auld man. He wouldn't like to be cut up. Nobody would.'

'He won't know anything about it, Nelly,' William said. 'He's dead. And he owed Hare money. Four pounds, nearly.'

'But won't he need his body ... after?' Helen had never managed to learn her scripture very well, but she had a notion folk needed their bodies whole at Judgement Day, or they would ... well, in truth she wasn't sure what would happen to them, she had always had enough to do keeping body and soul together in this life, to worry over much about the next one. She knew it was a bad thing, though, to cut up a dead body and do them out of a right burial.

'I don't know, Nelly,' Burke said. 'I've been looking in my Bible and I can't see where it says anything about anatomists. The Doctor said we need the bodies to help doctors learn to heal the sick, and there's plenty about helping folk in the Bible, Nelly. Knox, his name was, the Doctor.'

'How much did he give you?' Helen asked. She still felt queasy, but it made sense, what William said, doctors did need to learn on someone, and maybe better on the dead than on the living.

'He gave us seven pounds and ten shillings,' William said. 'Hare took the greater share, because of all that Donald owed. I got three pounds and five shillings. I've got two pounds and twelve shillings left.'

'And the rest down your throat in drink,' said Helen.

William coloured at that, and she felt her heart soften. She cuffed him gently round the ear. 'And a fine meal you stood me, too,' she said. 'But, William ... Let this be the last time you do such a thing. Do you promise me?'

'I do,' said William. He looked much happier now he had relieved himself of his burden. He allowed Helen to take him by the hand and lead him to bed, bringing his Bible with him and placing it in a drawer.

'Take care around Margaret and William Hare, though, William,' Helen said, once they were in bed. 'I don't trust them.

Even if it's not in the Bible, it's against the law to sell a body, it must be. You could be taken up, and there where would your Nelly be? Do you hear me? William?'

But William was fast asleep.

The next day, Helen woke to find William gone. There was a small parcel on the pillow. She sat up and unwrapped it to find a brooch made of gold metal framing a piece of stone with bands and lines of brown in crystal the colour of tea.

Helen had never had any jewellery of her own, not even a wedding ring. She held the brooch up to the light. It glistened like ice on a peaty loch. Carefully, she opened the drawer in the dresser where William kept his Bible and slipped the brooch inside. Then she said a brief word of prayer for the old soldier called Donald, and got up to face the cold December day.

10

Abigail

IT WAS DARK WHEN ABIGAIL SIMPSON LEFT to meet the carter at the crossroads in the village, and cold; the sun rose late in February and it would be an hour and more till dawn. But Abigail had been up and working for long enough to dispel any stiffness in her bones, finishing the business of packaging salt in twists of cloth to sell for thruppence, and wrapping pennyworths of clay for the housewives of Edinburgh to whiten their flagstones and the steps to their door. She bought the clay from a quarry, and the salt came from her daughter Bess. Bess was married to a salter in Joppa and carried the salt on her back up through Niddrie Marischal and Craigmillar, Little France, and Liberton, skirting the southern edges of the city and calling at every house she passed until her wares were gone. If anything was left by Gilmerton, she sold it half-price to Abigail, and rested a while by the fire before she shouldered her empty creel and began the long trek home. Salt wives, they called the women who did this work and they were a hardy crew indeed, second only in reputation to the fishwives who hauled the catch each week from Fisherrow and Newhaven. There were fewer and fewer of the salt wives on the road now, though, since the salt duties had ended and cheap stuff begun to pour in from England and France. Abigail didn't know how much longer Bessie would be able to pass on a share of her meagre margin; perhaps the day would come that she would stop her tramping altogether. Abigail didn't like to think of that; her pension wouldn't keep her on its own, and she looked forward to Bess's visits more than she owned even to herself.

Foolish old woman to dwell on things that might never happen, Abigail scolded herself, as she loaded her wares into baskets, smoored the fire and happed herself in her blue and white shawl. She bided only a few minutes' walk from the crossroads and as she approached she saw the horse in the lamplight, breath steaming in the chilly air. The cart was well laden and as she heaved up her baskets and then herself, the carter told her they would make their first stop at the big house at Gracemount, where he was to deliver flour and malt.

The carter was a taciturn man and said nothing to Abigail as they made their way west and then north towards the city. They turned off the main road after a mile or so and followed a long drive to a house where lamps burned and a serving laddie scuttled out to direct the carter to a door in back. Abigail had never been there before and was a little disappointed by the house itself, truth be told, for it was squat and square and she had imagined something much taller and grander, with turrets perhaps, or a great stair tower. She was more interested in what she took to be a walled garden a little way down the drive, and while the carter was busy unloading, she wandered down to investigate. The gate was ajar and Abigail stepped inside, seeing signs of industry everywhere in the pre-dawn light, fruit trees with their roots bound in sacking, ready for planting, beds half dug and neat piles of branches and twigs bundled up for burning from the winter pruning. The place was deserted and had there been anything to take Abigail would have had it in her pocket, quick as you like, but there was nothing this early in the year that might supplant her meagre diet. As she breathed in the smell of the soil, a thought stirred that perhaps she could turn forager, and mix herbs in with her salt to sell. That could add a ha'penny to the price at no extra cost but time. She mulled this over as she wandered back up the drive to the cart.

The carter was hauling himself up and turned to offer Abigail a hand into her own perch behind him. He clicked his tongue to the horse and they made their steady way down the drive. There was a mouthwatering smell of meat and pastry, and Abigail's stomach rumbled. They must have fed him his breakfast in the kitchen of the great house. By the smell of it, he had eaten better that morning than she had for many weeks together.

At the end of the drive they turned north again, towards the Kirk Brae, but before they began the steep descent, the carter directed the horse off to the side of the road. He reached into an inner pocket of his coat and brought out a kerchief which he unfolded to reveal two slices of meat pie. One of these he handed to Abigail.

'The cook is my father's sister,' he said. 'She always saves me something.' He pulled out a stoneware bottle and offered it, too. 'Ale,' he says. 'My own.'

They ate and drank in companiable silence, watching the sunrise from their vantage point high above the city. It cast its glow over the great hulking form of Arthur's Seat and the Salisbury Crags beyond, reaching west to light the skyline of the Old Town, perched precariously on the ridge of the High Street leading steeply up to the Castle Rock, and the low streets of the New Town beyond.

Abigail had meant to save some of the pie for later, but before she knew it, it was gone. The carter wiped his mouth and picked up the reins again, and they set off down the brae. Replete for the first time in as long as she could remember, Abigail nodded off as they climbed past Blackford Hill. When she awoke they were already past the common grazing land at the Meadows and almost in the West Port.

This was where they must part, and Abigail climbed down, stiff again after her sleep. She handed over the price of her journey, and then in thanks for the food she bound up the contents of two packs of salt tightly in cloth to make a lick for the horse. The carter nodded his gratitude.

'I'll tak ye hame the nicht an a, Mistress Simpson,' he said. 'Meet me here at five.'

'Och no, I'll walk,' said Abigail. 'After I've selt my salt it's easy. Nae weight tae cairry, and it's no even five miles hame. There wis a day I'd run the hale way and even noo I could walk as far again gin I had tae.'

'It'll be dark, though,' the carter protested. 'I dinna like tae think of ye walking alane in the dark.'

Abigail thanked him for his concern and agreed that if she was done by five, she would meet him in the same place, but she made him promise that if she wasn't there, he wouldn't wait. He frowned but he had no more time to argue, he had many more miles to travel before his day would be done. He turned his horse west and Abigail made her way through the narrow streets into the heart of the Old Town.

Although she was born and bred in the country, Abigail felt most alive on her incursions into the city and today, with her belly full of pie, she felt especially buoyed up by the life erupting on all sides of her. By the time she reached the Grassmarket she had already sold four twists of salt and one of clay, and met a regular customer and caught up on the woman's news. On the corner of King's Stables Road, a tavern brawl spilled out into the street and Abigail stood and watched until the innkeeper at last came out and broke it up. He was a massive individual who separated the combatants by dint of lifting one in each hand so their feet were fully off the ground. They glared at one another as they dangled, taking the occasional fruitless swing. Quite the crowd had gathered and they cheered the innkeeper who took a bow before sending one of the would-be antagonists on his way and ushering the other ahead of him into the tavern with stern admonishments about his future conduct.

The crowd dispersed and Abigail walked on, holding her wares above her head and announcing their quality for all to hear.

'Fine Scottish salt,' she proclaimed, 'fresh panned at Joppa. The best that money can buy.'

A well-dressed woman approached and asked for three twists and Abigail chanced her arm and asked for sixpence a packet.

'I'll gie ye anither ane for free, Mistress,' she said, and the woman professed herself delighted. Abigail couldn't believe her luck, for even with the free twist she had made sixpence more than the usual price. She had no need to buy herself a dinner now, either, and so the day looked set to be a profitable one.

And so it turned out. By late afternoon Abigail had made enough to buy a large can of dripping that would eke out bread and stews for weeks, and still she had money left over. All her salt had gone, although for some reason the clay had not shifted as well. The can of dripping was heavy and she was tempted to take the carter up on his offer of a ride home. It was only four o' clock, though, and so she decided to ask around the taverns for someone to take the clay at bulk price.

By the third tavern Abigail had given up hope of shifting the clay but she had decided she had a thirst that might be slaked by a cup of ale. She counted out the pennies for the tavern keeper, gratified to see she still had the well-to-do woman's shilling and sixpence and more, and took a seat to drink her drink. When she had sat down, she suddenly realised she was more tired than she had known. She downed a draft of the ale and rubbed her eyes.

When Abigail dropped her hands, she was looking directly at a couple at the next table. They were Bess's age, or younger, although when she looked again she saw the woman might be the elder and the man the younger, although it was clear that they were husband and wife, or might as well have been at any rate. They saw Abigail looking at them and the woman smiled. She nudged her partner and they both rose and came to sit with Abigail. He introduced himself as William and the woman said her name was Margaret. From their speech Abigail thought they were Irish.

The woman asked what Abigail's business was in town, and Abigail explained about the clay. The woman said that they might be able to take it, if it would help Abigail out and if she could give them a good price. They ran a boarding house, she explained, and so always had need of cleaning materials. She prattled on about the slovenly habits of their lodgers and the laziness of their cleaning woman until the man stood and said he was going to buy two more cups of ale. Could he buy one for Abigail too, he asked, to seal their agreement on the clay? Abigail started to say that she must go, she had to meet the carter who was to take her home at the West Port at five, she'd never manage to carry the can of dripping she had bought all the way back to Gilmerton without a lift. The woman sucked her teeth and said she didn't think Abigail could make it to the West Port for five, and was she sure the carter would wait? Abigail said no, she had told him to go if she wasn't there on the hour.

'A shame to go then,' the woman said, 'and risk missing him after carrying the can all that way.' And then her face lit up and she said she had an idea: Abigail could come home with them and sleep in their lodging house. They had spare beds that night, and if Abigail could give them a few pence off the clay, they could call it even. And their place was at the West Port, Abigail would be sure to find a carter going back to Gilmerton from there the next day.

By this time Abigail was halfway through her second glass of ale and she readily agreed – she couldn't run to the West Port if she wanted to, her legs seemed to be drunker than the rest of her. And so they stayed for another round – she used the last of her pennies to buy it and had only her shilling and sixpence left – and then William carried her dripping and Margaret carried her clay and each took one of her arms so she was supported between them as they wove their way along the Cowgate and through the Grassmarket and into a close past the West Port. It was full dark by then, but there were lights high above them in the sky and Abigail looked up and pointed and asked what that was, and Margaret laughed and said she must be half cut indeed, sure wasn't that the great Edinburgh Castle? And Abigail laughed at her own foolishness.

Inside they sat in the kitchen and called for their friend who was minding the lodging house, another William. He turned out to be a smallish man with a kindly face. He came and set out oatcakes for them all, and poured out tots of some awful-tasting stuff that made Abigail cough and splutter. And they had quite a merry night of it, all in all, exchanging stories of the village where Abigail lived and the places they grew up, far west of here and across the sea in Ireland. They asked about her family, and she said she had a daughter, Bess, a bonnie lass and strong, too, and the first William said perhaps he should marry her and inherit all Abigail's great wealth for himself. Abigail laughed and laughed, for wasn't Bessie already married to a salter, and William to Margaret, and what did Abigail have to leave in any case except the clothes she stood up in and a few sticks of furniture fit only for burning?

'I'll have your pension then,' William said, good-naturedly, 'although you're right there, Abigail, the fact that Bess has a husband and I have a wife is an obstacle right enough, no matter how you look at it. Or is it, William? Have you not a wife at home and a hoor here to warm your bed, for all you walk the streets of Edinburgh with a Bible under your arm like any good Presbyterian?' He roared with laughter although Abigail didn't think the other William enjoyed the joke much, nor even Margaret. She tried to ask the second William about his wife in Ireland, but it seemed her tongue would no longer do her bidding.

They fried some bread in dripping then, from Abigail's can, but she didn't mind, there was enough of it to go around. After that her memory went hazy, but somehow she found herself in bed, in her shift, in an unfamiliar room that spun till she thought she might be sick, but then that passed and she fell asleep.

Abigail wakes in panic, in the grey light of morning. Burning vomit fills her mouth. She catches what she can of the foul stream in her hand, but a dribble escapes through her fingers to stain the front of her shift. She sees a basin on a rough chest by the window and scrambles out of bed towards it, her joints creaking in protest. The vomit spatters into the basin and she coughs and coughs again. She tries to clean her mouth with water from the ewer, rinsing her hands and scrubbing at the mess on her front but before she can finish, her gorge rises and she vomits and vomits again until there is nothing left but bile.

Shaking, Abigail crawls back into the bed and closes her eyes. She remembers meeting William and Margaret, remembers coming with them to a close off the West Port, but she cannot remember what happened then. She should get up, get dressed, retrieve her things and go home, but she is worried she will void herself again. She closes her eyes and tries to focus on slowing the beat of her heart.

The door of the room opens and closes and Abigail hears a murmur of voices. Men – William and another. She thinks she has heard the voice before but she can't be sure. Had it been only William she might have spoken, but before a stranger she is embarrassed and so she feigns sleep, lying with her eyes closed, breathing as steadily as she can.

William exclaims in disgust at the mess in the basin. They confer in low voices – it seems William's companion is protesting about something – and then Abigail hears the sound of liquid sloshing in a cup. The smell of strong drink reaches her and she almost retches again, but then she feels a hand on her face. It slides down her forehead and the fingers pinch her nose closed. Her jaw is clamped in an iron grip and a crushing weight lands on her chest.

Abigail is an old woman, inebriated and dehydrated. In her already weakened state, shock takes hold quickly and spares her much of the horror of the few minutes of consciousness she has remaining. She does not relive her life. She does not think of her home, or her beloved Bess, or Tam who loved her and was taken from her so many years ago, when she was too young to know how good she had had it. Only one face comes to her in her final seconds, calm and comforting and kind. The carter. She knows he waited, long past five.

11
Jaundice

FOR SOME WEEKS NOW, WILLIAM HAD BEEN busy at the table from first light until dusk, his glasses pinched tight to his nose and a lamp pulled close, but not a single pair of shoes had he made. Instead, he seemed to have set up business as a conjurer, magicking up tiny, wonderful things – a roomful of furniture for a fairy, perhaps, or a very house-proud mouse.

The chairs and tables, beds and dressers William made looked tiny and as light as air, but the tools he used to produce them were solid enough – a sharp knife and a chisel, a plane and a sanding block, glue and files and clamps and a hammer for nailing. The materials were not dissimilar to those he used in his everyday trade – leather, wood, offcuts of metal – but he also took himself off to see a man in the High Street who made tables and chests decorated with all sorts of inlays and carvings, and from him he bought sheets of wood so thin it felt like paper, and scraps of ivory, and pieces of something he called 'mother-of-pearl', from the insides of shells, that glowed in lamplight like the sky at gloaming.

Helen was enchanted by this miniature world, and before long, she had persuaded William to let her help dress the tiny beds with hangings and eiderdowns, and cover the seats of the chairs and the backs of the settles with silk. She had never owned such fine stuff herself, and William gave her the money and sent her out to buy it special – but scraps only, he said, for the things they were making were so small, they had no need of anything larger than a handkerchief. That set Helen to thinking, and she suggested she embroidered some flowers on the back of a settle, in coloured silks. She practised on a rough piece of linen first, till she was pleased with her stitching and felt it wouldn't shame any pixie or fairy. When she showed William he was well pleased, and said she should begin on the settle directly; he had only a few days to finish the work before it would be gone to the customer, and delighted he would be with it, too. William had finished all of the carpentry, by that point, and all there was left to do was the last of the sanding, and varnish it with shellac, but first William planned to trace patterns on the wood with ink, to look like inlay or poker-work.

As they worked, William told her a story about a man who voyaged to a land of tiny people called Lilliputians, and went from being their prisoner to living happily amongst them for a while in a city they had there. Then he pissed on a fire to put it out and was sentenced to have his eyes put out, and so he ran off. This was part of a book written by an Irishman, William said, a clergyman called Swift who preached in Dublin long ago. Then he spoke a little of his mother, who had greatly loved this story. She took in piecework, he said, doing fine stitching on linen articles. Her own mother had taken in bales of flax and spun it for the linen merchants to weave on their great looms. Their work had helped keep a roof over the family's head, and they had a few shillings left over now and then as pin money moreover, to buy a thing they fancied at market. That was how his mother had bought her book about Lilliput.

His grandmother had been no reader, though, and instead she coveted items of fashion. He told a funny story about how, in her great age, she had wanted a pair of gloves with ears of corn embroidered on the fingertips in metal threads, but when she had saved enough money to buy them, she found they didn't fit her hands, worn and swollen as they were with spinning and with age.

Helen looked at her own rough hands and thought to ask about William's wife, whether she had a gift for fancy work or the stomach for plain honest labour, but in the end she kept her mouth buttoned closed – better not to ask a question if the answer could hurt you, she knew, for all your heart wished to do it, in the way your tongue always sought out a sore bit in your mouth and worried at it until it was worse.

When at last their work was finished and all the varnishes and finishes cured and hard, Helen wrapped the pieces in soft paper and packed them carefully in a box. As she picked up each piece to wrap it, she saw how William's skill had grown as he worked, so the first pieces seemed rough, almost, clumsy by comparison to those he had made last. She missed the sight of them on the dresser, when they were all packed away and ready for William to deliver.

'Where are they going?' she asked, thinking perhaps they were for a child.

'A doctor asked me to make them for his wife,' William said. 'To furnish a fine little house he has bought for her.'

'Why would a grown woman want a thing like that?' Helen asked. 'I thought it would be a plaything for a wee lass.'

William snorted. 'After all our hard work?' he said. 'Nah, Nelly, these are too good for play. They're to be admired, like a collection, only in a cabinet shaped like a house instead of a chest of drawers.'

Helen knew nothing of such things, and told him so. William told her about the clergyman he had worked for and how he had had a great glass-fronted cabinet filled with drawers, each only an inch or two deep, and there were scores of them, and in each there were shells and stones and rocks with strange things in them, that looked like bones.

'What did he want with dirt like that?' Helen wondered.

'He said there were things to learn from them,' William said. 'I never understood quite what, but then I was a young lad and I had lasses on the brain, Nelly! Come to think of it' – he snagged an arm around her waist – 'I've not changed mightily since then, have I now?'

The next day, around noon, William set off with his box and returned that evening well pleased with his payment.

'Did the wife like them?' Helen asked. She hoped her sewing had pleased.

'And how would I know that, Nelly?' William laughed. 'Sure I only gave them to the Doctor at his rooms in Surgeon's Square. I never saw his wife at all!'

With his words, something chimed in Helen's memory and all of a sudden, she felt uneasy.

'How did you come by the commission, William?' she asked. 'Who is the Doctor man?'

'Well, now . . .' William's ears had gone red, and he seemed to be having difficulty meeting her eye. Then he cleared his throat and looked at her. 'Knox, his name is,' he said.

'Knox . . .' Helen repeated. 'Is that not the man . . . When the auld man died, is that not the man that gave you the money for his corpse?'

'It was,' said William. He looked at his feet.

'How came you to take a commission from him?' Helen asked. 'The way you told it, he just came and gave you money

136

for the auld man's body. And that was half a year ago! You only started working on the dolls' house gear after the turn of the year. How can you have had such a commission from a man you never saw but once?'

William scratched his jaw. 'I did . . . see him more than once,' he said.

'Why? When?'

'Och, Nelly,' William said, after a second's pause. 'I didn't say anything because I knew you would worry. You see, there was a man from Cheshire lodging in the room upstairs, so there was. A miller, I think he was, and he took the jaundice. You know, where a man turns yellow? Well, Margaret was near distracted, worrying that word would get out and no one would want to lodge here, and so Hare and I went up to see him and—' He made a strange gesture with his hands, lifting them to the height of his chest with the palms turned upwards.

'And what?' Helen asked.

'Well, what do you think?' said William. 'When we went up there, he was dead. And we thought of Margaret, and the panic that was on her, and . . . we took him to Surgeon's Square that night.'

Helen felt as though her legs had turned to water suddenly, and she sank down in the chair. William crouched in front of her, rubbing her hands.

'Oh, Nelly, Nelly,' he said, 'I'm sorry. I never would have done it, but I wanted to help William and Margaret.'

'How much did you get?' Helen asked.

'Ten pounds,' William said. 'And . . . there was another one who—'

Helen goggled. 'Another one? Three of them?'

William didn't answer and instead stared at his feet, his face aflame. 'Ach, Nelly,' he said at last. 'They were poor folk, living in a lodging house. So what if they went off to help the anatomists in their work?'

'William,' Helen's voice sounded odd to her own ears, high somehow, but flat – 'we're poor. We live in a lodging house.'

'Och, that's different,' said William.

'How? How is it different?' Helen demanded. 'If I died, would you not send word to my father? So my own folk would know what had become of me?'

'Of course I would,' William said. 'But you live here with me, and William lives with Margaret. These folk had no one. We had no way of letting their people know what had happened. Surely you see that, Nelly! We didn't know their people or even their place. The best they could have hoped for was a pauper's grave, far from home.'

Helen didn't know what to say to that. It was true, and yet . . . 'There's no shame in a pauper's grave,' she said. 'And more than that, we should be thankful the city buries its dead when there's no one else to do it.'

'Well, I suppose so,' William said, 'but what of the harm to Margaret's business, Nelly? What of that? If the city were to have sent a coffin, and men to lift it, then it would have been all over Edinburgh that two folk had died in this house, and then three! Sure, no one would ever have wanted to stay here again, or they'd be after a room at half price for fear it held the plague.'

Helen took a deep breath.

'It's wrong, William,' she said. 'I don't care what you say. It's wrong, and that's all there is to it. Now you have a choice. You can promise me, right now, that this is the end of it. You'll make your living honestly, as you've told me your mother did, and your grandmother did, or you won't live with me anymore. Then you can do as you please.' Even as she said it, she thought the words rang hollow. Would she really have the courage to up and leave William?

But William didn't seem to have noticed. There were tears running down his face, and he laid his cheek on her knee.

'I promise, Nelly,' he said. 'I only did it to help William and Margaret, sure I did. I'm an honest man, Nelly, with an honest trade. I'll never do anything like it again.'

'And no more drinking,' Helen said. 'You'll do things in drink you'd never do sober. I know it, William, and so do you.'

'No more drinking,' said William, his voice muffled by her skirt. 'I promise.'

Helen sat there while his tears soaked into the poor fabric of her skirt. She could choose to believe him, or she could leave. She thought of the little chairs and tables and dressers and beds. The man that had made those was not a bad man. Maybe a weak one, but not bad. She would choose to believe him, but she would do her level best to get them out of this house, out of the influence of William Hare. Until then, she would watch William like a hawk.

12
Splinter

J OHN HELPED SUSAN UNPACK THE DOLLS' HOUSE, which was wrapped in sacking and blankets and secured with string and leather strapping. It was not really a dolls' house, Susan learned from a note in the wrapping, but something called a 'baby house', never meant to be a plaything for a child but instead a woman's precious possession, where she might showcase miniature furniture and paintings, tiny silverware and exquisite needlework. This note was written by the antiquarian who had sold it to Robert, and in turn he had discovered it mouldering in the damp and dirty attic of a great house, when visiting to value some pieces the family wished to sell to meet their death duties. He said the family maintained it was a copy of the real house, but it was clear to anyone with eyes in their head that this was not the case. They believed this was why it was called a 'baby house', but the antiquarian said this was nonsense. He said that in the last century and the one before, little girls called their poppets 'Flanders babies', while a 'doll' was a word for a strumpet. This baby house dated from that time and so could not have been named so, its Mistress would not have countenanced such a thing.

Whatever it was called, the house stood five feet tall and four feet wide. It was built of wood, painted to resemble pale stone blocks, and modelled as a three-storied house of perhaps six score years before. The door was situated strangely in the middle of the second floor, with a twelve-paned window either side, and a fanlight above. Two pillars flanked the door, and two others each side of the façade. On the upper floor were three windows, quite ornate, and on the floor below were three more, quite plain, with only nine panes apiece. The bottom floor was painted with closer blocks than the others, and Susan thought perhaps it was a basement, like those in the New Town, although the steps from the doors there led to little bridges to the street, and this door led to thin air only. Along the top was a balustrade, with great sections missing, and underneath the house itself was a drawer with much-worn paint that showed the ghost of a place in the Orient.

The façade opened by a strange mechanism – Susan was glad of the antiquarian's note – which required that the tiny front door first be unlocked with a key, a hand inserted, and a catch unclipped. It took all Susan's courage to reach inside, for it had been untouched for so long that the dust had taken on a furry, clinging quality and she thought at first she had touched the remains of a mouse or a bat that had died inside. Then the whole front swung outwards with an alarming creak so Susan thought it might fall, but the hinges seemed sturdy enough, and she could see there were no corpses, only dust in the webs of generations of spiders that had lived there, festooned with great ropes of moth eggs, thick as the roes of fish.

There were six rooms, on three floors, but Susan could see no details past the swags of filth and while she gathered her courage to sweep them out, she turned to unfastening a separate box that had been delivered with the house, wrapped in paper and bound up in string and seals. This contained various pieces of furniture and chattels. There were a number of small pewter plates, embossed with pictures of fish and fowl and vegetables, and two larger plates made of earthenware, glazed in cream and modelled to seem to hold a leg of mutton, with a great slice cut out, and an enormous mound of peas. There was a dainty basket containing a dozen bone fish game-counters, far larger and cruder than the tableware but pleasing nonetheless with their staring eyes and incised scales. A birdcage, an assortment of bottles, and a number of other small pieces were also made from bone, finely worked – a label hanging from the cage said that it was made by prisoners from Napoleon's armies, using the lamb bones from their meals. There were four wooden pieces only – a dresser with ivory pull-handles, a little table with flaps to either side, a corner washstand with no bowl or ewer, and a little chair. A tiny needlework rug with a lion on a red ground and a gaily-coloured fringe had survived the moths' attentions, although it seemed nothing else had, even the seat of the chair was more than half gone. There were two brass items and one of steel she did not recognise, and set to one side, and, lastly, a dark metal chandelier, quite beautiful, and a curious item with four prongs pointing upwards from a round base, standing on three little legs.

Once she had examined these pieces and noted the many repairs required – the table was missing a leg, the pewter plates were curled here and there, and everything wooden needed reglued – Susan fetched a great apron from the kitchen and a scarf for her hair and set about the filthy task of clearing the rooms of dirt. Under the heavy wreaths of dust and debris, she found the mouldering remains of carpets and curtains, eaten by moth and rotted by damp. In one room a mouse appeared to have taken up residence, leaving its droppings in what seemed once to have been a finely worked carpet – perhaps it had come down the chimney. Susan ripped out the horrible things and deposited the lot in a bucket for John to empty outside.

Gradually the rooms appeared from the filth, dingy and grey but with charming mouldings visible now, and pleasing proportions. There were two low-ceilinged bedchambers on the top floor with curious corner fireplaces, and two taller rooms on the first floor, with panelling, heavy chimney breasts, and pretty mantelpieces with overmantels. She recognised then, that the mysterious metal items were grates, and she wiggled two of these into place in the first-floor fireplaces. There was no staircase, but each room and its adjoining fellow shared a little two-panelled door, with neat triangular pediments above both sides of the one on the first floor. Susan liked the ground floor best of all, or the basement it might be; it had one room with nothing in it at all but a corner cabinet with a glazed door to the top fixed on with too-large butterfly hinges, and the other was a kitchen, with a dresser fixed to one wall, a large fireplace in the centre with a spit rack on the wall above, and a copper off to one side. She fitted the steel grate into the fireplace; it was a strange, old-fashioned thing but it looked very fine when it was in place.

Mrs Scott bustled in then, clearly desperate to see Susan's progress, and she startled herself, it seemed, as much as Susan by giving a barking laugh in her shock at Susan's appearance. Susan went to the mirror and saw that she was as dirty as any chimney sweep's boy. She swept her hand across her face and felt the grime smear greasily under her fingers – the attic where the house had stood must have been a sooty place. She said she would do no more today, she would need to bathe before she tried to clean the house any further, or she would make it worse. Mrs Scott peered inside and said it was a wonder, just like a real house in miniature. She picked up the strange silver item and smiled at it, saying it had been many years since she had seen such a thing or thought of it, and even then it had been very old-fashioned, and ten times larger, of course.

Susan said she didn't recognise it, and Mrs Scott said it was a plate holder, so a serving man or woman could carry a great number of heavy plates to table all at once, metal plates made from pewter. She offered to take it and the chandelier and shine them herself – they were silver, she said, and the tarnish would come away so that they shone once more – and she would polish the brass grates and the steel range while she was at it. Susan thanked her, and Mrs Scott said she would have the bath brought up to Susan's room and filled and get John to clear away the dirt and close the house, but it seemed to Susan she really wanted to go back to her room with the miniature metalwork and admire it.

The next day, Susan didn't even have to ask for buckets and bowls of warm water, and soap and cloths, all were ready and waiting for her after breakfast. She set to cleaning the rooms of the house, beginning at the top and working towards the bottom. The grime on the walls of the top rooms came off slowly, and revealed pale green paint in the right-hand room, with cream panelling and delicate painted veining on the fire surround to simulate marble. The left-hand room had been papered, with a garish design of blue and white stripes with coral spots – the sort of thing Jessie would like, too modern for the house – and slowly Susan soaked and peeled, and soaked and peeled, until the whole of one wall came off and she could see the pale blue paint underneath. She had to leave the rest of it for another day, it hurt her neck to lean so far into the house and her thumbnail was blunt. Instead she began to wash down the exterior of the house, changing the water again and again until at last the soot was gone and the glass in the windows shone. Mrs Scott came in with a plate of cold pie for her in the early afternoon, although it was clear that what she really wanted was to see the house. She proclaimed herself amazed at the difference in its appearance, she said it was as though the stones had been wet and now were dry, so much lighter did they appear, and she offered to polish the outside walls with beeswax so that it would shine.

In the afternoon Susan got a little more of the wallpaper off in the upper floor, and the next day she got the middle rooms cleaned. The paint in there was a kind of distemper and washed off, but she could see what the colours had been clearly enough, and Mrs Scott went off to ask John to bring her fresh distemper mixed to the right shades, pale pink in one room and a rich middling blue in the other. John had done much of the decorating of Lillypot, it seemed, when Robert had bought it, and he had a good eye; the colours looked too dark to Susan but he promised they would dry lighter, and indeed they did. Mrs Scott had somehow become Susan's assistant in the task of rescuing the house, and she wanted to know which was the drawing room and which was the dining room so they would know what furniture would go where. They didn't really know the answer, so they decided that the dining room should be above the kitchen for ease of serving, and then Susan suggested the empty room with the corner cupboard should be the housekeeper's room, since it was by the kitchen, and Mrs Scott seemed delighted at the thought of that.

As it happened, the housekeeper's room was the first to be furnished. Robert had commissioned two boxes of furniture for Susan, which came down by cart in the middle of the next week with a note to say he hoped they would be of use, and enclosing a list from a toy-man's shop with drawings of the things he supplied that Robert thought she might wish to order. By then they had finished the cleaning and the stripping of the bright wallpaper, and the repainting of the rooms where the distemper had washed away. They had left the drawers on the stand alone; they did not see how they could paint the Chinese motifs in gold, but Susan thought it looked well with the marks of age on it. She had placed the house's own items back inside, the chest and the washstand in a bedroom and the little folding table in the dining room with the creamware food on top, the pewter on the dresser in the kitchen, and the plate rack and the fish basket on the floor. Mrs Scott offered to mend the seat of the chair, and until that was done they placed it in the dining room behind the table, which was in turn propped up against the wall so the missing leg did not matter. John put a hook in the ceiling of the drawing room so they could hang the chandelier, and Mrs Scott found some tiny tapers they cut into even tinier slivers to fill it.

Susan and Mrs Scott opened the boxes of furniture together and looked over the items. Mrs Scott clucked over them like a broody hen, but Susan found most of them wrong; they seemed too recent in style and too bright for the old house, and some were rough in their finish – a bead of blood rose on her thumb as a splinter from a sofa pierced the flesh. In the end she selected a small number of items – two four-poster beds, an inlaid table, a second washstand and chest, a little settle, and a plain dining table – and placed them in the bedrooms and the dining room, saying she would redress the beds in time to match the colours of the rooms, but she would like to choose her own furniture for the drawing room from the toy-man's list. Then she asked Mrs Scott to make her own selection from the remainder for the housekeeper's room. Mrs Scott selected a little round table, and two matching chairs, a sturdy wooden bed dressed with an eiderdown, a washstand and a linen press, and she arranged and rearranged them until the room was exactly to her liking.

'We'll need to find some bonnie things for your cupboard,' Susan said. 'And a basin and ewer, and candlesticks, and a picture for the wall.'

Mrs Scott was delighted and immediately offered to sew a sampler with a Bible quote. She left Susan with the toy-man's catalogue and said she would arrange for John to go and order the pieces she wanted when she had made her choice, and then she took herself off to design her wallhanging. Susan packed the pieces of furniture she did not want in the Chinese drawers and then she began to peruse the pages of precious things: pewter pressed into the shapes of chairs with rush seats and carved stretchers, or painted to resemble bamboo, tin moulded and painted with lacquer to resemble wooden tables and clocks, and white glass made to appear like tiny tea sets, so fragile that you might think they would shatter with a breath.

Once she had made her lists and received her items, Susan was less satisfied than ever with the furnishings Robert had procured for her. She said to Mrs Scott that she would like to make her own: did she think she could write to Robert to ask for some tools capable of producing finer pieces to her own designs? She was worried Mrs Scott would say no, files and chisels and the like were not suitable, but perhaps Mrs Scott knew fine that Susan would not have the skill to prise open a lock, and surely she knew she would do herself and the children no damage? Indeed, she agreed readily enough, and in a few weeks Susan had a fine set of equipment she had no idea how to use. Mrs Scott told John to show her how to cut wood and metal, and how to mix up glue and make a joint and brace it. John did so well enough, although without much enthusiasm, he was a man of few words who liked his own company best of all. Even after his tuition was finished, Susan remained less than proficient, but there was no rush, she could practise to her heart's content.

It was a curious thing, the house. Susan's world had narrowed so completely to Lillypot, the handful of humans who lived there, that she had imagined the tiny house would somehow imprison her even more closely. Instead, it had worked an uncanny magic and made Mrs Scott an ally, if not quite a friend. Somehow, too, it had opened up companionship of a different sort to Susan. As she lit tiny tapers in the wall sconces, she felt herself in the company of a century and more of other women, and their friends, and their children, all of whom had performed the same ritual of lighting the little candles and peering through the green, bubbled glass, to see the little house come to life. As she reached inside to nudge a tiny treasure this way or that, she felt their hands, heard their laughter echo in the little rooms. The signs of them were everywhere, from the soot marks on the ceilings to a miniature shell in the chest of drawers, a tiny print pasted above the fireplace in a bedroom upstairs, a tin pot jammed up the kitchen chimney. It had been theirs and now it was hers.

Oddest of all, the house gave her a sense of freedom, as though it took her back again to the time when she was young and hopeful, waiting for her life to begin, wondering where she might make her home, and with whom, and what sort of place it might be. There was no doubt left now in her world, of course she knew that she would only ever have Lillypot, on and on and on until she died. But the little house gave her back that sense of having a future, as though she were waiting for something to happen but knowing not what it might be, and thinking after all that there might be wonder, and beauty and comfort and care.

13

Laceration

IN THE WEEKS THAT FOLLOWED William's confession, Helen kept a weather eye on him, conniving excuses to be nearby while he worked and going with him to his prayer meetings at night, although she was hard-pressed to keep from dozing as they yawed on.

In the daytime, William seemed much as he ever had been, an upstanding, sober man who worked hard and maintained a cheerful demeanour at all times. He had taken up his cobbling again, tying on his apron and tool belt with seeming pleasure, and he sang to his customers as he mended their shoes in the close or out on the street, the Castle looming above them, earning himself a few pence more for a verse of 'The Minstrel Boy' or 'Whisky in the Jar'. He had given Helen all the money he had from the corpses, so he would have the knowledge, he said, that all his own coin was honestly earned. Helen wore it in a cotton pocket tied round her waist under her skirts, thinking to keep it until such time as she could get them out of Tanner's Close and into rooms of their own.

At night, though, it seemed that William's misdeeds returned to torment him. He would say his prayers in the usual way and fall into sleep, but then it seemed almost as though something pricked him awake, so he started up with a cry of pain. He couldn't bear the dark then, and so they had taken to sleeping with a tuppenny candle lit beside the bed. The only thing that could get him back over into sleep was a draught of whisky, else he would lie awake the rest of the night whispering to himself and shivering so Helen was driven near distracted, passing days and days in a stupor of tiredness that William never seemed to feel; he was driven by a sort of nervous energy that never seemed sapped by the long nights of wakefulness.

That was how Helen finally let him escape from her sight. It was a night near the start of April, and in the wee hours of the morning, William had started out of his sleep with the usual sounds of distress. Helen had turned to soothe him with a hand on his back, trying not to wake fully from her own sleep so she might have a hope of proper rest. She heard him uncork a bottle and pour out a tot of spirit, the smell of it tickling her own nostrils. Then it seemed to her that he was quiet again, the whisky must have done its job, and she slipped back into a deep sleep.

When next Helen woke, the candle was guttering, and William was gone.

Wearily, Helen climbed out of bed and began to dress, cursing the woollen stockings that seemed to tangle round her legs as she fumbled to get them on, and the laces on her corset that defied her cold fingers as she fought to tie them. She still had her pocket – she slept with it on, always, not that she didn't trust William around money, mind, but the Hares and the other lodgers were always on the prowl. Looking in the drawer of the dresser, she found William's Bible, but not his cobbling money. That likely meant he had gone to a tavern.

Helen lit a lantern and set out into the dark. Early as it was, there were plenty of folk about, setting up stalls and toiling over cooking fires, rolling barrels up closes and lugging hides into the tanneries. The taverns were open and doing a good business, it seemed, between the early birds and the stragglers from the night before.

First Helen tried the places nearest home, in the West Port and the Grassmarket, but no one had seen William, or if they had, they weren't admitting it. She puffed up the hill then to a place she knew he liked on the High Street, but they said he hadn't been there that night. There were some folk in that Helen knew, and she decided to lighten her foul mood by sitting a while to crack over a cup of ale and a breakfast of pie.

Once Helen was fed and rested and in a better humour, she bade her companions farewell and set off again in search of William. She tried a couple of howffs in the darker closes to no avail, and another two taverns on the High Street, and then she reached Swanston's place in the Canongate. There was no sign of Swanston this early in the day, and the lad he had working there said he wouldn't know Burke the cobbler from Adam himself. Helen described him, and the lad said there had been an Irishman of about that height in early that morning, but he didn't think that was William, this man had been a pensioner. Helen asked how he came to know that, and the lad explained that the Irishman had been sat with two young lasses, a rough pair they were, that had been arrested for some wildness the night before and had come here straight from the police station when they were let go. They all had several rounds of rum and bitters bought by the man, and then he invited the lassies to break their fast in his lodging house and share two bottles of whisky he had bought to take with him. That was how the lad had come to know he was a pensioner; one of the lasses had come away with some cheek about going nowhere with an Irishman, and he had said she might do as she pleased, but it was a shame as his pension was enough to keep them all handsomely for life. The one who had resisted went happily enough when she heard that, he said, and his mouth twisted in disgust, as if he would spit.

Helen was stuck then, not knowing if the man had been William or not, though her blood steamed at the thought it might be, and she so daft as to think him hers, and faithful forby. She ordered herself a rum and bitters, to see what it tasted of, this treat the Irishman had bought for the girls. It was good, and she ordered another and another and another, dipping into the coins in her pocket to pay the barman. At last she got up and made for the door, a trifle unsteady on her feet and not entirely sure of her next move.

Outside, Helen breathed in gulps of air and looked around her. It was full light now, had been for some time, and the place was alive with trade and traffic. As she looked up and down the road, contemplating her next move, who should her eyes light on but William himself, a little way ahead of her and walking alongside a woman. They turned down Gibb's Close and Helen realised they were making for the apartment where William's brother Constantine lived with his wife and bairnies. She felt winded, for a second, but then her blood rose and she lifted her skirts to run after them.

Constantine Burke's place was in a dirty tenement, up a narrow wooden stair and along a dark passageway. As she rushed along in her fury, Helen heard the sounds of merriment – William's voice raised in a story and women laughing. She lifted the latch of the door and stormed inside.

William started at this intrusion and half-rose, his mouth hanging open so he looked like a fish on a market stall. 'Nelly!' he said. 'Is it you?'

Helen looked around. The place was a midden, as ever, with the shutters half open, rubbish strewn about, and great rents and tears in the curtains on the bed. There was no sign of Constantine, but his slatternly wife Peggy was sitting at the table with William and two girls. One of these was a small, dark-haired lass Helen had never seen before but one she knew well enough – Mary Patterson. She was from out near Helen's home-place and Helen had met her a time or two in Edinburgh, where she'd got in trouble and spent time with the Magdalenes. Now Mary was asleep in a spindle-back chair, her head lolling back and curling papers in her long red hair.

'Come away in and sit down, Nelly,' said Peggy, as though there was nothing at all odd about the gathering she was presiding over. She brandished a spoon. 'There's plenty breakfast left. Will you take some haddock?'

'Or an egg?' the dark-haired lass suggested.

'No, I will not have an egg,' said Helen, almost choking on her fury, and she turned and raised her hand to slap the lass across the face. 'I will not sit and take an egg with a tuppenny hoor who would make a play for my husband.'

'Hoy!' the girl shouted, grabbing Helen's hand and struggling to hold it. 'I'm no a hoor and I never made a play for anyone! And even if I had, how was I to ken this was your man? It's him you should be skelping, no me!' Helen tried to slap her with the other hand and the lass grabbed that as well.

'It's true, Nelly,' William said. 'This is Janet, we met in Swanston's, she's just breaking her fast with us, that's all.'

'I'll break your face,' Helen said, feeling the rage flame through her blood. All these weeks of worry that he might be discovered and taken up, all the nights of calming him and soothing him, and this was to be her thanks! She picked up a dish with the remains of a haddock on it and threw it at him, followed immediately by a dish of butter.

'Mind my dishes!' Peggy said, as a bowl smashed against the wall, leaving a dent in the damp plaster.

Helen threw another plate and then, moved to anger at last, William threw a glass back at her. It struck her hard on the forehead, stupefying her for a moment. Blood poured down into her eye and she put up a hand to staunch it.

'Jesus God,' Peggy shouted, and she grabbed her shawl and ran out of the house. William got to his feet and grabbed hold of Helen, dragging her to the door while she thumped his back and head, leaving bloody marks all over his jacket. She tried to knee him between the legs for good measure, but he was too strong for her and, at last, she found herself locked outside in the dark passageway. She turned and hammered on the door, shouting that William was dirt, a whoreson and a meater, and demanding that he open the door and face her.

In a few minutes, Peggy returned with a man – not Constantine, as Helen had expected, but William Hare. Behind him came Margaret, her eyes glistening like a rat's at the thought of trouble.

'What's to do, Nelly?' Hare demanded. 'What's the reason for all this shouting and bawling?'

Helen opened her mouth to tell him he had ruined William, made him into a drunkard and a sinner, but before she could get the words out, a great heaving sob escaped her chest, and then she was blind with tears and blood.

William Hare shook his head, but Margaret stepped forward with a sigh.

'Come on, Helen,' she said. 'You've had a bit much to drink. Let's get you away home and clean you up. You need some food in you as well.'

Helen allowed the woman to lead her away. As she turned to climb down the narrow stairs, she saw Peggy let William Hare into the apartment.

Back at Tanner's Close, Margaret cleaned Helen's wound with whisky while Helen sobbed out the whole story, and then she helped her out of her clothes and put her to bed. It was barely gone midday, but Helen fell immediately into a deep sleep, or perhaps it was a stupor. The last thing she heard was Margaret closing the door behind her.

Helen slept right through that day, and the night, waking at dawn with the wound on her forehead pounding in time with the thumping of her heart. She had a raging thirst on her, a terrible sourness in her mouth, and her teeth seemed to be coated with something strange and metallic, but those were the least of her worries. William had not returned, and when she thought of the events of the previous day, great red waves of shame crashed over her. Had she really smashed Peggy Burke's dishes in her fury? Had she called William a cheat and a meater and a whoreson? What if he left her? Surely it would be no worse than she deserved, abusing him in front of all those folk, when now she could see that it might be that he had done nothing worse than she had, many's the night, sitting in drink with pleasant company. The lasses were rough types, right enough, but Helen herself was none too fancy, and they had often kept company with worse.

Save for a trip to the pot, Helen managed to stay abed until it was full light outside, and then she crawled out from under the blankets and got herself washed and dressed. She thought about eating, but her stomach was queasy and she knew she would puke if she tried. She pulled her shawl about her and took herself out, meaning to go directly to Constantine's, find William and throw herself on her knees before him.

Helen had got no further than locking the door when she heard Margaret's step behind her. She closed her eyes and took a breath – did the craitur never sleep at all?

'I was coming to see if you needed anything,' Margaret said. 'You were so upset last night, I was worried about you, so I was.'

Helen cursed her luck; she could bear Margaret in one of her 'good' humours even less than she could bear the woman in a temper or in her cups. She was like a sugared plum made with rotten fruit, the sugar so sweet it set your teeth to aching, but still not sweet enough to hide the taint of foulness behind it. Still, she had looked after Helen the day before, and so she gritted her teeth and turned, with her own attempt at a smile.

'I'm feeling a bit foolish this morning,' she said. 'I shouldna have said the things I said yesterday morning. In truth, I had taken too much in drink, looking for William in the taverns on an empty stomach, and I shouldn't have gone to Constantine's, let alone carried on like that. I owe William an apology, Margaret, and Peggy, and you and William.'

But Margaret snorted. 'No need to apologise to me,' she said. 'I thought you spoke the truth. They were hoors, the pair of them.'

Helen found herself wrong-footed, she had expected Margaret to glory in her misfortune. But she felt it was only fair to admit her own mistake.

'They're not hoors,' she said. 'I've kent Mary since she was a wee lass, on and off. She came to the town to work as a maid, but one of the lads in the house got her in the family way. She got a place in the Magdalene Asylum, after that, to learn a trade.'

'A trade!' Margaret snorted again. 'Aye, she's learnt a trade, right enough. Don't be a simpleton, Helen. You saw rightly yesterday how it was, and I understand why you were so angry. Now come into my room with me,' she went on. 'William left at the crack of dawn to attend to some business, and I'm all alone. I have tea, do you like it? It'll set you right in an instant.'

Helen shook her head. 'I'm on my way to Constantine's,' she said, 'to find my William.'

'Sure, they're away together to get some breakfast,' Margaret said. 'They came back just an hour or two behind us yesterday to fetch the horse and cart, and off they went on some business or other. Your William slept here in the kitchen, last night. You must have put the frighteners on him, Helen! I'd say he took too much himself and he's feeling the worse for it now. So they're getting themselves set up with a good feed, and we can stay here and have a good crack.'

Helen felt light-headed with relief – William hadn't left her! He had come home, and he would come home again. She would tell him she was sorry, and he might storm and bluster and sulk, but in the end he would forgive her. Numbly, she allowed Margaret to bustle her into her room, where Margaret took a key from about her neck and unlocked a wooden box she had on a dresser. She took out a scoop of dried leaves and put them in a pot. Then she took herself off to the kitchen to boil a kettle of water, and Helen had a few minutes to look about her.

The room was no finer than Helen and William's, really, with the same small window and mean furnishings, and it was even more crowded than their own with baskets and bundles of clothes. That surprised Helen – she and William had piles of clothes and gear because it was their trade, but Margaret had no trade in such things and seemed to own twice as much. Helen stirred through a few of the baskets with a curious finger to see what there was – if it was the right sort of stuff, she might offer to hawk it on Margaret's behalf for a share of the profits. Surely the woman had no need of all this?

It turned out to be a right gallimaufry – one basket was all men's things, poor and worn, and another women's, clarty but serviceable enough, but too wide and too short for Margaret, who was as thin as a rake for all she was almost as tall as a man. There were piles and piles of bairnies' bits – shawls and wee dresses and napkins and bonnets. Nothing was fine, but most of it seemed to have been made with care – folk tried their best for their bairnies, after all. Helen couldn't see why Margaret had it, she had no children of her own, and the wee ones she cared for came with their own things and left with them – at least, Helen had always assumed they took their belongings with them, when they went back to their mothers or onwards to new homes. But now she understood that Margaret must keep them, meaning to sell them on, perhaps, and wring a drop more profit out of the poor wee souls and their families. Or perhaps more of them died than Helen had realised. She shuddered at the thought of that – Margaret seemed to have laid off on the baby care trade for the moment, and Helen wasn't in any way sorry.

When Margaret came back in with the hot water, Helen asked her about the clothes.

'Left behind,' Margaret said, as she poured the water on the tea and stirred it. 'By lodgers when they move on. Some of them skip out on us, you know, Helen, do a moonlight flit and leave owing us rent. An auld man died back in November owing us four pounds – can you credit that? He said he was due an army pension, but then he died before we saw a penny.'

Helen did know about that old man, who had turned a profit for William Hare and her own William in the end, as others had done after, but she said nothing of that. She had no idea if Margaret knew. She probably did, the woman was shameless, but Helen thought it best to play dumb.

'Funny you should be asking me about the clothes,' Margaret said. 'I've been keeping a few bits aside for you, Helen. You're a bit bigger than me round the middle, and I've a fine skirt here I think would suit you.' She raked in a sack lying on the floor by the bed and pulled out a plaid skirt made of good, thick stuff.

'It's bonnie,' Helen said, 'but are you sure, Margaret? That's a fine piece of wool.' She stroked it between thumb and fore-finger, frowning. She had seen the pattern before, but she couldn't place it.

Margaret was grinning now. 'Christ, you were in your cups yesterday!' she said. 'Do you not know it? That hoor was wearing it, the one with the red hair!'

It came back to Helen in a flash then, the scene at Constantine's the previous day. She felt her face grow red, remembering it all again, but then her wits caught up with her.

'What . . . how do you come to have it?' she asked.

Margaret crowed with laughter. 'When William and Peggy went in, they found the redhead clambering onto your William's knee,' she said. 'My William threw her out of the house in her shift, what do you think of that?'

'In her shift?' Helen was horrified. 'Mary?'

'Ach, don't waste a moment thinking of her,' Margaret said. 'Her kind always fall on their feet. She said she would sleep at her friend's place and get a finer dress there. She was bound for Glasgow, that's what she said, she has some idea of making her fortune there. I heard tell she poses for artists in the nip.'

While Helen struggled to imagine that, Margaret poured them two bowls of steaming liquid. Helen cupped her hands round hers, grateful for the warmth, and sipped. Margaret was right, it did help, her stomach felt more settled already.

'What about the other one?' she asked. 'The other lass who was at Constantine's. Janet, I think William said her name was.'

'I don't know anything about her,' Margaret said. 'William said she walked out the minute he came in. Maybe she meant to rob them, Helen, do you think? That would explain why she left so fast when William arrived.'

Helen shuddered, but then she shook her head and took the skirt, thanking Margaret for the gift.

'Do you have anything else you don't need?' Helen asked. 'I could sell it for you and pass you the money.'

Margaret's eye glittered. 'What cut would you take?' she asked.

'A third,' said Helen. 'Half if anything needed mended.'

'I'll think on it,' said Margaret, and then she turned at a sound in the close outside. 'That's your man back, I think, Helen,' she said. 'On you go and see him. Take your cup and bring it back to me later.'

Helen couldn't face William out in the close, where so many windows looked on, and so she hurried along the corridor to her own room, feeling her belly gripe with nerves. She waited behind the door, full ready to throw herself on her knees before him, but when the door opened all that was forgotten – William's arms were laden with boxes and parcels so he could barely move, let alone get inside, and she grabbed at a box as it fell from his grasp.

When at last all was safely lain down, and William inside, he opened his arms to her. 'Oh Nelly!' he said, 'can you forgive me?'

Nelly's mouth fell open. 'Forgive you?' she said. 'Surely it's me who needs to ask forgiveness for the things I said. And for breaking Peggy's plates.' She tasted bile in her mouth again.

'What she must think of me,' she said. 'The shame I've brought on you, William!'

'Ach, never mind that,' said William, indicating his parcels, 'sure, haven't I bought Peggy a fine new set of crocks? She'll be glad to be rid of that old hotchpotch she had. Now if we're talking of shame, it's Peggy that should have been embarrassed to serve anyone their victuals on those chipped and cracked articles! And look, Nelly' – he pulled out his pocketknife and began to cut through the string tying a box – 'I bought a set for us too. Not so many pieces, for we don't have any babbies, or at least not living here with us.'

He began to unpack the box, lifting out blue and white plates, cups, bowls and, lastly, a big-bellied tureen with its own lid and ladle. 'What do you think of that, now, Nelly?' he asked. 'Won't you be proud to carry that in your basket to fetch home a few ladles of stew or soup?'

'I couldn't take that out to the street, William,' Helen said. 'It's too fine.' It was true, the things were finer than any gear she'd ever had, or even seen.

William chuckled in delight. 'We'll go to Peggy's tomorrow,' he said. 'But for now, let's hansel that soup pot and fetch ourselves some stew. I've a fair hankering for some meat.' He crooked his arm, and after a moment's hesitation, Helen took it.

It seemed any and all unpleasantness between them was forgotten, and they passed a pleasant afternoon and evening together playing cards and chasing off their sore heads with some cups of ale. Peggy was in a fine humour too when they visited her the next day. As well as the tableware, William gave her some money – for the breakfast, he said, although it looked to be a large sum for some eggs and haddock – and he brought her a bottle of whisky too. Peggy insisted they all drink it together, and by the time they left it was as though there had

never been any ill-feeling between them. Helen tried to apologise a time or two, but Peggy brushed her off, saying it was
nothing, sure hadn't she and Constantine had their fallings-out
too, over the years?

Helen and William returned to Tanner's Close in good spirits,
and the next morning William left early for a prayer meeting.
Helen lay in bed a while longer, and then took her time in
dressing and packing her wares. The gash on her head looked
to be healing, from what she could see in the small mirror they
had, although the skin was bruised purple and yellow all around,
so she pulled her frilled cap lower to cover it before she tied
on her bonnet.

As she stepped out the door to the close, Helen near about
fell over a figure on the doorstep. When she had righted herself,
she saw it was the lass from Peggy's, the one called Janet.

'I don't want any trouble,' the lass said quickly. 'I'm just
looking for Mary, that's all.'

'Mary?' Helen said. 'Why would I ken where Mary is? She's
your pal, is she no?'

'Aye,' said Janet, 'we lodge thegether. With Mrs Worthington,
and before that with Mrs Laurie. When I left Mary at yon
Mrs Burke's house, I went to Mrs Laurie's, for she's a kind
old wife and I was shaken by . . .' – she stopped, apparently
choosing her next words – 'by the things that happened. Mrs
Laurie sent her servant mannie back with me, but at first we
couldna find the place. We asked in the tavern, in the end,
and auld Swanston told us where to go. But when we got
there, Mary was gone. They said she was with Wi—with your
man, out fetching whisky. So we sat and waited a while with
Mrs Burke and yon other man, but they never came, and then
Mrs Laurie's serving-man said we had to go, he had to get
back to his work. I went back again that night and chapped

the door, but Mrs Burke said they never came back. And Mary has never come home since.'

'I heard that she had gone to Glasgow,' said Helen. She was still sore at the thought of Mary climbing onto William's knee, or trying to.

'What would she do in Glasgow?' Janet asked. 'She has no folk there.'

'How should I know?' said Helen.

Just then, Janet's eyes lighted on Helen's skirt. 'That's Mary's!' she said, grabbing at the fabric. 'How have you got it?'

Helen stepped back. 'She left it behind,' she said. 'After she stripped it off and climbed on my man's knee.'

'She wouldna do a thing like that,' Janet said. 'No if she kent he was a married man.'

'She kent fine he was a married man,' Helen said. 'She's kent me for some time.'

'What?' Janet looked confused. 'But when we met Will ... I mean, your man, in the tavern, she never let on she kent him.'

'Well, it seems she's maybe had us all on,' said Helen. 'I'm sorry, Janet, it must be sore to think she's done a flit on you. Does she owe money? For her rent?'

Janet looked miserable. 'A wee bit,' she said. 'No a lot.'

'Here.' Helen reached into her pocket and pulled out a few shillings. 'Put that against it. I've aye liked Mary and I'd no see her shamed as a debtor. Or you.'

Janet looked like she was about to start crying. She nodded her head, turned on her heel, and ran out of the close. Helen let out a breath, shouldered her basket, and prepared herself for her day of trade.

14

Elizabeth

ELIZABETH HALDANE COULD DATE the beginning of her misfortunes very precisely; she may not have known the hour, but she knew the day. All had been well until the nineteenth of August in the Year Of Our Lord 1745. Elizabeth herself was not yet born, indeed would not be born for a score more years, almost, but that was the day that Charles Edward Stuart climbed a hill at Glenfinnan, raised his standard, and claimed the throne of Britain in the name of his father James. Both sides of Elizabeth's family had rallied to the cause.

Elizabeth's mother was descended from minor gentry in Angus, the daughter of a younger son who had grown his scant portion many times over as a merchant bringing French wine and cambric into Scotland through Montrose. Her father's people were Haldanes, of course, descended from a cadet branch of that clan and living quite comfortably in Perthshire as tacksmen, although some might have mocked them and called them Bonnet Lairds.

The two families' allegiance to the Stuarts had different roots: Elizabeth's maternal grandfather disgruntled with the union and keen to build his trading links with France; her father's folk following blindly in the path of their Laird. In the end it made little difference, when it all ended for Prince Charles in a hail of cannonballs on Culloden Moor. Mother's father was taken to Tilbury with other prisoners, and died there of typhus, leaving his widow almost nothing to pass to her children when she followed just months behind him. John Haldane fled to France, and the vassals who had flocked to his standard were swiftly cleared from his lands as his children sought to win back royal favour, transforming themselves into the very model of a Lowland family loyal to the crown.

Mother and Father's marriage had been brought about through the Stuart links between the two families; if you believed Mother, it was all clandestine meetings and white roses and toasting over a finger bowl as code for the 'King across the water'.

Mother and Father took all that they had and made their way to Edinburgh, where they hoped they could live with some dignity on very little silver. Father took work as a teacher, and Mother did fine work, she was a skilled embroideress and had learned to make needle-lace as a girl. Her collars sold by the piece, for a pittance really, when you thought about the work that went into them, but any money helped.

Two sons were born in the early years of the marriage, called James and Charles for the Old and the Young Pretender, but neither survived infancy. It seemed there would be no more but then, in Mother's thirty-eighth year, the year James Stuart died in Rome, Elizabeth was born.

Elizabeth grew up quite unaware they lived in a sort of poverty that was painful to her parents, having known nothing else. She had no schooling; Father taught her her letters and her numbers and Mother taught her to sew. She was alone but not lonely, she had Mother and Father to herself and she wanted for nothing; Mother kept her beautifully dressed with the work of her needle, even as Mother's own fine gowns grew faded and worn and she had to patch and darn, turn collars and cuffs and let down hems to snip a bit of fabric for a repair.

Father's circles in Edinburgh included those still loyal to the Stuarts, even so long after the cause was lost. He frequented particular coffee houses and inns where much coded talk took place. Sometimes he took Elizabeth, and one of the men made a pet of her, an older man who had lost his fortune and his family name. He told Elizabeth she should call him 'Uncle', for her father was like a brother to him and he would do anything for him, anything at all.

Mother preferred to stay at home, but she too entertained ladies of a loyal persuasion, although they spent more time discussing the scandalous carryings on of Prince Charles and his mistress Clementina. She had fled his clutches and was traipsing from nunnery to nunnery in France with a child the Prince did not acknowledge as his own, leaving it to his brother to maintain them.

Charles was a bitter drunk by then, and a lout, but Father remained loyal to him until his death in the winter of the same year the Prince himself died. Elizabeth was twenty-two then, and almost as accomplished a needlewoman as Mother, but without Father's salary it was not enough, they were forced to begin selling off the few pieces Mother had treasured as relics of her past life. Elizabeth was charged with this task, going to call on Father's friend for help, the one she had called Uncle, for many of their valuables were of a nature that could not be sold openly, even after all this time, but were very desirable in the right circles.

Uncle was as good as the promise he had made, seeking bids for Elizabeth's artefacts among his circle, helping make sure they realised the best price. He would take no payment for his help, saying he had loved her father too dearly to profit from his widow and daughter.

Mother's treasure went first – a silver brooch set with garnets that formed the number '45' for the year of the Rising. That, and a few collars, kept them going a good while.

Next Mother unlocked a cupboard Elizabeth had never seen open before and brought out a set of six glasses, with twisted coils of red and white in their stems and white roses carved into the goblets. Those caused a stir in the coffee houses and Mother and Elizabeth lived a long time on the proceeds. Last of Mother's pieces was a pretty paper fan painted with a portrait of Prince Charles on one side. It could be opened quite innocently, the Prince's face to the user's bosom, so all an onlooker might see was the design of roses decorating the other side.

After that there was a glass Father had used that said 'Hanover to the Devil', and his most treasured possession, a ring that commemorated the four peers sentenced to death for their parts in the Rising, the Englishman Derwentwater, Balmerino and Kilmarnock who died so bravely, and Lord Lovat the Old Fox. He had gone laughing to his death, they said; the seating collapsed under the weight of spectators, and some of the ghouls were killed for their trouble. Uncle bought that for himself and said he would always wear it and think of Father.

Mother and Elizabeth sewed and sewed and spent as little as they could, and in this way they eked their money out a good few years more. Then they had to begin selling the furniture, and clothes, all the things that made their shabby room a home. Eventually, there was nothing left to sell.

Mother was growing frailer by then, her eyesight fading so she struggled to sew and complained of a pain in her head in the evenings when the light was low. Elizabeth said nothing to Mother, let her believe they still had a little money put by. She said she must go out one night to meet a man Uncle had found that was interested in a that glass of Father's, the one that said 'Hanover to the Devil', Mother might remember it. It had been sold years before, of course, but Mother didn't argue, perhaps she really had forgotten, or she wished to believe it was true.

Elizabeth dressed with care, in a gown of Mother's that was so threadbare they had never sold it. It was what they called a round gown, cut in one piece, and although it was fifty years out of date, it had been fine once and Elizabeth was pretty enough to wear it. Some fancy took her when she had it on and she put a dot of black high up on her cheek, like the patches they used to wear. It felt like war paint.

At the club where she had met Uncle, Elizabeth knocked and looked the skinny lad in the eye who answered the door and said she was looking for company, for any man that wanted company and could afford it. The lad blushed bright red but then he recovered and brought her in and took her to a side room and went away again. And then a man came in – it wasn't Uncle, she had a horror that it might be Uncle – and he did what he wanted with her and gave her six shillings.

Elizabeth left then, holding back tears, and bought a pie from a seller on the street to take home. Mother tried to make her eat some of it but she couldn't, she was sick to her stomach. They slept in the same bed, for warmth, had done for months, and she had to turn her face to the wall, she couldn't bear to look at Mother, having done what she had done. When she woke to ice on the window, though, and knew she had the means of buying firewood, she felt a little better.

Elizabeth visited the other places she knew, over that winter and the next spring, and her money and the lace money kept them in rent and food and firewood. She thought Mother didn't know but of course she did; when Elizabeth found herself sick in the mornings and the bodice of Mother's dress too tight, Mother wasn't surprised at all. Perhaps it came from being part of a family of traitors – in the government's lights, that was – that reticence of Mother's to put into words the things they all knew fine well.

'We need to leave,' Mother said. 'We can't let the neighbours see how low we have fallen. We'll go west, to Glasgow. No one knows us there and we can live more cheaply still.'

And so Jeanie was born that autumn in Glasgow, a bonnie wee scrap. Mother and Elizabeth took a room in a lodging house, shared the care of Jeanie and took in sewing, not fine work as they had once done, but mending and alterations. They bought worn-out clothing from the ragmen, too, and made smaller garments out of such fabric as they could salvage, women's blouses and children's smocks from men's shirts, that sort of thing. With the sale of these, they could almost cover their rent and their food, and Elizabeth needed to go out of a night less often. She got away with it for five years and more without getting with child or a pox, but then her luck ran out and Peggy was born when Jeanie was six, and Mary Ann when she was eight.

Jeanie and Peggy were good lassies, but Mary Ann was a demon, it seemed, from the moment she could toddle. She was bonnie and blithe, but she fibbed and lied without compunction, pinching her sisters and stealing their ribbons, messing Mother's work and pulling the tail of the cat they kept for mousing till it screeched. By the time she was twelve she had already been brought home by a policeman, having attempted to steal a pair of gloves from a stallholder at the Lammas fair.

Mother died that winter, worn out with work and worry, and Elizabeth took herself and her girls back to Edinburgh.

Jeanie married a good man, the next year, a tinsmith with a shop on the High Street. Elizabeth and the other lasses lodged with them there, for a time, and it seemed Mary Ann had calmed down, but then she palled up with another girl, a weaver's daughter called Margaret Finlayson, and soon she was up to her tricks again. They spent their days in the New Town, where basement steps and busy servants afforded them the opportunity of stepping unseen into this fine house or that and leaving with their aprons full of booty. Margaret served sixty days in the Tolbooth, for the stealing of some coats, but although it seemed Mary Ann had done the actual thieving, she escaped punishment as she had passed the loot to Margaret and absconded. She missed Margaret sorely and visited her often, but no sooner was Margaret out but they had stolen a gown, a hat and a half-pound of tea from a house in Dublin Street, and both had been arrested. They had learned a lesson of sorts, however, and had handed the loot off to someone else entirely in the hullabaloo as the servants of the house gave chase, and so they were released without charge for lack of evidence.

Both girls' luck gave out after that, though, and they were sentenced to transportation, first Margaret for a theft in Melville Street and then Mary Ann for the same crime in Elder Street. Elizabeth wondered if Mary Ann had done it on purpose, once Margaret had had her sentence, they were that devoted to each other. Elizabeth, on the other hand, had found out her devotion to her daughter had its limits and she really didn't mind very much being relieved of Mary Ann.

When the girls were gone, first to London and thence to Van Diemen's Land, Elizabeth took herself away from Jeanie's house and found herself lodgings in a place in Tanner's Close. Jeanie gave her enough to live on – they could well afford it, her man's shop was doing fine – and Elizabeth gave herself over to grief and drink and long days spent abed. The grief was not for Mary Ann, but for Mother and for herself, the things she had had to do and give up. She saw it all clearly now, how in her caring for Mother, and helping Mother cling to the pretence of dignity she held so dear, Elizabeth had never had a chance at a man or a home of her own, and now she was old and fat and had one tooth left in her head and no one would want her anymore. It pained her, but the drink dulled the pain along with the other senses. And that was how Elizabeth found herself here, lying in the stable of the lodging house; she had gone out for more drink, and fallen asleep somehow. The cobbler man who worked in the cellar found her there, and she began to thank him, thinking he was going to help her back to her room, but then all was confusion, his hands were over her mouth and nose and all of it running before her eyes, thoughts like stars exploding, there and gone in an instant, Father in the coffee houses, and kind old Uncle, and crystal glasses, and stitches, so many stitches, like the white tips of the waves under the ship carrying Mary Ann across the ocean with the girl she loved – of course Mary Ann loved Margaret, Elizabeth sees that now – and Mother's hands holding baby Jeanie who had her own babes now, and Peggy—

But at that, Elizabeth's thoughts still, the flow of blood to her brain is not enough, the bright pictures flicker and go dark.

15
Effy

THE FAMILY LIVING IN THE OLD vault storage room in the deaf arch adjoining the middle arch of Edinburgh's South Bridge had no idea there was a room below their own. They came and went in the dark, stifling in the heat and freezing in the cold, for there was no opening to admit light or air, and the fire seemed to have been installed for the look of the thing only; it had neither flue nor hearth, just an iron fireback, flush with the wall and a useless fret in front. They had never thought to explore it, even if they had had enough light, and so they had no idea the fireback was really a door, with a ladder behind it, leading down to a lower room. This room had no other door, for that had been nailed shut and plastered over long ago. In this quiet and private space, Effy had made her nest.

Aside from the challenge of access – which required her to listen at the top of the ladder until she was quite sure the room on the other side was empty – Effy's conditions were rather better than her neighbours'. She had a pipe siphoning water off the town's supply, a waste pipe and even a flue, so she could light a fire if ever the place became damp, without choking herself to death. These improvements had been added by some enterprising citizens years back, so that the place might support an illegal still. For well over a year the distillers had worked here, defying the Revenue and making a tidy fortune in the process, but they had become greedy, in the end, and flooded the taverns of the Old Town with their illegal liquor. The authorities had noticed, and set about tracing the source. They set watch where they knew the moonshine was sold, and soon enough they noticed a woman come and go, heavily cloaked, and seeming always to leave lighter of foot than she arrived. They followed her back to the vaults, and at last the jig was up for the moonshiners, though their profits had been salted away long syne.

Effy's brother had known these men, and helped once or twice to carry mash tubs and other items into the place, receiving generous payment for his service and his silence. After the distillers were lifted, he had remembered the place, and kept watch until he was sure that he and Effy could move in without being noticed. That was years ago, and Effy had stayed ever since, living alone now since Davie had fallen from scaffolding on a tenement where he was working and died. It wasn't the handiest of places, but it was safe. There were times when she couldn't get out or in, right enough, but she kept enough food there to see her through, and she could always spend the occasional night in a stable or doorway. Anywhere but the Poorhouse, she had a horror of that place.

The great value to Effy of her secret vault, besides that it was free and she knew she wouldn't be set upon in her sleep, was that she could leave her belongings there in safety. She had a great collection of treasures she loved above all things, and these she displayed on an old wooden pail, turned upside down. There were shards of pottery in every colour, a white piece dense with red leaves and flowers in shiny paint the colour

of blood, half a saucer with flowers in pink and green between
dots and flashes of gold, a dozen green-glazed fragments, various
shard painted with birds, and part of a mug showing an animal
she knew to be an elephant, for all she had never seen one.
Two pieces of a broken tile showed a girl milking a cow, and
one with its corner off showed a ship in full sail. Now and
then, when Effy found a ring or a brooch or an earring – it
was amazing how careless folk were and what they would
lose – she would bring it here and treasure it a while before
she sold it. She had plenty of light, for the stubs of candles
were plentiful in the ashpits and cinder heaps and around the
stables and yards of the coach houses, and Effy gathered so
many she could afford to burn a few herself.

This was Effy's trade, raking in the middens to find anything
of value, no matter how small. Almost everything was of use
to someone – scraps of leather let cobblers patch shoes, and
broken metal did the same for a jeweller. Peddlers could sell
buttons or marbles or old pipes. Even bits of paper could have
value to someone – Effy took any letters or papers she found
to a man with a wee booth in the steep lanes north of the
High Street, and he would look to see if the words contained
any secrets the writer might pay him to keep. In this way Effy
managed to keep food in her belly, blankets on her bed and
shoes on her feet.

The weather in June was fine and Effy was in high good
spirits. It was easy to come and go as the stifling heat of the
vaults meant the family who lived above her stayed out of
doors as long as they could, returning only to sleep. She had
had a good month, and today she had been raking not half
an hour before she had found two treasures – a medal of
some sort and a fine bone needle. The metal she took straight
to a peddler she knew, but the man said he would make

nothing from it, instead she should take it to one of the stalls on the High Street where he reckoned it would fetch a fine price. Thanking him for his advice, Effy had zig-zagged up the West Bow to the place he named and, just as he said, the dealer was pleased with her find and gave her two shillings. She bought some fried fish for her meal and then she began to wander back down the West Bow and through the Grassmarket to Tanner's Close where she thought she might kill two birds with one stone, selling the last few days' worth of leather scraps to Burke the cobbler and the bone needle to his woman.

The close was narrow, and as soon as Effy was halfway up she could hear Burke singing; he had a fine voice and she stopped a moment to listen. When the song was done, she chapped on the open door and called out.

'Mr Burke? It's me, Effy. I've a fine pile of scraps for ye, and a bonnie thing for your wife forby.'

Burke came out, wiping his hands on a rag, and stirred through the pieces of leather in her sack.

'I'll take the lot,' he said. 'How much will that be, Effy?'

Effy named her price, he countered, and she named a figure in between.

'Grand,' said Burke, and he gestured towards the stable. 'Come in and take a seat while I go to fetch the coin. Will you take a cup of ale?'

'I will,' said Effy, sitting herself on a stool, 'and a dram if you have one.'

Burke laughed but there was no scorn in it. He poured the ale from a jug into a horn cup, and then he handed her a stone piggy.

'See you don't finish the whole bottle,' he said. 'What was it you had for Nelly?'

Effy gave him the needle. 'Tell her it's a gift from me,' she said, raising the whisky bottle. 'As thanks for your generosity.'

Burke laughed again. 'Have as much as you like then, Effy,' he said, and he turned and left.

Effy took him at his word, finishing the ale in one draught – she had a thirst on her from the heat – and refilling the cup almost to the brim with whisky. She was halfway down it, leaning back on a bale of hay with her eyes closed and half-dozing, when she heard his step and made to open her eyes. But somehow, she couldn't move, she had had too much to drink and the bale had fallen on her, it seemed. She raised her left hand to move it, holding fast to the horn cup in her right, but she couldn't move either, her arms were held fast.

It lasts a minute, little more, and in her panic and struggle, the horn cup breaks in Effy's hand, cutting her palm and her pinkie finger. The sting of the spirit in the wound is the last thing she knows.

16
Tympanic Membrane

H ELEN'S BAD EAR SOMETIMES PAINED HER, and so she thought little of it when she woke on the first day of August to a mess on the bedclothes where she had lain her head. She tilted it experimentally a time or two, but the pain wasn't very bad and there was no discharge, so she washed and dressed and loaded the shoes William had repaired for sale into her hawking basket. William said there was no need, they had no need of money right now and she should rest, but Helen couldn't see the sense in letting his work go to waste. Cold and wet as the last fortnight had been, harvest time was near, and thousands of city folk would be tramping out to the Borders and Falkirk and Berwickshire to work at the reaping and the stooking. They would be wanting shoes, at last a fair day had come, and Helen could clear out William's stock and make a pretty penny for her troubles.

In the Grassmarket she found a spot between a coffee seller and an oyster stall and she began to call out to passing women – she always preferred to talk to the women. She had some early success, selling a pair of stout shoes to an old wife for her grandson and a pair of slippers to a lass she thought most likely a hoor. *Good luck to her*, Helen thought, though she felt her usual shudder of fear that someday she might have to take up such a trade. She put the thought firmly from her mind; William would keep her, so long as he was living, surely he would, they had come through so much already and it hadn't broken them.

Trade was quiet after that for an hour or so, folk rushing here and there on business with no time to stop and crack. Then a woman a bit younger than Helen stopped to look. She had a babe strapped to herself in a shawl, tied so it looked out at the world, and Helen chucked its cheek and laughed to see it smile. The woman admired a fine pair of black boots, trying them on her feet and strutting up and down fair trickit with herself. Helen named the price, and the woman turned out her pocket and made to count her money, but it was clear from the slump of her shoulders that she knew she hadn't enough. Indeed she was short some shillings.

'I'll tell you what,' Helen said, surprising herself, 'I'm feeling a cold and shivery way and I could use a hot cup of coffee and an oatcake. If I give you the boots for what you have, and you keep back enough to bring us both coffee and food to share from that stall over there, then I'll be well pleased with the bargain.'

The woman didn't need to be offered twice. She handed over her money to Helen, less a few coins, and scurried off in her new boots to haggle with the coffee seller.

When she returned, they sat themselves in the lee of the old wellhead at the foot of the West Bow and the woman – her name was Jenny – fed the babe and drank her coffee while Helen ate her oatcake, and then Helen dandled the babe while its mother ate her share. Jenny kept stealing a look at her boots every now and then and Helen was gladder than ever that she'd more or less given them away. As William said, they had no pressing need of coin, and this woman's pleasure was payment enough.

The wellhead wasn't used any more, and so they sat undisturbed a good while talking of this and that until Jenny said she must be on her way, the babe was sleeping and she should use the time to get on with her own work. Helen bid her farewell and sat a while longer by herself, missing the warm weight of the babe in her arms. She felt less chilled now, but muzzy-headed and weary. When she stood she found her bones were aching, and she set off slowly for home.

As she passed the ruckle of stones that were all that remained of the Flodden Wall, a woman in the red cloak of a peddler came the other way, from the direction of the King's Stables. She had a fine basket of pretties, lace and buttons and a clutch of carved wooden dollies. Helen stopped her and asked the price of the one poppet she had that was dressed.

'That one's no for sale,' the peddler wife said. 'It's just to show how you can dress them, see? You can have one of the others and make it look every bit as fine for your wee lass at home. Get her to help you, it's a fine way to learn.'

Helen looked at the dressed doll again. She had dark painted hair, a yellow hair comb, and a pretty, sulky face.

'I do so much plain work, my eyes are too tired for fine,' she said. 'And my wee lasses are no longer with me. Please can I have your dressed doll? I can pay you enough to make it worth your while to make another.'

The peddler woman sighed. 'I lost four bairns myself,' she said, and she named a price. Helen didn't bother to haggle, just handed over the money and tucked the doll in her basket. She bid the peddler wife farewell and climbed up the rise of the West Port to Tanner's Close, dodging as best she could the pigs that seemed ever more numerous in the streets and closes. By the time she had closed the door of their room behind her and set down her basket, she was chilled again, and sweating. She took off her cloak and bonnet, kicked off her shoes, and climbed into bed fully clothed. She hugged the little doll to her and drifted off into an uneasy sleep.

The next time she woke, it was night and William was there, sitting on the bed, asking what was the matter. His voice sounded strange, like she was hearing him from under water. Helen tried to speak, but her tongue seemed stuck to the roof of her mouth. William's hand felt for her forehead then, and he jerked it back.

'Christ, woman,' he said, 'you've the heat of the Devil in you! What ails you, Nelly?'

'My ear,' Nelly managed, thickly, and he turned her head and grimaced at the sight of the mess that had returned, crusted on her neck and the pillow.

'I'll fetch an apothecary,' he said, and hied him out of the room.

Helen drifted back into an uneasy sleep, haunted by memories of fists and blows and fire. She thought she heard a woman scream, and she started awake, her heart pounding, to see William and another man she didn't know standing over her. This was the apothecary, it seemed. He was a small man, dark-haired, and his touch was gentle as he turned Helen's head this way and that.

The man said the ear had gone bad right enough, and he prescribed a tea of bark powder to bring down the fever, laudanum for sleep, and a poultice of turkey rhubarb to draw out the infection. William said he would write it down, and even in her fevered state Helen saw the surprise with which the man heard that; he must have thought William unlettered like so many of the Irish. He looked at him appraisingly and asked, 'Have you the money for a nurse? It would be best, if so, to have a woman in.'

William said they did, and the two men left Helen and sat at the table so the apothecary could write his instructions and measure out his potions from the case he carried. Then the man dosed Helen with foul-tasting stuff and strapped her ear up with a hot rag of some sort against it – the bandage round her throat holding it in place made her feel sick at first. Then William settled the bill and the man told him where he could find a good nurse, a clean, efficient woman, and then he took his leave.

The hot compress was comforting and the draught seemed to do its work so Helen slept without dreams, or if she had them she couldn't remember after. When she woke in the middle of the morning, the nurse was there, a strong-looking creature with wiry grey hair and a wrinkled brow. Helen had a fiery pain in her ear, and was hotter than ever, and the woman set to right away and made her draught with hot water and honey, it didn't taste so bad when it was hot and sweetened. Then she cleaned the mess and dressed the ear again, and after that she made Helen drink a glass of ale. Helen tried to say she didn't want it but the woman insisted and in the end Helen got most of it down. The woman took up some needlework she had with her and made herself comfortable by the fire, and Helen drifted back into sleep.

Her dreams were filled with horrors, the walls of the room closing in and in about her until they enclosed her completely. When she tried to sit up, she found she couldn't, her arms were held tightly on each side and her legs pressed tightly together. She tried to raise her hands but there was no space above her either – her hands hit wood, she was in a coffin, buried alive. She began to hit it with her head, her knees, scratch it with her nails, anything to get free. At last it seemed the wood had cracked, but then earth began to pour in, and worms and all the crawling creatures of the ground, filling Helen's mouth and her eyes. When she thought at last she must choke, a hand reached down from somewhere above and grabbed at her, pulling her up and into the light.

'Don't let them!' she screamed, starting up into the arms of Margaret Hare. 'Don't let them cut me up!'

'Good Heavens, Nelly,' Margaret said, easing her back down. 'What are you saying?' She shot a look at the nurse, who was busying herself at the table.

The nurse laughed. 'We all rave, in fever,' she said. 'Pay her no heed.'

'Shall I dose her?' Margaret asked. 'Let you get out for a bite to eat?'

The nightmare still clung to Helen. 'Don't leave me with her,' she said to the nurse. 'They cut up Joseph. And the other man. Cut them up with their wee knives.'

Margaret looked furious but the nurse just kept on mixing her poultice.

'Did they now?' she said, unpeturbed. 'Well I never.' To Margaret she said, 'I thank you, but I'll stay here till the fever is broken. Her man said he'll bring me a bite at midday.'

Margaret looked put out and Helen turned her face to the wall, closing her eyes on more phantoms, birds this time, flying into the room and scratching at her face and arms, hurting her. Somewhere in the horror of it, she heard voices and a great bird rose up above her, but then it flapped its wings and it was gone. A warm pressure came at her ear, easing the worst of the pain of the birds' scratches, and Helen slept.

Afterwards, the nurse told Helen that she really had been in danger, those first days. She had known an ear infection go into the brain, she said, and there was no surviving that. But thanks to careful nursing – she took pains to emphasise that part – Helen's ear had drained, and she had fought off the infection. The apothecary's medicines had been good, the draught stopping Helen's body destroying itself while the poultice did its work.

Helen didn't feel very sure her body hadn't destroyed itself, in all honesty; she was as weak as a baby, almost unable to raise her head from the pillow. The nurse no longer stayed overnight but she came a time or two each day and fed Helen broths and jellies and eggy things to build up her strength, and checked the ear was no longer weeping. She turned out to be a right gossip, telling Helen she had heard raised voices two nights in a row in the kitchen, when Helen was at her illest, thon Margaret was a harpy and no mistake, but Helen's man had stood his ground right brawly.

Helen tried to ask William what the argy bargy had been about, but he didn't hear her, or at least he let on he didn't hear her. He said a strange thing though, one morning, that he would prefer Helen lock the door when he or the nurse weren't with her. Helen agreed, although it took almost all her strength to reach the door and her heart was pounding by the time she got herself back to bed. She didn't mind, though, with the door locked she knew there was no chance of waking up to discover Margaret sitting over her. The woman still gave her a curious feeling in her stomach. Indeed, a time or two she thought she heard Margaret try the door, and, finding it locked, go away.

Helen's strength built slowly, and by the middle of the month William asked if she might be well enough to go with him to Redding. She might finish her convalescing in her father's house, he said, and he could go to harvest. If she would mind the bairns, Peter might harvest too and William's money would all be his as well, to pay for the wee lassies' keep. Helen cried at the thought, she had missed the procession the village had to mark Robert Bruce's victory against the English, when she had often gone home to play her own part, and she had expected to pass the whole summer in Edinburgh. The nurse was done with her, by then, and had gone on her way content with her fee, and so it fell to William to make arrangements, packing their bundles and moving their other goods into the stables so the room could be let in their absence.

On the allotted day, two men came up the close with a sedan chair to convey Helen to the Falkirk coach. It was an odd feeling, swaying as the men hoisted her out across the setts and the muck in the cool dawn light, the soaring tenements seeming to sway overhead. They had a hard job, for the first part, to avoid the pigs who were rooting around for their breakfast, and once or twice it seemed almost that they would topple her. In the end, though, they cleared the West Port and made their way through the bustle of the Grassmarket – the place never slept – to the Cowgate. William walked alongside, lugging their bundles.

To travel by coach had never been within Helen's means before, and under normal circumstances might have been a wonder, but as it was it was something of a trial, and by the time they reached Polmont that afternoon, she could barely rouse herself to climb down. But somehow William had got word to Peter Gaff that they were coming, and he was waiting for them with a neighbour's cart and horse. He and William lifted Helen up into the cart for the short journey home, and at the other end they lifted her down and carried her into the house, laying her down on a pallet by the fire.

Helen slept away that entire first evening and night at home and only woke in the morning when the bairns gathered for their breakfast, but it was the good, healing sleep of exhaustion and not the uneasy rest of the fever. Before much more than a week had passed, she was on her feet, baking oatcakes and making porridge, and then mending clothes and setting the place to rights. Peter had acquired a cow, a nice beastie with a wee calf, and Maisie taught Helen to milk it, although she was handless at first compared to her daughter. Maisie was now a tall, confident stripling, and at first Helen was shy of her, feeling her a stranger, but Maisie attached herself to her from the first, calling her 'Mother' and talking quite easily with her as if they'd last seen each other the week before, not years ago.

Peter and William were off at the harvest, returning stiff and tired in the darkness. Some nights, William camped out in the fields, earning a night's shelter in a hut or tent with his piggy of whisky and a few songs. He met up with a cousin of Helen's – well, of James MacDougal's, really – a woman named Ann MacDougal, and he spent a night or two in the bow tent she shared with a gang of young folk. At first Helen felt a sting of jealousy, thinking of the strumpet Mary in Constantine's house and wondering if William had taken a fancy to Ann MacDougal. But she said nothing, and was mollified by the attention he paid to Maisie and wee Annie. Both lassies had become great favourites of his, and in his rest time he carved them a bonnie wooden doll, like Helen's, with proper pegged joints so the arms and legs could move. Peter mixed them up some kind of black paint with varnish and shoe-black and they painted a face and hair for her with a feather quill, and then they made her a frock from rags. Then Maisie led wee Annie in the making of a tiny bed of sticks tied together with strips of leather, and chairs made with the quills of feathers, pinned with nails purloined from Peter Gaff's cobbler's kit, and the two of them spent hours together imagining the goings-on of the dolls. When William slept in the fields, they crawled into bed with Helen, and she revelled in the unaccustomed closeness of her bairns, for all they wriggled and kicked and bruised her.

When at last the harvest was finished and their time in Redding drawing to an end, Helen noticed Peter watching the two lasses with a keen eye. On one of their last nights, it was unusually mild, and Helen and Peter and William sat outside by the door, the men smoking their pipes and all three of them enjoying a dram from William's piggy.

Peter tapped the ash from his pipe and began to fill it again. 'I've been thinking,' he said, peering closely at his task, 'that the lassies are fell fond of you, Helen. And you, William. This place you have in Edinburgh, your friends' lodging house, it sounds a grand place. Would you wish to take them back with you?'

Helen's heart leapt, but before she could speak, William stood up, knocking over the stool he'd been sitting on. He strode off into the darkness.

Peter was silent, Helen blinking hard to keep the tears from her eyes. There was no more talk of the lassies that night.

In the morning, Peter fed the bairns and shooed them out the door before he picked up his own tools and announced he'd a saddle to mend for a friend out by.

As soon as he was gone, Helen turned to William.

'Do you no want them?' she asked. 'My lasses?'

William stared at his feet.

Helen tasted blood in her mouth; in her anxiety, she had torn a strip from her lip with her teeth. 'Is it because they're another man's?' she asked.

William's head bobbed up.

'No,' he said, with a frown. 'James MacDougal doesn't trouble me. It's . . . Ach!' He punched his own thigh, his face dark.

'What is it?' Helen cried. 'Why can't I have them with me? Do you not trust me, is that it? You think I'd let harm come to them, like my father once thought!'

'No!' William stood up and strode over to the door, clenching and unclenching his fists. He took a deep breath and dropped his shoulders.

'I don't . . . I don't trust your woman,' he said, still not meeting her eye. 'Margaret. She doesn't like you, Nelly. Doesn't trust you. She thinks you'll blab. About the lodgers who . . . died and how we had the money for them.'

'I won't,' said Helen. 'Why would I? Anyway, I don't know anything about it. Just that there were three of them, and no one missed them, so it didn't matter, you said.'

William turned to look at her. 'You're not one of us, that's what she said. Not Irish.' He still seemed unable to hold her gaze. 'Ach, drink had been taken, Nelly. But it feared me a bit.'

Helen thought back to those days in their room at Tanner's Close, when she was sick and alone and Margaret always lurking outside.

'Is that why you had me lock the door?' she said. 'Did you think she would hurt me?'

'No!' William laughed, but it didn't reach his eyes. 'She joked about it, that's all. Said we'd get ten pounds for you if you died too.'

Helen thought about Margaret sitting over her in the bed, offering to let the nurse leave. Her wiry frame, the cold look in her eyes. She felt the hairs on her arms rise.

'How can we go back after that?' she asked flatly. 'We can't.'

William shook his head, like a dog coming out of a river. 'Och, we were all acting the maggot, Nelly, just a bit. It was the pressure of it, taking that money for the bodies. But now we've had some time away. When we get back, everyone'll be the master of themselves again, you'll see.'

'And the lassies?' Helen asked. Her lips were numb; she knew the answer.

'I'm not saying never, Nelly,' William said. 'But let's get ourselves settled first, before we bring them into it. No sense upsetting things with two more mouths to feed.'

With that, he stood up and stretched and looked about him for some task to do, as though all was well again and he hadn't just suggested two minutes before that Margaret Hare might kill Helen's children if they brought them home. Helen sat on her stool and picked up Phemie – that was the name the girls had given their dolly. For a moment she thought of throwing herself on her father's charity, asking to stay here and keep house for him, but she knew she could not. Nothing had changed, and Peter still had need of any money they could earn him. She straightened the little doll's clothes, tucked her into her bed and went to pack her own bundle.

The Burke and Helen who left Redding the next day were not quite the same pair who had arrived three weeks before. William seemed lighter, somehow, as though by putting his fear of Margaret into words, he had divested himself of some awful burden. Helen, on the other hand, had arrived weak of body but light of spirit, and left strong of frame but sore of heart. Not only must she continue on without her children, but her trust in William was dented yet again. He would keep Maisie and wee Annie safe, for sure, but what of his Nelly?

The little girls put brave faces on it and neither cried, but Maisie had dark rings around her eyes and red patches on pale cheeks, and wee Annie held tight to Phemie and would not speak. Helen kissed them, and then William hugged them and pressed a coin into each of their hands. Then William shook Peter's hand, and Helen kissed him, and it was time to go and meet the coach to return to Edinburgh and Tanner's Close.

17

Fracture

ELEN'S LEGS FELT LIKE LEAD as they walked up the West Port to Tanner's Close, and she was none too cheered to see William Hare ahead of them by the close mouth, bending over a man who seemed passed out on the ground. They could smell this creature from twenty yards away, he seemed to have spilled a tankard of some strong liquor over himself, and pissed his breeks into the bargain.

As Hare straightened up, he spotted them and beckoned them over. 'Burke!' he shouted. 'Come and help me get this man into the stable. He's taken a dreadful skinful and we can't leave him here on the ground. Here, Nelly, hold my coat for me, he stinks.' Hare stripped off this article, a hideous garment of garish green in dandy style, and handed it to Nelly.

'I can't help you just now,' said William gruffly. 'I have my own gear to carry. We're only just home from the harvest.'

Hare looked askance. 'And what if he's robbed?' he demanded. 'Or worse?'

For a second it seemed that some unspoken message passed between the two men, and then, with ill-grace, William asked Helen if she would manage both their bundles and Hare's coat.

Then he took the man by the feet, and Hare lifted him under the arms, and they lugged him down into the close, William grumbling all the while at the dead weight of him.

'There, now,' Hare said, jovial again, when they'd deposited the man on the floor of the stable where he snored wheezily. 'That wasn't so hard, now, was it?' He rinsed his hands in a pail of water at the door and took his coat back from Helen. 'Welcome home, Nelly,' he said. 'The place has been mighty quiet without you both. Margaret's made up the room for you with some of our things; she thought you might like to wait to unpack your own gear till the morning.'

'Thank you,' Helen said, although it stuck in her craw to be indebted to the Hares. There was something in the air between William and William Hare, poisoning their return even further.

'Go up to the room, Nelly,' William said. 'I'd like a word with Hare.'

Helen took both the bundles and made her way up to the room. Margaret had made up the room, it was true, if what you meant by that was pushing the dust further into the corners and strewing a couple of blankets over a rough straw bolster on the bed. Helen missed the clean order of her father's house already. She sank down on the blankets, wondering whether the last person to sleep on the bolster had fleas. The next moment, the sound of raised voices in the close drew her to the window.

William was shouting at Hare, words Helen couldn't catch at this distance, but it was clear he was furious. Hare had his hands up, as if to placate William, but as Helen watched, William lowered his head and launched himself at Hare, punching him in the stomach so that he doubled over, and then locking an arm round his neck so that he was in a crouch, as William rained down blows on his head.

Helen ran down the corridor and clattered down the stairs to the door. By the time she got out into the close, Hare had got loose from William's grasp. Margaret had got there ahead of Helen, and she threw herself between William and Hare, shielding Hare with her body as she held an arm out to keep William at a distance. A small crowd had gathered, drawn by the excitement, but Margaret paid them no heed.

'What Devil's got into you, William?' she demanded.

William was panting from his exertions and there was a rip in the shoulder of his jacket. 'When we left, you two were in hock to your eyeballs,' he said. 'And now here *he* is with a new jacket and new boots and there's a new gown on you too, woman.'

'And what of it?' Margaret demanded.

'Margaret—' Hare began, but Margaret's dander was up and she put up her other hand to shush him, so that both men seemed held back by some force emitting from her palms. Hare shut his trap again and settled for pulling off the great flounce of his stock and wiping the blood from his lip with it. He tried his nose gingerly as he did so, finding it broken.

'Our business is no concern of yours, William Burke,' Margaret said, 'and I'll thank you to keep your nose out of it.'

William gave a scornful laugh. 'No business of mine, you say? We had an agreement, and now I find you've cheated me out of my share.'

'Your share?' Margaret demanded. '*Your share*? Who do you think you are, man? This is our place, and you have no right to any share of money we make in it when you're gone. I've had four babbies here while you were off sunning yourselves in the countryside, and what of it? Did you think you deserved some of the coin for wiping their arses? That's a neat trick, all the way from Falkirk.'

'Babbies!' William repeated. 'Do I look a fool, Margaret?'

'You surely do,' she said, and she stuck out her chin, evidently determined that the conversation was over. After a moment or two, when she saw that the fight had gone out of William, she hustled Hare inside with a glare for both Helen and William in parting. The door closed behind her with a bang.

The crowd began to disperse, disappointed in their hopes of a knife fight, or at least a broken crown.

Helen went over to William, who had sat himself on a wall.

'What's this all about?' she asked. 'What do you mean, he cheated you, William?'

William took a deep breath. 'He owed me money,' he said. 'We had an ... investment. And now I see they've spent my share. Him and Margaret, she always takes a cut. I won't stay here, Nelly, not one night longer. I can't be under the same roof as a low dog like him and a bitch like her.'

Helen's heart leapt. Whatever had happened, she wouldn't care a jot, if only it meant they could finally leave Tanner's Close.

'Where will we go?' she asked.

'My cousin's man Broggan's,' William said. 'I was half of a mind to say we should flit there anyway, when we came back. Let's get over there now and we can send for the rest of our gear to come after.'

'If they haven't sold it,' Helen said, and William laughed.

'You're a grand lass, Nelly, so you are,' he said, and he put an arm around her. She could feel the tension in him, and smell the copper tang of blood.

'I was frighted, William,' she said quietly, 'when I saw you angry like that.'

William sighed. 'I was frighted too, Nelly,' he said. 'I don't like to think of the harm that pair might do us. Come on, then. Let's get ourselves down to Broggan's.'

John Broggan lived only a close or two away, and even with their bundles the walk took just a few minutes. William banged on the door and opened it, shouting in that it was himself, and a minute or two later Broggan appeared, a great bear of a man he was, with a long grey beard that reached halfway down his chest. When William said they had need of a place to stay, for a few nights at least, he professed himself delighted, for didn't he have a room lying empty, with its own private access?

'The old soak who rented it off me up and died last week,' he said. 'He died happy though, I'd say, there were two dozen empty bottles in the room at least.'

He took them along straight away to look at the room. It was shabby, although once it might have been fine enough, when rich and poor lived cheek by jowl in the lands of the Old Town. There was a good large window, and a fireplace that might serve as a stove, two low beds and various chairs and stools. There was a press in the wall where they might keep their crocks if it turned out Margaret had not indeed sold them. What Helen liked best of all, though, was that it was secluded, the door being at the end of a hallway where none had cause to pass, it leading to nowhere but this very room. No longer would Helen have to lie in bed and listen to feet passing, her stomach in knots at the thought the steps might stop outside her own door and she would hear Margaret's knock.

With a quick glance of confirmation to Helen, William said they would take it and he and Broggan began to negotiate the rent. Soon they were settled on a sum that pleased them both, and Broggan was more delighted still when William offered him three months' money there and then, upfront. Broggan offered to go out and fetch a meal for them, since they had no pots or crocks, and a bottle to toast the deal. William said thank you, that would be very kind and Helen had need of food, but he himself would eat later, he had to go out on an urgent matter of business.

Fear flamed in Helen's breast then, for she thought he might mean he would go back to Tanner's Close, but William assured her he had no intention of ever setting foot in the place again. His business was in the town, with a man who had had the selling of some items he had made and owed him the coin. He kissed Helen and told her to rest, saying he would ask Broggan to send his lad tomorrow to fetch their gear from Tanner's Close, and if anything was missing, he vowed that William Hare and Margaret would pay for it in full.

Helen was worn out, by then, after the travel and the theatrics at Tanner's Close, and she was thankful to eat the stew John Broggan brought and sink into bed. William returned shortly after dark, ate a cold meal and slipped into bed beside her.

'Did you settle your business?' she asked drowsily.

'I did,' William said, 'and more than that, I put my own mind to rest on that business of Margaret and William. They did cheat me, Nelly. The man who had our . . . investment confirmed it. He's a vicious man, Hare, I see that now. Did I ever tell you he killed his own horse?'

'Old Dob?' Helen asked. 'Why did he do that?'

'It refused to obey him,' William said. 'It just plain refused to pull a cart with some . . . thing he was transporting. It just plain stopped in the meal-market and would go no further. Hare was wild. He lashed it and swore at it, but it was a dour beast – do you remember, Nelly? – and it stood there and took all he threw at it, the poor creature. In the end he had to get a barrowman to take his goods the rest of the way. After that, he took the horse to the tanner's and asked if he could shoot it himself. I didn't like that, Nelly, I don't see it's necessary to do harm to an animal in such a way. Then he had a row with the tanner, for the horse's hide was all damaged and the tanner wouldn't pay much for it. You couldn't see the sores, Nelly, for he had packed them with cotton and laid the hide of another beast on top.'

'Poor Dob,' Helen said. 'I don't like to think of that. He was a nice enough beast.'

But William seemed to have lost interest in Dob. 'It fears me, a bit,' he said. 'What if he should wish to do us harm, Nelly? Hare?'

'Why should he, now?' Helen said, wishing he would hush and let her sleep. 'And if you're thinking of the things you did long syne, well . . . did he not do those things with you? If you should be taken up, so should he be.'

'Do you really think so?' William asked.

'Yes,' Helen said. 'But you stay away from him, William. You may be foolish, oftentimes, and greedy, maybe, but you're not a vicious man.'

'I'm gladdened to hear you say that, Nelly,' William said.

'He'll get his comeuppance one day,' Nelly said, feeling her eyes close. 'It's like my father says: *the mills of God grind slowly, but they grind exceeding small.*'

That didn't seem to soothe William, though, but Helen was done for and as he stewed, she slipped into sleep.

The next day seemed to dawn brighter, in the new place, and in the middle of the morning Broggan's lad set off for Tanner's Close with a handcart and returned with William and Helen's stock, William's tools, and their other gear. Helen unpacked it all and filled the press with plates and pots, stacked her bags and sacks of stock on one side of the room and laid William's tools out neatly on a stool. Their linen was folded in an old kist her father had given her on her marriage, and she was pleased to see her sewing tools and her stock of candles still in the shuttle drawer where she had left them. There was a tea chest she didn't recognise, and when she managed to prise it open with one of William's tools, she found it was full of women's clothing – good pieces, not fancy in the main but made from decent cloth, and the occasional fine shawl or bonnet. At first, she thought Margaret had sent these in error, but then she thought perhaps the woman meant Helen to sell it all as they had arranged. Well, she thought, she'd see if she was minded to. Some of it she might keep for herself, since Hare had cheated William. With that thought, she pulled out a bonnie shawl and wrapped it round herself, thinking she would attract a fine trade, dressed in such a manner.

As it happened, though, Nelly didn't get her day's trading in. As she left Broggan's place with her basket, who should she meet in the close but Cousin Ann MacDougal, James's cousin that was, who had been at the harvest with William.

'Helen!' Cousin Ann shouted, 'I've found you! I've had a devil of a time. I went to the place William said, in Tanner's Close, but the woman Margaret said you'd flitted and they had no idea where.'

'Did she now?' Helen said. 'Well, she kent fine, cousin, but she's a hard-faced bitch and she'll say whatever comes up her back for the devilment of it. But I don't want to think of her any longer. What brings you to Edinburgh?'

It turned out that William had said to Cousin Ann that she might bed down with them a night or two if she fancied seeing whether Edinburgh might be to her liking.

'I thought I might look for work in a fine house,' she told Helen. 'I'm a hard worker.'

'Why here, though?' Helen asked.

Ann sighed. 'I've no hankering for marriage,' she said. 'And there's nothing for me at home unless I marry. You ken how it is, Helen.'

'Aye,' Helen said, remembering her first marriage. 'And I don't blame you for it, cousin. You're welcome here as long as you please.'

With that settled between them, Ann and Helen made up the second bed in the room and left Ann's bundle on it. Then they took themselves out to a tavern for a plate of oysters and a loaf of bread and a chance to share their news. Cousin Ann had seen Peter Gaff and Helen's brothers and sisters and her lassies, and she pulled out a wee package from her pocket, a piece of needlework wee Annie had done for her mother, with her own name and Maisie's, the date and a cat that was meant to be Jezebel. The cat looked nothing much like Jezebel at all, and the stitching was rough, but it brought a tear to Helen's eye just the same. Then Cousin Ann shared all the gossip of the harvest, and in that way they passed most of the day. By the evening, they were well in their cups and Helen was telling her about James MacDougal's vicious nature and his ready fists, when William came into the tavern, exclaiming in pleasure to meet Cousin Ann again. Helen thought he had no memory of inviting her to stay with them, he had probably done so in drink, but he readily agreed they should do all they could to help her find a situation, and it was a fine thing to have family nearby.

Helen made a sort of holiday of it, with Cousin Ann over the next few days, traipsing here and there across the city, up to the Castle and down past the great wall built after Flodden to the Palace at Holyrood with the ruins of the Abbey behind. They climbed the great mound of Arthur's Seat and walked round the path at the foot of the crags below it, careful to avoid the places where men were blasting the stone apart, to make setts to send to London and other foreign places.

They had brought with them an afternoon meal of bread and cheese, and they sat in the lee of a cairn of stones near the ruins of the old Abbey to eat. A beggar-mannie passed by and Ann cried to him to come and share their meal, and he agreed with alacrity, paying for it after with a great tale of deception and murder. Did they know what the stones here were set up here to mark, he asked. They said no, and he said the townsfolk of Edinburgh had raised them a hundred years before, in memory of a lass called Margaret Hall, the daughter of a burgess of the town. Poor Margaret had been married when she was just sixteen, to a landowning man called Nicol Muschet, from a place called Boghall, out on the road to Stirling.

This Muschet was a black-hearted rogue and he had tired of his young wife right promptly, planning to desert her and take himself off to France to live a life of debauchery there. It rankled with him, though, that he would have to maintain her and so the villain set about trying to trick Margaret into betraying him, in order that he might procure a divorce and save himself a few merks. He and his associates drugged her and tricked her, kidnapped her and imprisoned her, but still the lass held firm to her marriage vows. After that he decided he must kill her, and the poor lass endured more than a body could believe, poisoned with great drafts of a vicious dose for the French disease – this Muschet was a medical man, you see, the beggarman said – so she was tormented with retching and sickness until she seemed like to die. Not once, not twice, but three and more times they attacked her with this poison, but the poor lass clung to life, and in time recovered. After that, Muschet and his confederates planned to push her from her horse into a river, or hit her over the head with a hammer as she walked home of a night, but there were always too many folk about and never a chance. In the end, Muschet asked the lass to walk with him to Duddingston Kirk, and as they passed this place he took out a knife and attacked her, cutting her throat and stabbing her most grievously in all the soft places of her body. She must have been a rare lass, for even then she fought him, and so they found his sleeve under her body, torn off by her struggles, and embroidered with his initials. Muschet tried to flee but one of his conspirators betrayed him, and he swung by the neck in the Grassmarket, while the folk of Edinburgh set up this cairn to remember Margaret.

'What of the others who helped him?' Cousin Ann asked. 'Did they swing as well?'

'Two of them turned King's Evidence,' the beggar-mannie said, 'against the third. He was sentenced to be transported.'

'So the others never paid for it?' Helen asked, indignant. 'That's no fair!'

'I'm no sure the law is much concerned with fairness,' the beggar-man said, with some seeming bitterness, but then he smiled. 'My advice to you is to stay well clear of it, lassies.'

Cousin Ann laughed at the idea she would ever be taken up, and they parted with the beggar-man, giving him the last of their meal to take away.

Her cousin had enjoyed the story, it seemed, and prattled on about it as they walked home, but Helen found it unsettling, the thought of the awful things men did, and the dreadful price Muschet had paid, and the faithlessness of those who shared his evil. It put her in mind of Margaret Hare, and she began to see that William might have something to fear from the Hares, after all, perhaps her own belief that harming him would harm them had been foolish.

The holiday was at an end, and Cousin Ann turned in earnest to searching out a situation. William helped her decipher the notices posted for help in the great houses of the New Town, and Ann trailed down the Mound to enquire, returning low of spirit and resentful.

'They say I need references,' she told Helen and William. 'I've told them I'm newly come frae the country, but they say it doesnae matter, if I've no letters to recommend me, they'll no take me on.'

'Can we not give you a reference?' William asked. 'You've lived in his house, and we've seen you're a trustworthy lass. I can vouch that you're a hard worker, I've seen you at harvest.'

'You dinna own the house, though,' said Cousin Ann, and William had to agree that was true.

'Broggan then,' he said. 'He'll be happy to do it. He can say you've been a serving lass here, working for him.'

'It's a lie, though,' said Helen.

'And so what if it is?' said William. 'It's no fair, saying Cousin Ann can't have work because she's never had work before. Sure, I'd never worked in a fine house before I went to work for the preacher in Ireland. Where would I be now if he'd refused to take me? How can a lad or a lass get a start if it's forbidden them?'

'I suppose so,' said Ann doubtfully.

'They'd never find out, either,' said William. 'The folk over there have no business over here.'

Despite Helen's misgivings, it seemed it was settled between them. The next day, she shouldered her baskets and took herself out a-trading, and Cousin Ann stayed behind with William to talk to Broggan. William would be needed to write the reference, for Broggan could neither read nor write, and Ann was little better with her letters.

When Helen returned that night, all her cousin's gear was gone. She was surprised the plan had worked so fast, but then she had no knowledge of these things, perhaps that was the way of fine houses. There was no sign of William, and when she knocked on Broggan's door, only Broggan's wife Molly was home. Helen asked after Cousin Ann and Molly said she hadn't seen her since the morning when she had been sitting with William and Broggan, but a fine trunk had arrived in the late afternoon, it had been left out in the hall by Helen and William's door, and later a man had come in and helped William carry it out again. Could that have been the way they sent for her cousin's things, to take them to her new place? Helen had no idea, but she supposed it might have been.

After that, William and Broggan had been deep in conversation for a while, Molly said, and they had shared a few drams. William had given Broggan some money, for agreeing to the letter, it must have been. Broggan said he fancied taking a trip to Glasgow to visit some cousin of his there and had gone to arrange for a barrow boy to take their things to the coach in the morning. Molly was glad to see Helen, she said, she wanted to ask her to keep an eye on the place while they were gone.

Helen helped Molly bundle up a few things, gifting her a shawl from her basket to keep her warm on the journey, for the weather was turning chilly. Then she returned to her room to wait for William. When he came home he seemed exhausted, and was loath to speak, saying he felt unwell. Helen asked where Cousin Ann had gone and he said she had found a position, but he didn't know where, it was one of the houses she had gone to before and been turned away. Then he turned his face to the wall and Helen could get nothing else out of him; he was asleep, or at least pretending.

Helen sat in a chair by the fire and stared into the flames. She had trusted Cousin Ann, thought her a friend, and Ann had given her no reason to doubt that she felt the same way about Helen. How then, could she believe Ann would leave without telling her where she had gone? It troubled her that Broggan was leaving, too, she had felt safe from the Hares as long as she was under his roof, and now there was no one but William to protect her. What was the money William had given Broggan, and why? The more she thought about it, the more Helen felt the gnawing pains of worry in the base of her stomach. She uncorked the whisky bottle, poured a large tumblerful and, determinedly, drank.

18

Hyperventilation

IN THE WEEKS FOLLOWING BROGGAN'S LEAVING, Helen found herself unwell, worse even than in the time after James MacDougal's beating of her, or the fever that came from her damaged ear. This trouble was different somehow, it feared her more, for she had fits and turns when she couldn't draw her breath at all, it was as though a great hand had hold of her and was squeezing and pressing, and all the while her heart raced and pained her, and her belly and her legs seemed turned to water. It happened even when she was sleeping, wrenching her from her sleep, sweating and gasping, convinced that she had died and was in Hell. After a time or two of that, she became frightened even to sleep, so awful was that awakening.

Without Helen's knowledge, it seemed William had agreed they would take over Broggan's house and its business, renting out rooms to cover the rent, for which they seemed now pledged. They were sleeping in the Broggans' rooms, now, and their own room was rented out to an old soldier and his wife, John and Ann Gray, who had been with them a couple of weeks. They seemed a nice enough pair, happy to be home in the city of their birth after many years abroad, and often out of doors as they renewed their acquaintance in the city. They had a daughter, a nice wee creature, and Helen gave her a bonnet trimmed with lace.

Helen had plenty of time to make this article, for William seemed never at home, and when he was, he was in his cups or dosed with laudanum so he slept like the dead and didn't even waken when Helen started up and thought she was like to die. She tried the laudanum herself, and whisky, and that stopped the awful wakening, but it left her listless and exhausted in the day, her head pounding and her heart leaping at the slightest noise, as though it would jump clean out of her chest.

She dragged herself to the apothecary's shop, the same man who had saved her when her ear went bad. He put his ear to her back and told her there was nothing wrong with her heart, so far as he could tell, what he thought was that her nerves were to blame, they were the most likely culprits in disorders of this nature. He gave her wee pokes of herbs to steep in water, saying she should drink the infusion hot and be sure to take good, deep breaths to stave off the fear when she felt it approaching. He asked if anything troubled her, and she said no, but it wasn't true, she was troubled every which way she turned. William had made up his rift with Hare and was out with him at all hours of the day and night, returning drunk or morose or – once – bruised black and blue, refusing to say what had befallen him.

Even the city seemed in a sort of panic: a woman called Wilson was scouring the streets and closes for her son, a halfwit creature named Jamie who had disappeared, although it was whispered in the taverns that he had been recognised on the surgeons' table. Cousin Ann MacDougal's father was doing likewise, trudging through the New Town and down into Leith every weekend in search of his daughter, coming home to Broggan's house sore of foot and heart to report his lack of progress to Helen – it seemed

Cousin Ann had vanished into thin air. John MacDougal asked, one night, if Helen thought she had got herself into trouble and run off, and she couldn't answer him, she was afraid that something worse had befallen her, but she was too feared to let herself think what that might be.

Helen went back to the apothecary and asked if he had anything to slow her heart. He said he did, a tincture of foxglove could do that, but it was a powerful preparation and he didn't like to give it to her for fear it would do her more damage than good. Helen begged, but he wouldn't yield, and in the end she thought it was for the best; perhaps if he had given her a bottle of the stuff, she would have drunk it all, just to have some peace.

One night, William asked her, quite out of nowhere, if she would like to go with him to Ireland.

Helen stared at him.

'Ireland?' she said. 'What would we do there?'

'We could make our fortunes very well,' said William. He had a sort of nervous energy about him, and he wasn't quite looking her in the eye. 'Would you come with me, Nelly? I'd not like to go without you.'

'I don't know,' Nelly said. It was an honest answer and, as she said it, she realised that she rarely gave an honest answer to him, never had, she had always chosen her words carefully to make sure she wouldn't lose him. 'I might want to go home to my father and my lasses,' she said. 'And anyway, you have a wife in Ireland. How could we live together there?'

She saw his proud crest was fallen then, but somehow she didn't care. He didn't speak of Ireland any more that night, or in the days following.

The next week was the week of All Saints' Day. William came home on the Friday morning in fine fettle, with an old woman in tow, a poor soul who looked like she needed a good feed. He made a great fuss about how they had met in a shop and got to talking, and hadn't they discovered she was only a cousin of William's mother's – what did Helen think to that?

Helen thought she could see the woman far enough, but she knew she couldn't say so. Ann Gray, the soldier's wife, had been in with her when they arrived, and Helen saw her raise her nose in the air at the sight of William, merry already though it was not yet mid-morning. William's high good humour seemed to thaw her frostiness, though, and she agreed to put the child down and come back to join them for the breakfast William had brought. The old woman would take not a bite before noon, as it was Friday, but William and Ann Gray ate well enough and Ann had taken a large dram when William opened his arms to her and appealed to her to quit the house for a night or two with her man and her lass and stay elsewhere so that his mother's poor cousin could rest her head in the house of a relation. Helen expected her to refuse but to her surprise Ann Gray agreed, only she said she didn't know where to go, none of their connection had room enough for them to board.

'I have just the place,' William said, and he was on his feet helping the woman to pack her things and conveying her out the door on the way to Tanner's Close and the Hares, the wee lassie in her cradle carried in his arms.

Helen was left alone with the old woman, and tried her best to make conversation with her, but she couldn't make any sense of what she said, couldn't make out at all that she was from the same place as William's mother. Perhaps she was wandered, the poor soul, she certainly looked half-starved. After she had broken her fast, she sat nodding at the table, and Helen offered to take her to the Grays' bedchamber so she could take her rest. The woman agreed gratefully, and before Helen had closed the door of the chamber behind her, she heard her snores. Returning to their own rooms, she cleared away the breakfast things and sat down wearily to her sewing while she still had the light.

She must have nodded off, for the next she knew it was evening, and there were voices raised in merriment in the close outside. She shook herself awake and had just lit a lamp when William burst in, followed by Hare and Margaret, apparently in the highest of spirits. They carried great armfuls of bottles, a pie, bread, a dish of oysters and more, and these were set out on the table with great ceremony. William went off to wake the old woman, and Helen sat with Margaret and Hare, awkward still in their company, for all they seemed happy enough to see her and Margaret even asked to see wee Annie's sewing of the cat, which William had told her about, and admired it.

William returned with the old woman and they all tucked into the dinner and the drink. Hare asked William to give them a song and he readily obliged, with the 'Minstrel boy'. Margaret requested another, and he sang that, and then the old woman offered that she had been a fine singer in her youth, and although she had less of a voice now, in her old age, she would like to give them a song. She sang in the Irish language, and in a way Helen hadn't heard before, with all sorts of fine flourishes and ornaments. She was right that her voice was not the strongest, and Margaret whispered to Hare throughout her singing, but Helen listened rapt, feeling tears fill her eyes at the beauty and dignity of it.

William asked Helen to sing after that, and she did, feeling her own voice rusty from long years of no use but wanting to repay the woman for her efforts. She sang 'Auld Robin Gray', the ballad she had sung long years ago, in that far-off harvest field where William had called her his blackbird, and even Margaret Hare shut up for once and listened.

After that there was more singing and merriment, and William suggested they go down next door to the neighbours' where there was a squeezebox and they could have some dancing. Helen was tired, and said she would rather sleep, and so off they went while she went to her bed and drew the curtains about her – that was one good thing about sleeping here in Broggan's rooms instead of their own, where the beds were low and had no curtains. She slept like the dead, and wakened only once or twice when they came back in to fetch bottles and tumblers and then, by the sound of it, took the gathering to the old woman's room.

Helen slept on without any of her panicked waking, and in the morning she was roused only by a chap at the door. She opened it to see Broggan's son Will, and their neighbours Mrs Law and Mrs Connoway.

'Morning, Nelly!' Will said cheerily, as well he might, it seemed he was still a fair way in his cups for all it was a new day. He told her he had joined the company last night at Mrs Law's, and he had slept there. William had told them all there would be a fine breakfast waiting for them here this morning at Will's father's house, in thanks for their hospitality of the evening before.

'Come away in,' Helen said, in some confusion, for there was no sign of William and she had no real idea what food there might be to give them. Still, she sat them down and set water to boil with a mind to make coffee. In a moment or two there came another chap at the door and she opened it to discover James and Ann Gray and their daughter, come for the breakfast at the invitation of Margaret Hare.

'She said there was food aplenty here,' the Gray woman said.

'And sure there is!' boomed William's voice behind her, and to Helen's relief he followed the Grays through the door with an armful of bread and a basket that looked to contain butter and eggs, smoked haddock, a pie and a flask of coffee. She took the last off him and set about pouring mugs of it for her guests, to which young Broggan added liberal drams of whisky. Ann Gray asked for milk for the wee lass.

Helen soon had a pan of porridge on to hotter, and eggs fried and bread sliced, and the company seemed well enough pleased, half-cut as some of them still were from the night before; they'd be the better off with something in their stomachs. By this time Margaret and William Hare had arrived too, and they were hard-pressed to find seats for them all.

'Where's your old cousin, Burke?' Gray asked.

William said she was gone, she'd taken too much to drink and become impudent and they'd thrown her out.

'Isn't that right, Nelly?' he asked.

'How would I know?' Helen replied. 'I was dead to the world myself.'

'Not like you to miss a hoolie like thon,' Mrs Connoway said to Helen. 'Are you keeping alright, lass?'

Helen said she was, only she'd been a touch under the weather the last few days, but a good rest had seen her right. The haddocks were poached now, in their milk, and she began to serve them out, on great slices of bread since there weren't any more plates.

Ann Gray was finished before the others, being by far the most sober, and she said she would get the child dressed for the day. She stood up and made for her own room. Margaret said something sharply to William, and he rushed out after her. In a moment they were back, Ann Gray grumbling at William that she'd only been after some tatties she had in a sack under the bed, and her wee one's stockings, and William chiding her that she would kill them all, raking about in the bedstraw with a lit pipe in her mouth. She seemed put out by that, but William went back and fetched the stockings and the tatties and after that she appeared somewhat mollified.

At last the breakfast was over and the neighbours began to ready themselves to leave, back to their beds most likely, Helen thought. Will Broggan said he would stay there, and William asked him to keep an eye on the back room. Ann Gray looked askance at that, but her wee lass began to cry and she set about quieting the child.

William and William Hare said they had some business they had to see to, and both of them put on their coats and left. Margaret said they could set her as far as Tanner's Close, and she went with them. Helen was left with the Grays and Will Broggan, and she saw no harm in leaving them to their own devices while she cleared the night pots and the last of the mess from the meal. When at last she was done, she almost collided with James Gray in the doorway, carrying his bairnie.

'Beg your pardon,' she began, but Gray cut her off.

'What is that you have in our room?' he demanded. He had a look in his eye that feared Helen.

'I dinna ken,' she said. 'What is it? What have you found?'

'Ye ken fine well,' Gray said. 'That poor auld woman's body, naked as the day she was born and bloodied about the mouth and the lugs. Jesus wept, woman, she's been murdered!'

Helen felt the blood drain from her face, her breath cut short. What had William done? What had those Hares made him do?

'I . . . I . . .' she stuttered, her numb lips struggling to form the words. But then a calmness came over her and she found she could speak again quite clearly. 'Please, James,' she said, 'I beg you, whatever you've seen, just let William attend to it. He's a good man, is William, and he'll see you right. Here,

I have money, it'll pay for a bed somewhere else till William can come and speak with you, I'm sure he can explain—'

James Gray almost spat at her. 'Money? You're offering me money?'

Helen shook her head. 'Just for your bed,' she said. 'The auld wife, she must have . . . She had a skinful of drink, and she was a poor soul, half-starved, it must have done for her, William wouldna . . . ' She trailed off, unable to follow the thought to its conclusion.

Ann Gray appeared then, struggling out the door to the close with all their gear bundled up under her arms.

'What has she to say?' she demanded of her husband. There were tearstains on her dirty cheeks.

'She's offered me money,' James said. 'Till the man comes to see me.'

'There's no enough money in the world,' Ann Gray said.

Helen felt laughter bubble up through her, and she thought she might have gone clean mad.

'Ten pounds,' she said. 'You could be worth ten pounds a week.' Aye, she thought bitterly to herself, she could see now how things were, where William's money had come from.

'God forbid I should be worth money for dead folk,' Ann Gray said, with a twist to her mouth, and now Helen did laugh, out loud.

'I couldna help it, I didna ken,' she said.

'You can help it,' Ann Gray shouted, 'or you wouldna stay in that house.' She began to sob noisily, her husband patting her back awkwardly with the hand that wasn't holding the child.

'You're right,' said Helen, and she watched them rush out of the close. At its mouth, though, they met Margaret Hare, come back, Helen saw now, to check on them. One glance at their faces, and Helen standing behind them, and it seemed Margaret had the measure of things.

'What's all this noise about?' she demanded. 'Get you back into the house and sort out whatever dispute you have with each other in there, like decent folk.'

'I can't,' said Ann Gray. 'I can't go anywhere with her.'

'Never mind her then,' said Margaret, with a poisonous glance at Helen. 'Come with me and tell me what's to do. I have no doubt I can help.'

They left with Margaret then, and Helen could see nothing else for it but to go back into the house. She didn't go near the back room; instead she began to pack her belongings in bundles, ready to flee. She had no idea where to go. Redding wouldn't be far enough, if the Grays went to the constables, everyone knew that was her home place and they'd find her there straight away. Perhaps they could go to Ireland, after all, or over the seas to the New World. Helen had no notion of the New World, she couldn't imagine what might be there and she was greatly afraid it was a place of wild beasts and violent men. The thought of a journey of days or weeks terrified her, an ocean between herself and wee Annie and Maisie. She thought she might rather die.

When she was done with her packing, still William hadn't come back, and there was no sign of Margaret Hare. The day wore on, and she sat in the room as it grew dark. Around five, she heard voices in the corridor outside, and a great noise of dragging and swearing, and then there was quiet. She sat and waited. For William, for the constables, for Margaret – she had no idea.

For the first time, Helen understood she was completely alone.

19
Petechiae

MARGARET AND WILLIAM AND WILLIAM HARE went through the story Helen was to tell with her a dozen times or more, until Helen had it by heart, like a bairn with a catechism, only Helen had never managed to say her catechism – any time the dominie asked her she grew red and breathless and then there was no room in her mind for the words, she stuttered and stumbled over them and earned the strap for her troubles. She got it wrong over and over, so Margaret swore under her breath and said they should have killed Helen instead, she had always said so. That terrified Helen into getting it right, but by the time she was questioned in their room by the man Fisher who was a Sergeant-Major or some sort, and the constable called Finlay who was young with big sticking-out lugs, she had it all muddled again.

She was to say she and William had turned the Grays out for bad conduct, and ever since then the pair had had a spite against William. She got that bit right, but then when they asked about the little old woman, she was to say they had turned her out of the house about seven o'clock in the morning, which was a lie because Helen was asleep at seven o' clock in the morning, and the old woman was dead, and Helen's head was so busy with thoughts of that that she became muddled and said that it was seven o' clock at night, and that was wrong, she saw Fisher look at the constable and knew she had said the wrong thing. So she tried to save it, and said she had seen the old wife in the Vennel the very next night, on her way to the Pleasance, and the old wife had said sorry for the things she had said and done, but she could see they didn't believe it, she never was any good at lying. They asked then why there were marks of blood on the bed, and Helen said it was women's blood, that they had when their curse was on them, and the bedding hadn't been washed since last a woman lay in it, Ann Gray that must have been or even Helen herself, she couldn't remember. Their nostrils went white at that, they weren't used to hearing women speak of such things, although Helen couldn't think why they were so scandalised, after all they had wives and mothers, unless they thought they were born like Christ of a virgin.

They took them to the police office then, due to the differences in the accounts they had given, not the Hares but William and Helen, and put them in cells apart from each other. It seemed they had returned to the house then, with a surgeon, and they had found the old wife's bed-gown and a quantity of blood in the straw.

Helen had no idea of that at the time, her mind was full of awful imaginings of what William might have done under the influence of the Hares. The next thing she knew, Margaret and William Hare were arrested too; that was the morning of the Sabbath and the constable told her when he brought her bread and water to break her fast. Helen was afraid Margaret might be put in with her, and said so, but the constable laughed and said she wasn't to worry about that, they would all be kept well apart so they couldn't put their heads together and go over their story. 'I don't have a story,' Helen said. 'I was asleep while they drank with the old wife.' The constable wrote that down in a wee book he had, before he locked the door again and went away.

After that Helen saw no other soul the rest of the day. She fancied she could hear Margaret Hare's step outside the cell door, but it couldn't be her, she must be locked up or with the policemen. At one point they came and got her and showed her a body; it was the old wife's and no doubt, although she had that strange, waxen look the dead always have, when whatever spark it was that made them a man or a woman has gone out and only the clay remains. She had marks on her, a print like a hand on the neck and other bruises on the parts Helen could see.

She shook her head and said she had no idea who this body was, she had never seen the woman before in her life. The old wife Docherty had thick dark hair and this body was grey.

After that, they took her back to her cell. She thought she should say her prayers, it was the Sabbath and her father would wish her to, but she found she couldn't even keep her mind on that – the marks on the old wife's neck haunted her, it was clear enough she had been done a harm. Helen felt her own neck, remembering the feeling of James MacDougal throttling her, all those years ago. She couldn't imagine William doing such a thing to any man or woman; he might be a weak man but she didn't think he had that in him.

The next day they took her to make her declaration and she did her level best to remember the story Margaret had dinned into her. The old woman Docherty came into their house, as far as she remembered, about ten o'clock on the Friday morning, to join them for breakfast, and when she and William got to cracking they discovered a family connection on his mother's side. William went out for whisky, as far as she remembered, and they all had a glass to mark Hallowe'en in the Irish manner. About two o' clock, Helen remembered she was to say, Mrs Docherty went out to go to St Mary's Wynd to enquire for her son, and that was the last Helen saw her that night. They took dinner and drams with William Hare and Margaret, and the Grays. Then Helen was to say she had had a falling out with Ann Gray over a gown the woman had stolen – that was a lie, Ann Gray had never had anything from Helen except a bonnet Helen had given her freely for her lass, but she managed to remember it well enough and said it as best she could. Then she said that the Grays had taken a scunner against herself and William and had made up a story about a body being in their house, to bring the police down on them. Helen said she knew nothing of any body, and that part was almost true, she had been asleep the whole time, only the next bit was a lie, and that was when she said she still hadn't seen the body of the old woman – the body she had been shown here in the police office was of a woman she had never seen before in her life, God rest her poor old soul.

Helen knew William had a different story to tell, one they hadn't trusted her with, that would explain how the old woman had come to be lying dead in their house, and she thought they might ask her about that, but they didn't. Still, they seemed quite ill-satisfied with her own account of proceedings, but in truth she had none other to offer, and no matter how much they pressed her, she could say no more.

As they took her back to her cell, a woman was brought in by a different constable, writhing and spitting like a cat. As Helen passed her she stopped her struggles and asked, 'Is thon the murderess Mistress Burke? The one that killed the puir auld Irish wife and the daft laddie?' and she spat a great glob of spit onto Helen's cheek. That was how Helen knew that the news was out, the whole town was talking of murder. She felt the spit on her cheek the whole way back to her cell, only wiping it off there on the blanket, they had taken her bonnet and her hankie for fear she would somehow do herself a damage with them. This was the first she had heard of the daft laddie – at least, she knew who the woman spoke of, the wife Wilson's son who was missing, but what was he to do with William?

The days dragged on and Helen stewed in the cell. Ten days later, they told her that she and William, and Margaret and Hare, had been committed by the Sheriff to stand trial for the murder of Mary Docherty. Will Broggan had been released, they said, which was a relief to Helen, for all she had never known he had been arrested, he was just a young lad and she didn't like to think of facing his father and mother if any harm had come to him.

All this long while no one had troubled Helen, she had bed and board in the police office, but after they were committed to trial, they sent for her again and asked her to tell them yet again the events of that afternoon. She tried to remember Margaret's instructions, but the time was so long, and she was near distracted wanting to see William and know how it went with him. She tried her best to say the same thing as before, but she couldn't remember the reason she was to give for Mary Docherty going away, and got muddled with Ann Gray and the stolen gown that never existed, and in the end she said that the old woman had given her no end of trouble, asking for salt to wash herself – Helen was desperate for the same, never had she gone so long without a proper wash – and tea, which Helen and William rarely had in the house, it was too expensive. So she said she had thrown the old woman out of the house about four o' clock in the afternoon – that seemed as good an explanation as any, after all Helen really did have no idea what had happened to her.

After that Helen was moved to another place, a jail this time that she soon understood was the Tolbooth, but again she was kept on her own, and the woman who came with the slop bucket and water and porridge and bread told her the whole town was aflame with word of the awful things she had done and they couldn't risk putting anyone else in with her for fear they would do her an injury. Helen said she had done nothing wrong, and the woman laughed and said, 'That's right, pet, you stick to your story,' and then she told Helen some amazing tales of the goings-on of resurrectionists. It seemed the city was desperate for news of their crimes and the papers were full of it: a dead woman stolen from the infirmary by men claiming to be her brothers and later discovered on the surgeon's table, a mob chasing a carriage down the North Bridge because someone said it had a stolen corpse in the back. She said the mood had turned against the anatomists; someone had had money off them for a body, but when the box was opened, it was found to contain nothing but rubbish.

'My man did sell bodies to the surgeons,' Helen said then. 'That much is true. Four, I think, though I never saw them. But he never murdered anybody, I would swear to it.'

'If you'll take my advice, you'll swear to nothing for any man,' the woman said. 'You look to yourself first, pet – if you don't, then no one else will.' She pinched Helen's cheek in a kindly way and left, locking the great lock behind her.

This same woman brought Helen a letter, a day in December, and helped her read it, for it was a great long document and Helen's own skills were not up to the task. It said she was to appear before the High Court on the 24th of December, at ten o'clock in the forenoon, to answer for the crime of murder.

Helen felt faint at that, for she had trusted that, whatever happened, she could not be accused of any such crime, for she had never laid a hand on another person. After a moment she asked the woman to read on, and she did, stumbling over the name of the lawmen who had sent the letter, and the great words they used, but then she was on surer ground as she reached the accusation, and that was when Helen found she was accused of murdering Mary Patterson.

'Mary!' she cried. 'But Mary is gone away to Glasgow! How can I have killed her?'

The woman said she didn't know, and she seemed to fair pity Helen in her distress. She asked if she should read on, and Helen said *yes*, and she found that the letter accused her and William, or just William, neither she nor the woman could make that out, of lying on Mary so that she couldn't breathe and covering her mouth, and in that way bringing about her death. Helen wept to think of that; she had known Mary since she was a child and it pained her to think of anyone hurting her so.

The woman read on, and Helen heard again the name of the daftie lad, Jamie Wilson, whose mother had tramped the streets and closes all those months in search of him. She knew the lad by sight, everyone did, but she had never spent a moment in his company, and she told the woman so, and again the woman seemed to believe her.

'You will have to tell them as you've told me, pet,' she said, and she gave Helen a shot of her own handkerchief, even though it was forbidden, and said she could keep it. She asked if she should read more, and when Helen was ready she nodded, and the women reached the murder of Mary Docherty, or

McGonegal, or Duffie, or Campbell; it seemed she had a great raft of names she was known by, and as well as Mary she was sometimes called Madgy or Margery. There was a great long description of how the old wife died, and then of all sorts of articles of clothing and other gear that the police had found in Helen and William's house. Most of it she recognised but some not, and she told the woman that the clothes had come from Margaret Hare.

'Does it say nothing of her?' Helen asked. 'If it truly happened that William did these awful things, then it was she and her man led him to it, for they were as thick as thieves, and she always had a great many articles in her rooms, that she said guests had left behind when they quit the place.'

'There's no word of her,' the woman said. 'No, wait, here she is on the list of witnesses. She must be coming to court to speak for you Helen, that's what it'll be.'

Helen thanked the woman for her service and asked if she could be left alone. The woman – Jamesina her name was, she had told Helen that long syne – squeezed her hand and told her to be brave, she must just tell the truth and trust in God. Then she left, and Helen turned her face to the wall. If Margaret Hare was the best hope she had of a person to speak for her, she knew she might meet her Maker very soon indeed.

* * *

On the day fixed for the trial, Jamesina brought Helen her own clothes, washed and pressed, and gave her back her bonnet that had been taken from her eight weeks before for fear she might hang herself with its strings. She said there was a right to-do out on the streets, had been since the night before, with folk thronging to see Helen and William, and Margaret and Hare, go into the court. There were policemen everywhere, brought in from every town in the country, it seemed, and the cavalry were mustered in case of an emergency.

'So you'll be perfectly safe, Helen,' said Jamesina, although her account to that point had given Helen quite the opposite impression.

She had been woken early, and it was still full dark when she was taken to the court in Parliament Square and placed in a cell below. At last she was taken upstairs and into the court, where there was a clock that showed twenty to ten. Beside her in the dock was William, the first time she had seen him in all those weeks, except for a glimpse maybe, from the window of her cell in the police office, when he had been taken for questioning. He looked pale and tired, and he seemed smaller than she remembered; she hadn't known how to think of him in all those weeks, reading the things he was accused of and half-believing them to be true. He smiled when he saw her, though, and she found herself smiling back, though her face was little accustomed to it and she felt she made a poor job of it. As she sat by him, he found a way to squeeze her hand and she felt her heart leap, for all this trouble she would still wish to be his, if only they could be in Redding and never have come to this place or met the Hares.

They sat there a while waiting for something, which turned out to be the arrival of the judges. There were three of them, and a great many more lawmen; some would be speaking for Helen – she had met with three who had explained it to her – and some for William. Others would speak against them. Jamesina said she was lucky, these men would have no pay for defending her but they were famous lawmen and she was fortunate to have them on her side. She didn't feel fortunate, she felt afraid, and the men made her uncomfortable, she saw how they pitied and despised her.

The middle judge spoke to them at last, saying they must listen to the indictment against them, but he didn't manage to finish this instruction, as one of their own men said there was an objection to the way it was all being carried out, and he wished to object. There was some argy-bargy then, but the judge held sway and the whole awful list of accusations was read out, bringing tears to Helen's eyes again to think of poor Mary and the Wilson woman's lad.

Then the lawmen spoke for Helen and William, and although they might as well have been speaking in Latin for all the words meant to Helen, she had had it explained to her that they planned to argue that it was improper for William to be tried for three deaths that occurred at different times and in different places, with no connection proven between them at all, and moreover it was worse that he was to be tried with Helen, who no one was suggesting had any idea of the first of these crimes at all. Indeed, when they had explained this stratagem to Helen, she had asked them, 'Is Mary dead then, right enough?' and had wept a little when they said aye, there was ample evidence she was, enough of the students had known her to recognise her corpse.

The lawman spoke for a long time on this count, and Helen found herself drifting off, she hadn't expected that, thinking she would be riveted to the spot in terror. That turned out to be the way in which she passed most of the trial, by turns panicked and bored, struggling to keep awake or listen to them yaw on. The crowd in court seemed more entertained, making faces of approval at some of the arguments and scowls at others. Helen wished to watch them, in hope she might gain some idea of how the matter was going, but she was too afraid to catch anyone's eye.

The main man that was to speak against them rose up after that, and he seemed to make out that the arrangement her own man thought so unfair was actually a good one for Helen, for if William was tried and found guilty, and she tried after, she might have cause for complaint. He argued then that he had no choice but to try William for all three of the murders laid against him, although his reasons why were listed in language Helen could make no sense of at all. After that one of their own men spoke to say *he* was wrong, and Helen thought she might go distracted, it was like listening to old men in their cups, arguing to and fro. At last the judges made their own speeches, and it seemed they had thrown out the objection to Helen being tried with William, but on the matter of the three charges, their men had won, and William would be tried for one murder only. The opposition seemed put out by that, but at length he said he would choose that William be tried for the murder of the old wife Docherty.

Helen had her chance to speak then, but only to say she was not guilty, and she heard what a small and coarse voice she had, among these types who sounded to have been weaned on portwine and partridges. William said he was not guilty too, and then they started to sort out the jury of fifteen men who would pronounce judgement on them.

After that it was fell dry stuff for a while, with a man coming in to speak to some drawings he had done of their lodgings and the houses around, although how that mattered Helen could not understand. Then a woman called Stewart came to swear that Mrs Docherty had spent the night before Hallowe'en in her house in the Pleasance, where her son also lodged. This woman said Mary Docherty was in fine health, which Helen thought a clear lie, the woman was skin and bone and looked like to blow over at the slightest gust of wind. The Stewart woman said the bedgown found in their house was Mrs Docherty's, and so did a man named McLachlan, who also lodged in the house, although what business he had looking at auld wives in their bedgowns was anyone's guess. A shop lad came to say he had seen William meet Mrs Docherty, which no one was denying and so seemed a pointless exercise, but then he said William had bought a tea-chest from him the very next day, and he thought the tea-chest was the same one in which one Dr Knox had taken delivery of the old woman's body. Helen looked at William when she heard that; she remembered the name Knox, he was the one William had sold the old man's body to the year before.

Next came Mrs Connoway, their neighbour, who yawed on about how she had met Mrs Docherty on the day of Hallowe'en, and then that evening they had all come to her house. She said Helen was in the company, which wasn't true, but judging by the state of the old biddy the next day, she had taken a good skinful herself and it might be that she didn't remember. She said the Docherty woman had hurt her feet at the dancing, which didn't surprise Helen, given the state of her. She told of the breakfast they had all eaten together the next day and that Helen had said she had kicked the old woman out for being over-familiar with William, although as Helen remembered it, William had said he had kicked her out for being impudent. The woman had to admit she had heard no disturbance in the night – *Faith, no surprise*, Helen thought, *she was passed out with drink!* – or imagined anything amiss at all. On her way down from the place where she gave her evidence, she looked over at Helen, and Helen thought she seemed sorry. Mrs Connoway's great mucker Mrs Law was next, and she said much the same thing, and it was boring listening to everyone trot out the same accounts with no differences, although the lawmen had explained why, all the evidence had to be corroborated. At the end, though, her account differed, and she said she had heard shuffling or fighting from the house.

Another neighbour came next, and he said he had heard a noise on Hallowe'en as he went along the close, like two men fighting and then a woman's voice crying 'murder'. Then he heard a cry which he kent was a person or an animal being strangled, and the same woman's voice cried 'murder'. He was much afraid of fire, he said, which made no sense at all, and so he went to find a policeman, but he didn't, and so he went to his bed and forgot the whole thing. The lawman speaking for Helen rolled his eyes at this, which did seem to be patent nonsense.

Next came a man Helen had never seen in her life before. This man, one Davie Paterson, was the keeper of the museum of Dr Knox, whatever that might mean, and it was clear the courtroom was hanging on his evidence. He said that William had come to fetch him on the first of November, to say he had a subject for him, by which he meant a body for cutting up. He said he went with William to the house and paid him an instalment for the body. The lawman asked him this question and that about the state of the body, which he had given up to the police, and he said it was clear the woman had never seen the inside of a grave, the corpse was as fresh as could be, and it had marks of violence on it and a terrible look on the face that told him it had been strangled. He said he knew William and William Hare well, and had paid them for many bodies, and not one of those showed any signs of having been buried at all. He tried to cover for himself, since that made him look bad too, by saying that he knew of men that would go to a sick-house and carry off the body as soon as the poor unfortunate expired, and this was what he had thought William and Hare were doing.

Will Broggan came next, and the policemen, who made much of the differences in the accounts Helen and William had given of the events of Hallowe'en and the next day, although Helen thought the folk in the court found it wearing after the excitement of Paterson's evidence, with its suggestion that the doctors were as much to blame as anyone.

The effect of the next witness was like wind through barley; a murmur passed through the court, almost too low to be heard. This was William Hare, who seemed not to turn a hair, coming to the place where he was to speak with his usual smirk on his scarred face and his green jacket on. One of the judges spoke to him, saying whatever share he had had in the transaction, if he spoke the truth he could never again be questioned in a court of law. Helen knew he would speak against them, and pay no price himself for all that he had done, but still it stuck in her throat and she felt her face flush red and she had to stare at her feet until she could control her breathing again.

Hare swore his oath in a different way from most, on a cross, as he was a Catholic. He was reminded he would only need to speak about Mary Docherty, and he cheerfully told the court that he and William had taken a dram together on Hallowe'en, when William told him he had an old woman in his house he had found on the streets, and she would be a good 'shot' to take to the doctors. Hare understood, he said, that this was code for murdering the old woman, and then he described the events of the evening more or less as Helen remembered them, except he never said that she went to bed. He said he and William had had a fight – he couldn't remember why – and the old woman tried to intervene, but in the confusion she tripped over a stool and fell. Then he said William sat astride her, and she cried out, but William kept in her breath.

The lawman asked if William did anything else and Hare said yes, he pressed down her head with his breast.

The lawman asked if she had cried out and Hare said she had, one cry and then some moaning. William had put one hand under her nose, and the other under her chin, so her mouth was closed. In this way he had stopped her breath. Hare could not say how long he had done this for, perhaps ten or fifteen minutes.

The lawman kept up his questions and Hare claimed that the whole while he was sitting on a chair, as William got off the woman and put his hand over her mouth for two or three minutes more. He could not say for certain whether or not she was dead at this point.

Then he said that William had stripped the body and tied it in a sheet, so it was doubled over. He maintained that Helen and his own wife had run from the room while this all happened, and did not return until the woman was dead.

Helen tasted vomit in the back of her throat and swallowed it down. Weasel though he was, there was a ring of truth to Hare's words and she could see the scene before her, although she would bet that William had sat on the woman and it was Hare who had held her mouth and nose pinched shut. She couldn't look at William, who she knew would see in her eyes that she believed it.

Their own lawmen had a chance at Hare then, and there was some argy-bargy when they tried to get him to tell them whether he had sold other bodies to the doctors. Hare was taken out while the lawmen settled the matter amongst themselves, so that William and Helen's lawmen were allowed to ask the question, but Hare was equally allowed not to answer. He did, however, flat out denying that he had ever been involved with any corpse except Mrs Docherty's. He lied with such ease, if Helen hadn't known it to be untrue, she might have believed him.

The lawmen had another go then, and another, asking if Hare had seen William selling other bodies, or if he had been involved in any other murders, but Hare said he wouldn't answer. The lawmen pressed him, all but accusing him of murders on his own property, but again he wouldn't answer. He went through it all again, sticking to his story in every detail, and then was taken out to a cell, for he was still being held by the courts.

Next came the witness Helen was dreading, but still her mouth fell open when she appeared. Margaret Hare carried a babe in her arms, that she claimed was her own although Helen knew fine the woman had no bairns of her own – this one must have been procured from its unsuspecting parents for the charade. The poor creature was creasing and kinking with the whooping cough, and Margaret made much of this, especially when it seemed the questioning was going against her. Helen was sure she had a pin or some other sharp article in her hand to prick the child, so neatly did it interrupt proceedings when it suited Margaret, and moreover let her play the picture of maternal solicitude. Helen wondered how they could all fall for it; had this really been the woman's child then she would have been going about her murdering with it in her belly!

Margaret lied almost as smoothly as Hare; only once did she seem to have made an error. When the lawmen asked her what she thought when she returned to the house and found Mrs Docherty gone, she readily admitted she had thought the old wife murdered, for she had seen such tricks before. The lawmen asked no more on that front, though, leaving Helen near biting through her lip in frustration.

The last of the witnesses were doctors, a surgeon working for the police and other medical men, and they gave all sorts of evidence about the state of the old wife's body, and it was awful at first but then Helen was nodding by the time they were done; they had sat all day listening, into the evening and through the night with only a break for an hour for a meal at six she could not eat. Then her own statement and William's were read, and there was no more evidence, the lawmen stepped up to begin their addresses to the jury, who looked near as tired now as Helen herself. The first to speak praised the policemen and the witnesses, and he spoke at some length of the decision to allow Hare to give evidence against his own confederates, which seemed to Helen to be more about protecting his own reputation than anything else. He asked the jury to find William and Helen guilty and it seemed the courtroom was swayed by him, for their eyes turned to Helen and William with no kindness.

William's man spoke next, and he had less style about him, but still he laboured on behalf of William, arguing that this piece of evidence or that was faulty, and the only real testimony against William came from a man who admitted he was as much to blame as William was. He said William and Helen could have made just as good a case against Hare and Margaret, were the tables turned, and he called Hare a ruffian, with hands steeped in blood.

Helen's man came last, and he asked the jury to think of Hare's evidence again, that he had sat in a chair and watched while William killed a woman over fifteen minutes nearly, without so much as raising a cry for help. His wife, the lawman said, admitted that she had seen such tricks before, and Helen's heart lifted that he had noticed, she wasn't alone in realising Margaret Hare had given herself away. He had sharp words for both Hare and Margaret, which was balm to Helen's wounded heart, and he even said Margaret's show of motherly care had been a charade. He ended by saying the jury could put no trust in Hare or Margaret, and could not send Helen to her death on the basis of their lies. He asked them to find the case against Helen not proven, and let the public rage as it pleased.

There was one more speech, guidance to the jury, and then they went out. It was morning now, and Helen felt faint with tiredness and lack of food. William turned to her and said they must comport themselves well, even if the worst were to happen, and must not cry or call out. The hands of the clock made almost an hour's turn, and the jury were back. Helen's heart pounded as the man stood and she heard such a rushing in her ears that she couldn't hear the verdict. She only knew what it was when William turned to her and said, 'Nelly, you're out of the scrape.'

There was a great round of applause, but it wasn't for Helen, it was for William who had been found guilty, and in a moment they could hear an echo from the street outside, for it seemed the whole city was there and cheering. Helen looked at William and he seemed calm enough, only his face was smoother than usual and she knew he was holding himself rigid so as not to shake or cry. He would not look at her, after that one thing he said to her, and instead kept his eyes fixed on the judges as they pronounced sentence upon him. They spoke at length of his coldness and depravity, and said he must die, for it was the rule of God and the law of Scotland, and after that they said he should be given to the surgeons for dissection. One of the judges put on the black cap and William got on his feet and the judge said that he must prepare himself to appear before the throne of Almighty God to answer for his crime.

He said he had considered recommending that William's body be exhibited in chains, to deter others from such base and alarming crimes, but that the public should be spared the sight, and instead William's body would be publicly anatomised and his skeleton preserved so that his crimes might be remembered, if such a thing was possible.

He turned to Helen then, as William's sentence was written in a great book they had, and told her she had not been found not guilty, but the charge was not proven, and he said he left it to her conscience to know whether or not she was guilty of the crime. Helen knew she had done no killing, but she had no idea how to feel, for William stood rigid and unmoving beside her, and she knew now all that he had done in her house, and how he had lied, and betrayed her, but he was her man, he had been her man these many years, and the tears flowed down her cheeks for him.

20

Puncture Wound

SUSAN WAS HELPING YOUNG ROBERT make the words 'COW' and 'SHEEP' with letter blocks on the floor when Mrs Scott entered in a panic and thrust a silver tray at her. For a moment, Susan could make no sense of it but then she peered closer at the item on the tray. It was a neat white calling card.

'A visitor?' Susan said. 'Here – now?'

Mrs Scott nodded, confusion writ plain on her face. 'A lady,' she said. 'Very finely dressed.'

Susan picked up the card. It said 'Miss Jessica Knox'.

'She's downstairs,' Mrs Scott said. 'What do I do?'

Susan almost laughed. 'What do you mean, "what do I do?" Surely you worked in a house before where there were visitors?'

'No,' said Mrs Scott. 'I've always minded folk who were a danger to themselves.'

'I see,' said Susan, and now she did laugh. 'So now you're here with me, and we neither of us are used to social niceties. Well, I'm sure we'll manage between us. The lady is Doctor Knox's sister. Have you sat her on the sofa?'

'Aye,' said Mrs Scott. 'I asked if I could take her hat but she said no. And I've given her nothing. Do I give her tea?'

'No,' Susan said. 'I go down. At least, in other houses I would go down. But I wouldn't seek to place you in a difficult position, Mrs Scott. Are you sure you're content I won't be a danger to her? Or myself?'

Mrs Scott's cheeks flamed and Susan almost pitied her. 'Of course I am,' she said.

'Well,' said Susan, 'you bring the tea on a tray and put the things on the table and then I will serve it.'

Mrs Scott looked relieved. 'Will you go down now, then? The woman is in a queer state.'

'I will,' Susan said. She got to her feet and straightened her dress. 'This is hardly suitable for an "at home", but I can't see it would be fair to expect that I would have been dressing for visitors for all these years, when none have ever come. Will you fetch Joanie, Mrs Scott? Someone will have to mind the children.'

Mrs Scott bustled off to fetch Joanie, and Susan made her way slowly down the stairs, pausing before the mirror to tuck a stray lock of hair back into her bun. She pinched her cheeks, so Jessie would not think her shocked, and held her head up high as she swept into the best room.

'Jessie,' she said.

Jessie sat stiffly upright on the sofa in her hat and coat. She watched warily as Susan came into the room and sat herself in the chair opposite.

'You look well, Susan,' she said, at last.

Susan said nothing. Even had she been minded to put the woman at her ease, she couldn't in honesty return the compliment. Jessie was scrawnier than ever, her hair thin and lank under her hat, her eyes red and her nose and lips chapped.

Jessie seemed uncomfortable under Susan's eyes, jumping to her feet after a few seconds and walking over to the window to look out at the wintry garden beyond.

'It's a bonnie place,' she said. 'Or must be in summer. I was never here before.'

No, thought Susan, *you were in my place, keeping house in the house that should be mine.*

Out loud, she said, 'Mary is not with you?'

'She is indisposed with her nerves,' Jessie said.

At that moment, Mrs Scott bustled in with the tea tray. She seemed on surer ground with this – tea was tea, after all, whether it was being served to a visitor or to a lunatic. Well, the lunatic might have it colder, and in a beaker, but the business with the tray was much the same.

'Cake, perhaps, Mrs Scott?' Susan said, more to give the woman an instruction to follow than because she thought either she or Jessie wanted it.

Jessie took her seat again and Susan poured the tea. They drank in silence. During this time Susan had another chance to observe her, and saw that she was even more finely dressed than before. Her high-waisted frock and coat were made of some glazed brown stuff, elegantly tucked and gathered, with sleek grey fur round the neck, matching a trim inside the edges of the hat. A muff of the same sat beside her on the sofa, with a small, beaded reticule and kid-leather gloves. The muff was trimmed with pink and grey ribbons to match the hat, which additionally had a great lace frill dangling down. The general effect, Susan thought, was less than becoming, but no doubt fashion moved on in the world outside, and she had lost her sense of what was considered comely.

Mrs Scott came with seed cake, cut in small slices. Susan handed it and Jessie took a slice. She put it down directly, though, and with a glare turned to Susan.

'You must do something about this business,' she said, without preamble.

Susan blinked. 'Business?' she repeated. 'What business?'

Jessie clucked her tongue. 'You can't be innocent of it,' she said. 'The whole city is in uproar, talking of nothing else.'

'We live a lonely life, here at Lillypot,' Susan said pointedly. 'No one visits. No one brings us letters, or news. I owe all my knowledge of the town to what Robert tells me, and that is very little.'

Jessie stood up again and walked to the window.

'There has been a great scandal,' she said, staring out. 'A pair of Irishmen and their wives have . . .' She seemed unable to go on for a moment, but then she set her shoulders and continued. 'They have killed a number of unfortunates, in the Old Town. One of the murderers turned King's Evidence, but the other will hang for it.'

'Horrid,' Susan said. 'But I don't understand, Jessie. What is this to do with me?'

Jessie sighed and paced in an agitated manner for a moment before she came to the point. 'They're saying brother Robert bought the bodies for his classes.'

'Oh,' said Susan. 'Is it true?'

'Well how should I know?' Jessie snapped.

'Have you asked Robert?'

'We've barely seen him,' Jessie said. 'He keeps to his rooms at Surgeon's Square.'

'How could they prove what bodies he had?' Susan asked. 'They'd all be cut up and buried, surely?' It was an awful thought, Robert buying the victims of murder, but she remembered the bodies of her babies gone from the house before she saw them, and she found she could easily believe it.

'They were, all but one,' Jessie said. 'But there's a horrid wee man named Paterson. He works for Robert. Davie Paterson. He stood up in the court and told them he had bought a dead woman off the Irishmen on behalf of Robert, and others too. Oh, he was careful enough to say he thought the other bodies had died of natural causes, but now he is going from pillar to post saying that Robert had a hand in it all. He says Robert set the prices for the bodies himself, though he knew the gang were murderers.' She made a strange gasping noise and buttoned her mouth tightly shut.

'Do people believe him?' Susan asked. 'This man Paterson?'

'They most certainly do,' Jessie said. 'A great gang of laddies attacked the house last night.' Tears sprung into her eyes at that, and she searched in her reticule for a handkerchief, which she pressed against her eyes. 'They smashed all the glass in the windows. We thought they meant to break the door down. They were only turned back by a great force of policemen.'

Susan found she cared little for the windows of the house in Newington, but she did wonder what this meant for her.

'Will Robert be arrested?' she asked. What would she and the children do, if there was no more money?

'I don't think so,' said Jessie. 'When the policemen came to demand he open his rooms so they could look at the bodies there, it seems he made great swearing at them and threatened to blow their brains out, but it seems he has been civil enough since then, and they have been civil with him. The scandal sheets are crying out that he should be taken up, but it seems to me they shout so loudly because they know there is no chance of it. I have heard that he has dismissed Davie Paterson, so he has been seen to deal with the guilty party.'

That sounded about right to Susan; Robert liked having servants do his dirty work for him.

'So what would you have me do, Jessie?' she asked. 'When I am kept here and know no one and see no one. What do you imagine I can do about the matter?'

'You can speak to brother Robert!' Jessie cried. 'Convince him we must leave Edinburgh for London, or Paris. He won't go while you are here with your ... children. But if you agree to come, or tell him you don't mind if he goes, then we can be away from this place and the damned mobs on the streets. You don't understand, Susan! I can't go out! I can't leave my own home!'

Susan stared at her for a moment, but found she could not be bothered even to hate her. She picked up the muff from the sofa and held it out.

'I can't help you, Jessie,' she said. 'Robert has done what he has done, and I suppose he must pay the price for that. And you have done what you have done, and you must live with that, too. Please go, and never come here again. I have no wish to see you.'

Jessie looked as though she would like to slap Susan, or pinch her, but she settled for snatching the muff from her hands and wrenching open the door. Hearing the commotion, Mrs Scott scuttled from the kitchen and opened the front door herself. Susan stood behind her as they watched Jessie make her way to the gate in the garden where her carriage waited.

'Where's John?' Susan asked, as Jessie stared at the gate for a moment, expecting it to be opened, before she realised she was expected to do this herself.

Mrs Scott looked helpless. 'John's gone, Ma'am. He says he won't stay here. He gave me this and told me to tell Doctor Knox to go to Hell.' She thrust a folded piece of paper at Susan, as though it was hot. 'He didn't even take his wages.'

Susan took the paper from her, noticing that the woman's hand shook. 'Have we wine, Mrs Scott?' she asked. 'Or something else to drink? I think we both need it.'

When they were settled in the best room and both had drunk a steadying draught, Susan unfolded John's paper. It was a horrible picture of a great Devil with garden shears, about to cut the stem of a plant on which grew a balding human head. The head was seen from the back, but the Devil held a lantern that cast its shadow on a wall to the side, and the profile was unmistakably Robert's. In the background was a gallows, and under the picture were the words 'CROPPING A NOX-I-OUS PLANT, OR, AN OLD VIRTUOSO APPROPRIATING A NEW CURIOSITY.'

'N-O-X,' Susan said. 'Or Knox. So everyone knows?'

'John said he was related to a wife named Wilson,' Mrs Scott said. 'She's a cousin of his, I think. She had a laddie that was daft, and they're saying these Irishmen killed him and Doctor Knox cut his body to pieces.'

'Good God,' Susan said, and she poured them both another glass of wine. 'I hope it's not true, Mrs Scott. But I'm afraid it is. I am very sorry for John and his family. What will you do now?'

Mrs Scott looked into her glass. 'This is my place, here,' she said, although she didn't sound happy about it.

'Looking after a "madwoman"?' Susan said. 'In the service of a doctor who has been buying the victims of murder? Passing on his own dead children's bodies to him to do with them we know not what?'

Mrs Scott's eyes filled with tears at the last. 'I didna mean any ill,' she said. 'Poor babbies.' Then she shook her head, business-like again. 'I have a sister in Leith. I could go to her. If I needed a place for a while.'

'I think it would be better,' Susan said. 'I don't know what will happen, but I know it will do you little good to be associated with us. Who knows what stories might yet come out?'

Mrs Scott wiped her eyes on the back of her hand. 'But how could you manage on your own?' she asked.

'I don't know,' said Susan. 'But I think I must learn. The keys, please, Mrs Scott.'

Mrs Scott fumbled at her belt and unhooked the great ring of keys. She handed them to Susan, and then she took a great pull of her wine. 'There's a great deal of money in the desk in my room,' she said. 'Doctor Knox always left at least six months' worth at any time, for there were such long spells when he didn't come, and all the wages and merchants to be paid. The wee silver key on the ring opens the desk, and this' – she fished under the neck of her blouse and pulled out a ribbon with a small brass key on it – 'this opens the money safe you will find there. It's fixed to the desk, you can't pull it out.'

'Thank you,' said Susan. She put the key around her own neck.

'Elsie has no situation yet,' Mrs Scott said then. 'Doctor Knox would give her no reference. She's at home with her father near the High Street, working some days in a shop. I could ask her to come. She can cook well enough, although I don't know if she would need to. I don't think Mrs Foster would see you and the bairnies go hungry.'

Susan felt her heart lift at the thought of Elsie's cheery face. 'I think Elsie and I would do very well together,' she said. 'Thank you, Mrs Scott.'

'I'll go there now,' Mrs Scott said, rising to her feet. 'You know . . . well, you don't know, but Doctor Knox keeps a pony trap at the big house along the road, the Bower, and pays for use of horses and a coachman whenever he might have need. If you want to go anywhere, you just have to go to the back door there and ask.'

'I see,' Susan said. 'I had no idea there was anyone in that house. I thought they only came in summer.'

'No,' Mrs Scott said, 'there are servants there all year round. I'll go there now and they'll take me to Elsie's. I'll bring her back with me, and bide till I've telt her all she needs to know.' She paused at the door to ask, 'Will you manage the fire and a bit of food for yourself while I'm gone? I'll be a good while.'

Susan laughed. 'I'm not an imbecile, Mrs Scott.' Then a thought came to her and she turned again to the other woman. 'Did you ever think I was?'

Mrs Scott stopped. 'Not for a long time, lass,' she said. 'Before Doctor Knox brought you here, they told me you had tried to put a hand in your own life. I had no reason to doubt it, I've seen many poor souls that seemed just fine one moment, and did themselves a dreadful damage the next. One lass took a paperknife from a table and opened a vein in her neck in front of me. I tried to staunch the blood, but it gushed out no matter what I did, and she died under my hands.' She shuddered. 'I'll never forget it as long as I live. When I first met you, you seemed frantic, but I see now that anyone would be, were they to be locked up in a place they didn't know, alone. That woman that came today, she was the one that told me you seemed fine enough most times, but now and then a mania took you. I did wonder why she never visited, and ...' She tailed off, but then she looked Susan in the eye. 'I never saw that it was right, if a woman suffered from mania, that her husband should be always getting her with child. But I liked it here, with the bairnies, and it was easy work, so I said nothing. I'm sorry, Mrs Knox.'

'Susan,' Susan said.

Mrs Scott nodded and went out. In a few moments, Susan heard the front door close behind her. She drank another glass of wine, and then she walked up the stairs to the children's room and began a great pantomime designed to tell Joanie she should go down and make them all some lunch. At last Joanie understood and took herself off. Susan sat with the bairnies until she came back with bannocks and butter and cheese. Then she went back downstairs, opened the front door and walked across the garden. She opened the gate and stepped outside. Then she walked up the road. She walked for perhaps fifteen minutes, and no one tried to stop her. By then she was cold, and so she turned and walked back to the house.

21
Panic Attack

H ELEN WASN'T ALLOWED TO WALK out the door after
the trial, she was taken back to a cell in the basement of the building and allowed to sleep. The man
who took her down shook his head, and looked as though he
thought her far from innocent. His nostrils flared as he said
she would be detained a few more days yet, but it was for her
own safety now, the mob was wild and whipping themselves
up still further by deciding every person missing in the town
had been murdered by William and Hare. Helen shuddered;
she could well believe it. He said the feeling was highest against
Hare, after the evidence he gave, most folk thought him the
guiltiest party.

'Can they be tried for the others?' Helen asked. 'The ones
the lawmen said, the Wilson lad and poor Mary Patterson?
Margaret Hare gave me Mary's skirt and told me she'd gone
to Glasgow.'

'They can't be tried for any of it,' the man said. 'That was
what they meant, in the court. Neither can the doctors. That's
half the reason folk are so angry, they don't think it's fair.

It wasn't fair, as far as Helen could see, but she didn't
say so.

242

'Are they released?' she asked. The man said no, they would remain in jail a while, until the court worked out what to do about them.

'Can I see William?' she asked, then.

'You can apply,' the man said. 'They'll take him to the Calton Jail and put him in the condemned cell there to prepare for his fate. When it's safe for you to leave, you can put in the request.'

'Will he have a Bible?' Helen asked. 'He was never without his Bible.'

The man snorted. 'Well, I fear his reading was deficient,' he said. 'But aye, he'll have a Bible, and holy men too, if he wants them.'

It was three days, in the end, before Helen was allowed out. They waited till after dark to release her, saying the streets were quiet enough, this close to the New Year folk would be holding back their drink and their strength. She kept to the shadows all the way down the West Bow and through the Grassmarket to Broggan's, with a key they had given her from William's things. She made straight for their own room and not the place at the back where the old wife Docherty had died. She nearly tripped over a pile of clothes right inside the door; they had made a right mess with their searching. She was too feared to light a fire or a lamp in case anyone should come, and so she wrapped herself in a great heap of shawls and blankets and lay on the bed, but sleep would not come – it was as though she had been drunk, and now must lie awake and think over all that had happened, no matter how it pained her. Towards dawn she dozed, but after an hour or so she started awake; in her dreams the old wife was here in the room in her bedgown, crying out for help, with blood round her nose and mouth. Helen found she could not draw breath for a few moments, thinking her heart would burst and she would die, but in time she calmed down and breathed easy again.

All the next day Helen hid in the room, but come evening she needed food and drink, there was no way she could pass another night, so it would be better with whisky. She tied her shawl over her head and went to the shop, but the man knew her, of course, and with a twist to his lip, he told her he wouldn't serve her. As she left the place to try another, a gang of laddies saw her and one of them shouted, 'It's the bitch MacDougal,' and they began to pelt her with muck from the street. She cowered against a wall as a crowd assembled, sure they meant to tear her limb from limb. A woman had just grabbed the bonnet off her head when she heard a whistle and a gang of policemen appeared, their staves drawn. One of them sheltered her with his body while the others shouted and bawled and threatened to leather the laddies. They took her to their watch-house, a few roads west, and the mob followed, screaming threats and obscenities at Helen and the policemen. At last they were in the door, but the crowd outside grew ever greater, hammering on the door and smashing the windows with stones. Helen was sure they would break down the walls and she would die, but one of the policemen took her to another room and gave her a set of men's clothes to put on, and a great coat lined with leather, such as a coachman might wear.

'Have you money?' he asked.

'I do,' Helen said. 'Twelve pounds.'

The policeman shook his head. 'I wonder which poor soul that was got for.'

Helen's face flamed red, but she changed into the clothes under his cold eye, and then he cut off her hair with a knife he had – it hurt her and she thought he was pleased. Then he told her to start walking and not to stop until she was out of the city, and if she knew what was good for her, she would never return. He said they would hold the mob off a while, and then tell them she was being held again to give evidence against Hare.

Then he lifted her out a window in the back. Helen walked through the dark streets of the Old Town, avoiding the lamp-light as best she could, and down the great slope of the Mound, along the wide sweep of Princes Street and down into Leith. Near the place she had lived with James MacDougal, she found a sailors' inn and paid for a room for the night.

The next day, Helen found a seat on a coach to Falkirk and by the darkening, she was at her father's house in Redding. When Peter Gaff opened the door, his wary look gave way to surprise as he recognised her, and then his face creased in pain.

'Wait there,' he said, and then she heard him call to the bairns to get themselves all up the stairs to the loft, they could all sleep up there that night. Then he came back and opened the door again, standing in silence while Helen came in and sat by the fire. Jezebel appeared and wound round her ankles, the first kind touch Helen had felt in days.

'Is it true, Helen?' he asked. 'Did William do these dreadful things? I canna think it true, but I canna think the courts would get the thing so wrong.'

Helen said nothing, but tears ran down her face.

'I see,' Peter Gaff said. 'Well, I don't know what to say to you, Helen. I thought I'd brought you up right. I ken there was the accident with Maisie, I kent you could be careless, but I never thought you could hurt another body on purpose. For money, Helen? For shame!'

'I didna,' Helen said. 'I never harmed anyone. I didna ken William had done it either.'

'And how can that be?' her father demanded. 'How big was this place you bided in, in Edinburgh, that your man could kill a woman and you no ken?'

'It was a lodging house,' Helen said. 'There were other rooms.' She took a deep breath, and she said, 'I kent he had done a wrong thing, and selt bodies to the doctors. He didna sleep because of it, and I said he should stop, and he said he had and I . . . I believed him.'

Her father shook his head. 'So you thought it was a different crime,' he said. 'One against God.'

'I telt him to stop.'

'You should have left him, Helen,' her father said. 'One bad man was bad enough.'

Helen began to cry in earnest. 'I didna see badness in him, just weakness. Did you? Did you see badness in him, Faither?'

Peter Gaff sighed. 'No,' he said, 'and it grieves me sair. To think he was here in my house, wi the bairns. To think I said you should tak Maisie and wee Annie hame. And now I read he has a wife in Ireland, to boot!'

'What do I do now?' Helen asked, through her tears. 'What do I do, Faither?'

Peter Gaff shook his head. 'You canna stay here,' he said. 'Have you money? I thought you were a lad when I opened the door – if you take a room in an inn and keep your head down, you'll be well enough hidden. But you can't stay long in these parts, you'll have to arrange to take yourself somewhere far from here.'

'Where?' Helen sobbed.

'England, maybe,' Peter Gaff said. 'Or America. Somewhere naebody kens ye, Helen. It's the only way. I canna see that you'd be safe, else. An I canna hae the bairns in danger.'

'What could I do in England or America?' Helen asked.

'Trust in God,' her father said. 'Think on what he did for Jacob. *He found him in a desert land, and in the waste howling wilderness; he led him about, he instructed him, he kept him as the apple of his eye.*'

Helen nodded, she could see she had no choice. 'Can I see the lassies?' she asked. 'To take my farewell?'

'No,' said Peter Gaff. 'They canna ken you're here, it's no safe. But as you leave, I'll bring them to stand in the door so you can see them.'

'Tell them I've died then,' Helen said numbly. 'I nearly did, in Edinburgh. There was a mob there that wanted to tear me limb from limb.'

'It's no a bad thought,' her father said, 'though it pains me to lie. But if I tell folk I've had word of your death, they might not look for you any longer. I'd no see you harmed, lassie.'

He wept then, and Helen wept, and then he packed up such food as he could spare in a cloth and gave it to her. Then they walked to the door and Helen took her farewell of him, knowing they would never meet again. A wee bit along the road, she stopped and looked back. He was as good as his word. Maisie and wee Annie were standing in the doorway, and she heard Maisie laugh at her grandfather and say he was daft, there was no snow at all. And Peter Gaff said she was right, he had been mistaken, but was it no a bonnie night, look at the stars. Helen stared at the three figures as if she could imprint the sight of them onto her eyes. When at last Annie said she was cold and they went back inside, she turned and walked on.

She was glad they had parted, so, a few days later. She was staying in a rooming house in Glasgow, waiting for passage to Ireland and then onward to America. There was an almighty hubbub below, and she risked poking her nose out of the room and asking a cleaning lass what was the to-do.

'The murderer Burke has made a confession!' the lass said, near beside herself with excitement. 'They've printed it in the paper today. He says he and Hare killed more than a dozen folk – near a score! Can ye imagine? A poor cinder wifie and a salt seller, and a daftie and a mother and daughter, and even an old woman and her wee grandson! Hare's wife was a part of it too, would you credit it? She took a pound a body for her trouble!'

Helen's gorge rose but she swallowed it down. 'Bring me up a copy,' she said, offering a coin. The lass ran off to fetch it. Helen uncorked a bottle of whisky and sat, ready to look him in the face at last, the man she had forgiven, and excused, and shared her life with for the last ten years.

22
Strawberry Mark

LILLYPOT WAS A CHEERFUL ENOUGH PLACE, when John and Mrs Scott were gone and with Elsie back in situ. Elsie sang as she worked, or whistled, and she took Joanie under her wing and steered her about more kindly than Mrs Scott had done, so Joanie lost her nervous manner and proved very useful, especially with the children and for running errands. Mrs Foster came as she had come before and cooked for them, and she saw to any ordering that had fallen by the wayside was sorted, so they wanted for nothing.

They saw in the New Year together, by the fire with a bottle of Robert's wine, Susan and Elsie and Joanie, with the children in bed and a great steak pie ready for the morrow.

Susan was very busy, now she had the keys, investigating Robert's room. There was a cabinet of unpleasant things, which she did not yet wish to tackle, and the table was piled high with folders and papers. She ignored those at first and made a start on his desk, reading through the bills and invoices – Robert had paid some amazing prices for items, perhaps as exhibits for the museum. Susan cleared all of the receipts into a folder and gave them to Elsie to take home on her next leave day, thinking it might be of use to her to have Robert's records in her possession. Towards the back of the desk, she found a thing that gave her both pleasure and pain – a large pile of letters from Lady Jane in Portnellan enquiring after Susan's health and sharing her own news, such as it was in the quiet place where she lived. Mrs Scott or John had evidently intercepted these, and Robert had read them, and it seemed too that he had sent brief notes to Lady Jane explaining that Susan was indisposed and sending word of the births of the children, on which occasions Lady Jane had written with fulsome kindness and congratulation.

Susan took a pen and wrote a letter to Lady Jane there and then, telling her quite frankly that she had not received her letters, Robert had kept them from her. She wrote that soon Lady Jane would hear dreadful things of Robert, if she had not already, but not to worry on Susan's account, Susan believed she saw a way through it all and expected she would be much happier going forward. She began to write about the children and their carryings-on, but then she put that aside, and took a fresh sheet and wrote down all that had happened, as best she could remember, from the marriage that was no marriage to her imprisonment here, the births and deaths of the children and all of the half-heard and half-remembered things she could muster. She sealed that letter and then returned to the first, completing the gladder tidings of the children and signing off with a note to Jane that she enclosed a sealed letter she hoped Jane would keep, and if anything befell Susan, then she would be grateful if Jane would make its contents public. She trusted Jane to decide whether she wished to read it immediately or simply put it away under its seal. She sealed the second letter within the first, then gave Joanie the necessary money to take it to Leith and post it, which she did immediately.

When Joanie returned, she brought with her a newspaper she gave to Susan, with a grave face. Susan took it back into Robert's room and read the awful thing printed within, the confession of the man Burke who now admitted to the taking of sixteen lives. Her heart beat oddly as she read and she sat for a while after she had finished it, quite unable to stir, as the room grew dark around her. Then she felt a great wave of fury rise up in her chest and she lit the lamps and began to rake through the mess on Robert's desk, looking for any papers that might relate to this horror, though she knew not whether she wished to find proof of his involvement, or the reverse.

Most of it was dry stuff, about the shelving in the museum and display jars, and suchlike, but then Susan opened a great box and found a folder of papers, and a book, with a letter tied round it with string. She cut the string and read the letter, and discovered the book was by the accoucheur who had been at Lillypot when the twins were born, and he was pleased to send it to Robert, with the original drawings as Robert had requested. She laid the book and the letter to one side and picked up the thick sheaf of drawings. The first few she could make no sense of, but then she reached the third and she almost dropped the pile.

It was a drawing of a woman's body, from the breasts down. She was great with child, and the legs were splayed apart so that the sex was revealed. There was a red mark on the thigh, the same mark that Susan had had from birth, like a heart broken in two. It was her.

Very slowly, Susan leafed through the drawings. These must all be her body, her breasts, her sex, her very inner parts, for there were drawings that showed some metal thing that held her open and showed the structures inside. Some showed the delivery of the twins, and she realised the assistant had not been a medical man, he had been an artist, and she remembered all the rustlings and holding up of lamps, and that night when she seemed to half-remember being lifted and turned and woke uncomfortable and uneasy, feeling a stranger to her own body.

She turned to the book then and saw a great many of the drawings reproduced therein, although they were reduced to black and white engravings only. She could not read the text, as it was in a language she could not understand, but it seemed to be an account of the delivery of the twins. There were a great lot of instruments illustrated, and Susan felt clammy just thinking about those – thank God they had never used them.

Underneath the drawings were a smaller set, quite ordinary sketches, beautiful in their way, of Susan with young Robert, or walking in the garden. In one she was throwing hoops. The artist had watched her, it seemed, by night and day, always without her knowledge. And Robert had let him – no, invited him into the house to do this.

Susan returned all to the box, found a pen, and wrote another version of her sealed letter to Lady Jane, but with more in it than ever before. She put it in the box with the drawings and the folder of papers from Robert's desk – the book she kept – and she sealed it all with string and wax. She gave the box to Elsie and bid her go home to her father and ask him to hide it somewhere safe. Elsie said she would go in the morning, but Susan told her to go to the Bower right now and ask for the pony trap, the lad would wait with it and bring her back by lamplight.

When Elsie was gone, Susan put the lamps on the table and turned to Robert's cabinet of horrors, prising the doors apart with a letter opener so that the wood around the lock splintered and broke. It pleased her, that sound, after all she had read and seen; the great fury was building within her again and she was ready to cleanse the house of Robert's filth.

It was worse than she had imagined. There was a blackened thing, wizened and desiccated, smaller than an infant, that appeared to be human from the waist up, and fish from the waist down. Robert had written on a card that this was a supposed 'mermaid', exhibited by a travelling showman for ha'penny a peek with the claim that it had been caught off Fiji, but in fact was the upper body of a juvenile monkey attached to the tail of a large fish. Susan set it aside with a shudder. She would ask Elsie to bury the poor creature – creatures – in the garden.

The next things were real enough, according to Robert's cards. There was a skull with a round hole in it, and the card said it had come from a burial site where folk had been laid to rest thousands of years ago, and many had had such holes put in their heads while they lived, and apparently survived it, for the bone could be seen to have grown back some way in more than half of cases. Then there was a tiny head, the size of a poppet's, only its face was that of an old man, and the leathery skin was blackened and shrivelled with the lips sewn together and glass beads where the eyes had been. Robert had labelled that one with a long explanation that it was a tribal token from the Pacific, the cut-off head of an enemy tribesman, and Robert had ascertained that the skull had been taken out, the head boiled until it shrunk, and stones put inside instead of the skull. She put it down quickly. Next, a box was labelled 'Fleshed human hand found in a bog, apparently preserved by the peat.' Susan chose not to open that. She placed the skull, the head and the box with the 'mermaid' for burying in the garden.

The other curiosities were less awful to handle, being made of wax and wood and other materials that didn't make her wish to wash their dusty decay from her hands as soon as she had touched them. There was a little carved ivory woman, like the most precious child's plaything ever seen, only her belly and torso lifted off to reveal all the organs of her body nestled inside, and an unborn child curled in her womb. These tiny carved items lifted out too, and all could be put back so she looked again as sweet and neat as a doll. Susan put her back in the cabinet, but a larger, wax version of the same, in which the woman lay splayed like a voluptuary, her hair curled, lips coloured red and pearls around her neck, went on the fire.

She spared a little bone skeleton in a wooden coffin that said it was made in memory of a lost loved one with the date 1797, and several other such things shaped like skulls or skel-etons, some in gold and enamel or carved stone and made to hang on a chain; they seemed wrong-headed but also harmless, somehow. There was also a strange little model of what appeared to be a house, but inside there was a tiny skeleton and it said it was a model of the Paestum Tomb, whatever that was. Susan peered closer and saw that the little carved bones were surrounded by all sorts of tiny models of things – bowls and beakers and metal bits that looked like weapons, or perhaps some were implements for tilling the soil. She put that back too, it wasn't haunted. Last on that shelf – and largest – was a wax model of a human face, horribly painted to Susan's eye so that it looked almost frantic, and bearing a label that said it was a copy of the death mask of Mary, Queen of Scots. She consigned that to the fire, thinking the woman might not wish to appear so, hundreds of years after her death; or perhaps she would, she was of the old faith and Susan remembered learning that she had seen herself a martyr, and her supporters had wished to dip their handkerchiefs in her blood.

The wax head burned brightly for a time, and Susan felt a little frantic herself, so she fetched a glass of wine to drink before the flame. She mulled over the newspaper reports, and Robert's collection, and after a while she saw something she might do to pay a tribute to the poor souls who had died, in her own way.

The next day, Susan had Elsie cover the dining table and bring wood-working tools and a piece of wood from John's shed. As she laid the tools out, she remembered Robert saying the man he had bought them from was a cobbler, and for a second, she wondered if that man had been William Burke, the murderer. But then she shook herself, what difference did it make if that man's hands had indeed touched these tools? She had touched them herself dozens of times since then and felt no evil in them. Worse by far to think of Robert's hands touching her, when they had cut up those poor folks' bodies for profit, although perhaps even that didn't matter – it was the man she hated, not the things he had touched before.

Next Susan fetched a set of wooden soldiers Robert had bought for young Robert, and scraps of metal, and her needlework tools, and then she opened the cabinet in Robert's room – almost empty now as the remains of the poor creatures that had resided there were, even then, being laid in a grave in the garden by Elsie. She had taken the children out with her, the kind lass, and given them trowels and sticks to poke at the cold ground. They'd be more a hindrance than a help, but Susan could at least get on with her work. She took out the little coffin that said '1797', for a pattern, and set it on the table.

She selected sixteen of the little soldiers, and set about dressing them in scraps of fabric from a sample book. When the first few were dressed to her satisfaction, she began to fashion a tiny coffin, from wood, with little metal fixings, based on the one from the cabinet. It was a difficult task and took a long time, but Susan was in no hurry, she would take as long as she required to make one for each of the figures. She scrutinised each newspaper article and scandal sheet as it appeared, writing a list, as best she could, of their names:

Donald, a retired solider, not murdered but his body stolen and anatomised
Abigail Simpson, an elderly salt-seller from Gilmerton
An Englishman
An old woman (unknown)
Mary Paterson, a young lass
A grandmother (unknown)
Her grandson (unknown), a boy about twelve
Joseph, a miller
An unknown woman lodger
Effy, a cinder-gatherer
A woman (unknown)
James Wilson, a young man with a limp, clever with numbers, daft in other ways
Ann MacDougal, a relative of Burke's wife
Mrs Haldane, an old woman
Margaret Haldane, her daughter
Mrs Ostler, a washerwoman
Mrs Margaret, or, Mary Docherty, or, Campbell

Although the order of the killings seemed to change again and again with each fresh account, Susan decided to approach the little figures in the order she had written, so as to hold each clear in her mind as she worked. She placed a cross against each name as she completed its figure and said a prayer for the departed soul.

She had completed the first eight when at last Robert came.

She had moved her things from the dining room to Robert's study, by then, so they could all eat together, and she was in there working when she heard the carriage outside. She sent Joanie to answer the door with some relish – two could play at the game of a deaf maid. Robert could catechise poor Joanie all he liked, it would not matter to her how he railed and ranted.

It seemed he was sufficiently shocked, however, to follow Joanie into the study quietly enough, although he visibly started to see Susan there. She laid the chisel she was using down. He buttoned his lip, sat down, and looked around.

'Where are the things from the cabinet?' he asked, after a moment, as though that could possibly be the most remarkable thing about the situation.

'Gone,' Susan said.

His lip twitched, whether in anger or amusement she couldn't tell. 'And John and Mrs Scott?'

'They're gone too,' Susan said. 'John is kin, it seems, to the Wilson woman whose laddie disappeared last year. "Daft Jamie", they called him. Did you recognise him, Robert, when you dissected him? I hear he was quite the well-kent face in the town.'

Robert's face was a picture but he answered light-heartedly enough. 'No,' he said. 'I don't spend my time in the slums. I've read some of the poems written on him since, though; they'd bring tears to a glass eye.'

Susan kept her own voice light. 'They are dreadful, those poems.'

'More sentiment than skill, I agree.'

Susan nodded. 'Speaking of sentiment,' she said, 'it seems the feeling in the town has fairly turned against you, Robert. Jessie came here, did you know that? She told me the mob had attacked the house and broken all the windows. That was the day John left. He said to tell you to go to Hell.'

'I see,' said Robert. 'And Mrs Scott? Did she do likewise?'

'She left the day Jessie came, or the next,' said Susan. 'By . . . mutual agreement. We reached an understanding, you see. She regretted what she had done to me. And helped others do to me.' She reached into the pocket of her apron and brought out the accoucheur's book, placing it on the table between them.

Robert's face was white as bone.

'I think there is quite an appetite for scandal involving you, at the present time,' Susan said, 'and so I have placed the letter and drawings I found with this book with a friend, for safe-keeping. Another has a letter, with an account of our life here, and my request that she publish it, should anything befall me. The other friend knows to do likewise with the drawings.'

'What did you think might befall you?' Robert asked, as though he had not kept her imprisoned here for years.

'Och, admission to an asylum or the like,' Susan said. 'Mrs Scott promises to vouch for the truth of it all, too, should it prove necessary. I am to send word to them regularly that all is well – personally, mind – and they will know to do nothing with the letters and papers.'

'I see,' said Robert. 'So . . .' He tailed off, apparently at a loss for what to say next.

'I think, Robert,' said Susan, 'that I will stay here at Lillypot, with the children, and I would like it if you would arrange for me to receive enough money to live here comfortably, no more and no less. I have two lasses working for me – Joanie and another – and I need enough for their wages, and food and fuel. The cook still comes as before and I will need to pay her too. I would wish to have use of the pony trap as it suits me, and a man now and then to attend to the heavy tasks in the garden. Beyond that, there is just clothing for myself and the children, and books and the like for them. I can entertain myself well enough, with what remains of your library and my dolls' house.' She picked up the chisel and examined it. 'These are Burke's tools, are they not, Robert? I certainly said so in my letters. It seems to me that you must have had a fair number of dealings with him, to discover he was a cobbler and commission my little toys. Davie Paterson would be glad to know it, I think; from what I read, he is furious that he is to carry the guilt of it all as you insist you never met them.'

Robert's eyes flashed at mention of Paterson, but he held on to his temper. 'What of the children?' he asked. 'May I see them?'

'Yes,' said Susan, 'I suppose you may see them. It would be my preference that you visit them here, at least until they are older, and then we can discuss the matter again. I'll need notice of your coming, none of this disappearing for months and then turning up on a whim. You can write to me so I can make plans.'

'What of their education?' Robert asked. 'May I have a hand in that?'

'Of course,' Susan said. 'Although I think we will need Masters to come here. I cannot think they will be able to attend any school in this town, they would be unfriendly places for "Nox-i-ous" children, don't you think?'

Robert looked pained at that – of course he had planned the best of schooling for his sons – but he said nothing.

'Will you stay in Edinburgh, do you think?' Susan asked. 'Can you?'

'I don't see why not,' Robert said. 'My classes are as popular as ever. More so, even. Notoriety does not seem to suppress interest – quite the opposite, in fact.'

Susan could well believe it. 'Perhaps they are hoping to see some interesting cadavers,' she said.

Robert snorted. 'There are "interesting cadavers" in every theatre,' he said. 'I'm not the only one to turn a blind eye, though

I may be the only one who has such an organ naturally. The killers have said themselves they were looking for Monro when they came to sell the first of their subjects. But they didn't find him, so he will be the one to dissect Burke while I am put through some pretence of a disciplinary committee at the Society. They won't find against me, it's all for show – *let he who is without sin cast the first stone*, and all that – but I may have to resign from the museum. The College of Surgeons are already pressuring me, but I won't make it easy for them. None of them ever wanted me, you know, they only took me because Barclay made it a condition of his will that I be curator, and they wanted his collection.'

Susan heard the bitterness in this, the schoolboy of no great family chafing at the ease with which others claimed titles and appointments with little or no effort while he strived and struggled, but she could find no pity in her heart for him.

'Well then,' she said, 'you will still have an ample fortune, and you will hardly miss what I ask of it. Jessie spends more on her wardrobe, I think, even if she is afraid to go abroad in it.'

She stuck out her hand then, like a man agreeing on a deal, and Robert looked at it for a moment, eyebrow raised, before he shook it.

'Will six-monthly payments suit?' he asked.

'Very well,' said Susan.

Then Robert lifted his hat and cane. Susan rang the bell and Elsie came. Robert stared, but he said nothing, following her out of the room. He paused at the door.

'Give my regards to the children,' he said, and then he left. Susan heard Elsie close the door after him and she crossed to the window to watch him make his way across the garden and out the gate. Then she sat down at the table and carried on with her work.

23

Hangman's Fracture

ELSIE SAID SHE WOULD COME to the hanging with Susan, she wanted to see the man die for herself. They arranged for the cart to come for them early, for they knew the roads would be busy, everyone in the city and the towns around would be making their way to the Lawnmarket, or as close as they could get. Elsie had heard that places at windows overlooking the gallows were selling for as much as twenty shillings apiece.

It was a dark morning, and damp, but they were well-wrapped in cloaks and mufflers and flannel petticoats. It had rained in the night, but until then there had been hard frosts, so the road to Leith was not too bad and they made good time, the coachman as excited as anyone else for news of the execution and keeping up a steady chatter with Elsie as he drove. He told them it was his day off in the week and he planned to go to the University in hope of seeing the dissection – folk were saying the professors would have to let the public in or there would be a riot. Elsie cast a glance at Susan then, in the lamplight, but Susan shook her head to show she wasn't troubled now by discussion of such things.

When they reached the slow upward climb of Leith Walk, it seemed the whole town was there, making their way up, most on foot and some in such vehicles as they could muster. The coachman navigated the throng with some skill, and at last they reached the eastern flank of the New Town. They turned into the wide streets there, but when they reached the foot of the Mound, they could go no further in the trap. They arranged a time to meet the driver – towards evening, for they had business after the hanging – and he set them down with a lantern to light their way. Susan thought he was disappointed not to see the hanging for himself, and she told him he could leave the trap at Robert's house in Newington, if he chose, but she understood he might not want to go near Dr Knox's house, or he might not be able to get there and then back to the Lawnmarket on time. He said he would give it a good try, and drove off at the best speed he could manage through the crowds towards the North Bridge.

As they walked up the Mound and past the great spires of the Assembly, chatter buzzed on all sides. They fell in step with a woman who said she was in service in the house of a court officer and his wife, and another servant had overheard them say the condemned man had been taken from the Calton Jail to a lock-up nearer to the gallows in the dead of night, in case the mob arrived to dispense their own justice before the hanging could take place. He had been very exercised about having no good jacket to wear, she said, and they had got him a suit to calm him. Someone else said it was a right cheek, to worry about his own appearance before his Maker, when he had thought little enough about the poor souls he had killed and seen desecrated. There was a great wave of agreement at that, and some spat on the ground. A man said it was only a shame the others had escaped his fate, Hare who had been guiltiest of all, it seemed, and the women who must be coarse bitches. Then someone else said the doctors should pay, too, especially the butcher Knox, and Susan felt her face flush red, for all she knew she bore no guilt for Robert's doings, in fact quite the opposite.

It wasn't yet seven in the morning and still full dark, and Susan felt panic bloom red through her as they reached the top of the Mound and the crowd grew tighter and tighter. She called out to Elsie not to leave her, and Elsie took her hand and held to it hard as they made their slow way forward, alternately moving with and between the press of bodies.

'We should turn back,' Susan called, 'we'll never see a thing,' but Elsie said to look, she could see the scaffold now. It was true, there were lights burning on the platform and Susan swallowed her fear and followed Elsie's lead. At last they had gone as far as they could and were by the entrance to Buchanan's Close – they could breathe again, and they could see the gibbet clearly enough.

'There must be ten thousand folk here,' said Elsie, and a man standing near them said nay, it was double that, at least. For all the press of bodies, it was a curiously quiet crowd; the horror of the killings and the solemnity of the occasion seemed to have hushed them, and they stood there waiting patiently as the winter sun raised its wan face.

'I wonder what the man is doing now,' Elsie said. 'I would hate to spend a night so, myself.'

'I should think he is with a priest, or a minister,' said Susan. 'At least, I hope it's so.'

They waited a while longer, glad now of the bodies near them, for it was cold and damp still, the pale sun doing little to warm the day. A psalm started up somewhere in the crowd, and they sang along, joining the great mass of voices. Susan found herself wondering whether it would be worse to die as Burke was about to, after days and weeks of dread of it, or as his victims had, going about their business merrily enough until they crossed his path. Would it be better to have time to prepare, all the services of the clergy, or to find your breath stopped in an instant, without time for regret or dread of the hereafter?

She was distracted from her musings by a sort of ripple through the crowd, not a sound, precisely, but almost a shiver of sorts. Then a great shout could be heard from further down the Lawnmarket. This continued for some minutes, rising in volume as those closer by joined in, and then the hanging party ascended the platform, the bailies first, then Burke all in black between two priests in robes, and the others coming after. They were small figures at this distance, of course, almost like marionettes in a puppet showman's theatre. Susan saw Burke look around, while shouts rang out here and there in the crowd: 'Burke him,' and 'Choke him, Hangie,' and similar. A man behind Susan bawled out, 'No mercy!'

Then Burke went down on his knees with one of the priests, and it was clear the other clergymen were praying as well, though Susan could hear none of the words at this distance. This did not please the crowd, who had lost their view of Burke, and there was much bawling and shouting to the clergymen and lawyers to get out of the way. The bailies held up their hands to appeal for peace while the rites were completed, and during that time the crowd began to shout for Hare to be brought forth too, and Robert, taking up a chant of 'Hang Knox, hang Knox, hang Knox.' The solemnity that had prevailed before seemed quite gone and Susan hoped the business would proceed before the crowd lost its patience entirely and violence broke out. But then Burke was on his feet, putting something in his pocket, and he stepped onto the gallows. The hangman placed the rope around his neck and adjusted it as one of the clergymen spoke more with Burke, perhaps giving him his last rites, or perhaps it was instructions on how to comport himself at the end. The crowd continued to shout that the hangman should give Burke no rope, that Hare should be hanged by his side, and more imprecations of a coarser style. The hangman put a white cotton cap on Burke's head and pulled it over his face. There was a pause then, the crowd quietened, the man's hand came up and he dropped. His body twitched on the rope, and the crowd yelled out.

'Is he dead?' Elsie asked. 'Or is it like when a chicken twitches with its head already off?'

Susan had thought it was almost as a dreamer might twitch in sleep, but now she saw he lived, still, his legs were kicking and some men below the gallows were pulling on him to end the thing. They twisted him round so the rope seemed to shorten and his body raised up, and now it seemed he was truly dead – when the rope released he hung there quite life-less. The crowd surged forward then, as if they would claim the body, and Elsie pulled Susan back into the mouth of the close. It seemed the crowd was held back, though, and when Elsie and Susan looked, still the body hung there on the rope.

'Shall we go, Mistress?' Elsie asked.

'Aye, Elsie,' said Susan. 'Let's make for the West Bow.'

It was slow going, for the crowd filled half the West Bow and those that had not seen the hanging itself were determ-inedly pressing uphill in hope of seeing the body before it was cut down and conveyed away. Slowly Elsie and Susan wove through the throng, only able to breathe easy again when they were at the bottom of the Bow and almost in the Grassmarket. Then they made their way along the Cowgate towards Holyrood, making for the Salisbury Crags and the great hill of Arthur's Seat beyond.

There were others walking the same way, and at the bottom of St Mary's Wynd they met a larger crowd moving in the same direction, having watched the hanging from further down the Lawnmarket. More came down St John's Street and again the going was slow, but Susan said to Elsie it didn't matter, they were in no hurry, the coachman wasn't expecting to meet them until late in the afternoon. As they passed Horse Wynd, they saw two women supporting another, who seemed collapsed, and Elsie said they should help if they could. She was already untying the bag she had strapped to herself and taking out a stone bottle of ale.

The women thanked them for the offer of assistance, but they said their friend wasn't ill, only distressed at the awful business. Her mother was one of the victims, they said, the old woman called Abigail Simpson, and this daughter had been sorely grieved, never knowing what had befallen her mother until the brute Burke's confessions were published. She had simply left her house one day on business and never returned. The daughter had tramped the miles asking after her, for near a year, but nothing could be found out. They stood for a moment with their heads bowed, and then Elsie said to the weeping woman – her name was Bess – that they should go to the old Well of the Cross and say a prayer for her mother's soul. The woman seemed to like the thought of that, though her tears still flowed, and they made their way there, led by Elsie who knew her way around, as she had grown up nearby, after all. It wasn't easy to find, Elsie poking here and there in the tall grasses, but at last she crowed in triumph, and there was the well, bubbling up from some rocks. Elsie asked Susan to say the prayer, and Susan did her best, although she was no great speaker, asking God to look after the soul of the poor lady Abigail and her daughter Bess in all her sorrow. And then she surprised herself, saying she knew what it was to lose a loved one and never know where their body lay, or to live with the knowledge their body had been desecrated, and she asked God for peace for herself as well as Bess.

The women looked at her curiously then, even Bess whose weeping ceased, but none of them asked her any more; perhaps they had enough to do minding their own sorrows to take on some wealthier woman's as well. Susan was grateful for that, and they all drank from the spring and Elsie brought out the food that she and Susan had brought, and they shared it amongst them and were almost merry, talking of other days they had spent here on the hill, a high day or holiday here or there, when they were children, or in Elsie's case rabbiting with the boys. Then Bess said she and her friends should be going, they had a long walk back to Joppa where they lived, though the way would be easier with food in their wames, and they were glad to have met with kindness on such a day.

'If the world was run by women, there would be more kindness and less strife,' said Elsie, and they all found that thought pleasing, although Susan wasn't sure: weren't two of the killers women too, and Mrs Scott who had been her jailer all these years, and Robert's sisters who had put her away so they might have her place? But she said nothing, just bid Bess and her friends farewell, and then she and Elsie stood up and hitched up their skirts and petticoats and made their way up the hill. They climbed up past the ruined chapel to St Anthony, then dipped down past a rise that Elsie said was called the Whinny Hill, and upwards again towards the summit of the volcano.

It was hard going, Susan wasn't used to exercise after so long, so she had to stop again and again to catch her breath, but at last they reached the top and stood looking out to the city at a little distance and the sea beyond, so small it all seemed from here. When they had caught their breath they looked around and Susan found a place that would suit her purposes, a little cleft in the rocks. She reached beneath her kilted skirts and untied the bag she wore below; an old-fashioned idea it was to wear a pocket in such a way, but useful in a crowd. She took out the little coffins and stacked them in three rows, two tiers of eight for the poor murdered souls, and the last alone on top for the man whose death – if the sinner Burke was to be believed – was God's will but who was nonetheless deprived a proper burial. Then she searched around for something to cover them, and found some pieces of slate, and laid them over all, adjusting them a time or two till she was satisfied that it looked as though no one had ever been in the place before.

Elsie asked if they should say something, but Susan said no, the prayer they had said earlier would suffice. Then they drank some of the water they had refilled the bottle with at the spring, and began to walk down. Elsie said they should take a different route, along the crags; it was a bonnie walk although the miners had made such a mess with their blasting. It was beautiful, and easier than the ascent, although Susan had a moment of crisis, halfway across, when she wondered if she should step from the cliff out onto the air and allow herself to fall, one glorious moment in the sun and wind, unweighted by the things Robert had done to her and to others, and then nothing. But she shook herself. She couldn't do that to the children, and she stepped back from the brink.

Elsie didn't notice, or if she did she didn't let on, she just chattered away in her usual fashion and walked on. At one point she said something about Joanie that made Susan wonder – there was less in her tone of the way a woman might speak of a friend, and more of the way a lass might speak of her young man. It confused her, for a moment, but then she saw that might indeed be the way of it, and she realised it would suit her very well. She could go on, if Elsie and Joanie didn't leave her to marry, and as long as Robert kept his word and they had what money they needed and the coachman to fetch and carry, she could do as she was doing now and put one foot in front of the other, on and on each hour, until the hours became days and the days, became years, and the whole, God willing, became a life.

Epilogue
New York City, 1854

S NOW HAD BEEN FALLING ALL DAY, and Helen was glad of the open doors at Grace Church, where she could sit for a while when she became too cold where she was begging under the awnings further along Broadway. The pickings were slim, passers-by bundled up against the cold, rushing to get home to their warm fires. Helen would give it half an hour, no longer, and then she would head for Union Park where she knew a watchman who would let her huddle by his brazier for warmth, and share his dinner with her too, taking his payment in kind.

A team of horses struggled past in the slush, pulling an omnibus, and Helen watched as a group of passengers dismounted further up the street. Among those who walked her way was a little girl of perhaps six or seven, dressed in a velvet cloak the colour of a sugar plum, with fluffy white fur around her hood and throat. She had neat leather boots buttoned on her feet and her hands were thrust deep inside a furry muff. As Helen watched, she stopped and stared upwards into the sky.

Helen looked up, herself, to see snowflakes falling again, thick and soft. She looked at the little girl again, just in time to see her put out her tongue and catch a flake. The child laughed at her cleverness, looking round to see whether anyone had seen, and caught Helen's eye. Helen waved and she grinned, twirling round as she walked towards her.

'My name's Olive,' she said, without preamble.

'Hello, Olive,' said Helen. 'It's nice to meet you. But where are your parents?'

'Mama is dead,' the child said, 'and Papa is on his deathbed. Do you have any children?'

'I did,' Helen said. 'Two little girls, although they aren't little anymore. And I am sorry to hear about your parents. What ails your Papa?'

'No one knows,' the child said, with a weary puff of her cheeks she must have seen an adult do. The effect was comical, even if the words were sad. 'Mama sickened suddenly, and no one knows why. Papa was strong and vigorous, but then he began to sicken too, and now the doctors say he is like to die, but they are baffled why and cannot explain it.'

'You're not on your own, though, are you?' Helen asked. 'It'll be dark in half an hour.'

The child laughed. 'No, I'm with Peggy. Peggy is my nurse-maid. She says Papa will leave the house to me, and in his will he has said she can care for me there till I am grown. I'll always be safe with Peggy, that's what Peggy says.'

'Where is Peggy, then?' Helen asked.

The little girl's eyes sparkled. 'Peggy has a gentleman,' she whispered, 'but we mustn't tell!' She pointed over Helen's shoulder and Helen turned to see a woman in a dark cloak break away from an embrace. The woman looked over towards them, and Helen's heart thudded in her breast, so hard she might believe it had stopped forever. She stood there, frozen, a mouse trapped in the gaze of a snake.

She would know them anywhere.

'Peggy' is Margaret Laird. Margaret Logue. And the man is William Hare.

Helen turns and runs, slipping and sliding in the slush. She doesn't see the omnibus until it is too late. The last thing she knows are the great hooves of the horses, Clydesdales like the long-ago plough-teams of Redding, and it seems to her she is there again, tumbling back through the years to a place before pain or fear or regret, where there is only the hush of the snow and the iron of the sky.

Author's Note

The Specimens is a work of fiction. It observes the basic facts of the 'West Port Murders' of 1828 – where these are known – but fictionalises lives and experiences. The timeline has been adapted in some cases, in larger and smaller ways, so, for example, the early years of Helen and Burke's relationship are telescoped, or Susan sees the famous 'Nox-i-ous plant' cartoon a few weeks or months before it was published.

Accounts of the murders have tended to focus on the actions and motivations of the murderers, and their 'clients' the doctors. The victims themselves seem almost secondary to the narrative, a sort of grubby mass of people 'of the degraded class', to borrow a description of Helen MacDougal. The murderers themselves did not know the names of some of the victims, and could not be certain as to the order of the killings. Of course it helped their project to select victims from among people whose lives were precarious, and would not be missed, or if they were, whose connections could have few resources at their disposal to attempt to establish what had befallen them.

As far as we know, there were sixteen victims, and one man died a natural death and was sold. Eleven of the victims were women (including a mother and her daughter, killed at different times). One was a child, the grandson of one of the adult women. Four were men. The best remembered are probably James 'Daft Jamie' Wilson and Mary Paterson. Aside from Mrs Docherty, the last victim, their bodies disappeared into the anatomy theatre and left no trace. This reminded me of the end of another group of abused people about whom I have written – Scotland's 'witches' – and it struck me that Scotland's long-standing misogyny issues were again on show in the ways in which the female victims were described, at the time and afterwards. Aside from James Wilson, we hear little of the men beyond a place of origin or a trade. Of the women, we read of drunkenness, degradation, wild behaviour, and prostitution. No link is made between James Wilson's behaviours and his death, and he is viewed with pity, while poor Mary Paterson seems, in the view of some commentators, to have met an end she risked, if not actively deserving it. This has sad echoes in police attitudes to victims through the centuries, as in the 'Bible John' killings or the 'Yorkshire Ripper' investigation.

In fact, there is no actual evidence that Mary Paterson was a prostitute, and her friend Janet Brown insisted she was not. Again, this happens often in the historical record, including in the case of Helen MacDougal herself. More than one commentator mentions that Helen might have met Burke while working as a prostitute on the Union Canal. There is no apparent evidence to underpin this suggestion either.

In truth, Helen's life before meeting Burke is something of a mystery. She told the Sheriff (court officer) that she was born in Redding in Falkirk, was thirty-three years old, was unmarried, and had been with William Burke for about ten years. Prior to meeting Burke, she had been the partner of a sawyer, who had died, and had two children with him. 'MacDougal' may have been that man's name. Burke's confessions tell us that they had lived an itinerant life in the years between their meeting and taking up residence in Edinburgh, and the early sections of this novel broadly follow this account. In a pamphlet on the Falkirk Local History Society pages, John Walker of Stenhousemuir lists a number of possible contenders from the parish records of the time, including Helens Gaff, Nimmo, Brown and Galloway (although Helen's birth could equally have been unregistered, especially if she was Catholic). I chose 'my' Helen from amongst these, although Walker believes that Helen Gaff was probably the same woman as a Helen of the same name who died in Edinburgh in 1818 and so could not have been Helen MacDougal. I intended to fictionalise the details of Helen's father and wider family and so this suited my purposes.

It is difficult to ascertain to what degree Helen was complicit in the West Port murders. Many commentators consider that she was implicated and even helped, for example by staging the 'fight' with Burke that resulted in Janet Brown leaving Mary Paterson with Burke, who then killed her. The case against Helen, however, was found Not Proven – Walter Scott's 'bastard verdict' – despite the heat of public feeling at the time. This related only to the death of Mrs Docherty, of course, and the record very much suggests Helen was aware of that, at least after the fact, as she attempted to bribe her lodgers to stay silent. On the other hand, Burke insisted she knew he was a 'resurrectionist' but not a murderer, and the claim that the Hares wished for Burke to kill her does suggest she was not a fully accepted or trusted member of the 'gang'. Hare committed one killing while Helen and Burke were away, and she cannot have been implicated in that. She did not take payment, as Margaret Hare did – a pound a victim for the use of her house in the commission of the crimes. One of the victims was a relative of Helen's, and human nature recoils at the idea she condoned or connived at that killing, although of course it is not impossible that she did. In creating 'my' Helen, I was interested in the dynamics of her relationship with Burke, and the ways in which this might have influenced what she knew, or chose to know, at different points.

The ultimate origins of Margaret Laird/Logue/Hare are also unclear (as is the case with both Burke and Hare). Rumours of child murder attached themselves to her in the period following the trial, but this might well be attributed to a thirst for horror in the broadsides. Her 'baby farming' in the novel is a fiction, as is the suggestion that the child she brought to the trial was not her own.

We know how Burke's life ended, and indeed can view his skeleton today in the University of Edinburgh's Anatomical Museum should we so wish. The fates of the other three are not known. Margaret was reported to have returned to Ireland, and some accounts have her travelling onward to Australia. Different violent deaths were reported for Helen, but no account can be verified and there may be an element of wishful thinking in the broadsides. Hare was assisted in leaving Edinburgh and travelled to Dumfries, but was recognised and met by an angry mob. He was last reported to be making his way to the English border. The idea that the survivors all met again later is entirely a fiction.

The backstories given to the victims are entirely fictional. For Abigail Simpson, the salt-seller, and her daughter (my creation), I was inspired by the history of salt-panning at Joppa, very near my own home in Portobello, and I popped in a nod to Gracemount House in South Edinburgh, which the community there is working hard to save as a local facility – I wish them luck; many years ago I had an office there and have many memories of the kids who used 'The Mansion', as it was fondly known. Mrs Haldane's name set off an echo in my mind of Naomi Mitchison's masterful novel *The Bull Calves*, which in turn set me thinking about Jacobitism and how recent the aftermath of the '45 was in the early years of the nineteenth century. Effy's 'nest' was inspired by a real illicit distilling operation of a few years previously, in the vaults of the South Bridge. I find earlier incarnations of Edinburgh quite difficult to picture – rather like a modern tourist bewildered to appear to be in the right place but in reality standing 100 feet below it, I find a map doesn't quite tell the story of the bridges and closes. I did my best to work out how the characters might have got around, but might be quite wrong.

Susan's story is almost entirely fictional – we know nothing of her beyond the bare fact that Knox had a wife called Susan, of whose existence few were aware, and those who were seemed to have understood that she was not of sufficient social standing to be publicly associated with Knox. She lived at Lilliput or Lillypot – now in Trinity/Summerside, then entirely outside the city on the lands of the Masters of Trinity House, which still stands on the Kirkgate in Leith. There were seven children, of whom four survived.

Robert's treatment of Susan and their children is fiction, albeit inspired in part by the rumours that circulated of Mary Paterson's corpse being used as an artist's model for a study of the biological basis of beauty. There has recently been some controversy about the methods used by those studying female reproductive anatomy around this time, to the degree that a recent article accused William Hunter of anatomy murder in creating his 'Gravid Uterus' series, on the basis of statistical analysis to support the thesis that not enough subjects could have died of natural causes (this has been strongly rebutted elsewhere). The textbook Robert shows Susan is

William Smellie's – the book she unwittingly features in does not exist. Other women were most certainly used as living subjects without their consent, perhaps most infamously by James Marion Sims in the American South, who carried out experimental fistula repairs on enslaved women without anaesthesia.

The idea that Susan received miniatures made by Burke, and that she used tools of his to make the Arthur Seat coffins, is fancy only. The coffins are real – seventeen of them were discovered on the hill by a group of boys out rabbiting in 1836, and today eight survive, housed in the Museum of Scotland on Chambers Street. The theory that they are connected to the West Port killings is popular, particularly as the numbers tally so well. The museum has published research dating the fabric wrapping the figures to the early 1830s – Susan uses a sample book from 1829 – and suggesting they were made with cobblers' tools, which is woven into the fiction of their making in this book. The miniature house Susan restores is inspired by the writer Denton Welch's 1940s restoration of the eighteenth-century baby house that now bears his name and is held in the collections of the V&A Museum.

Robert Knox did not stand trial and was not officially censured for his part in the affair, because Burke's confession exonerated him to a sufficient degree, and he had enough power and wealth to ensure newspaper editors and others had libel laws in mind when publishing commentary. He was pressured into resigning from the museum – he had indeed gained the role in large part through the machinations of his partner Barclay – and eventually he left Edinburgh in 1842, finding his career effectively stalled. It never recovered, although he worked on, adding several works of scientific racism to his infamous legacy. He died in London in 1862.

The Anatomy Act 1832 finally made cadavers available for dissection in the sort of numbers required by medical schools, and ended the practices of graverobbing and anatomy murder. Horror at the West Port killings helped its passage through parliament.

Acknowledgments

From the earliest germ of an idea, many people encouraged me to write *The Specimens*, or more generally, a novel. Among the first were Sara Sheridan, whose work I admire and whose words of encouragement meant a great deal, and Torcuil Crichton MP, in whose company I learned much of what I know about writing. Many friends listened to me work through ideas, particularly Geraldine Bradley in the earliest days. I wrote the manuscript over quite an intense few months, while also working in a challenging full-time job and serving on a public body board, and other friends and family members were understanding when I vanished for a while. When the first draft was ready, Dr. Viccy Adams was the kindest and most insightful first reader. Thanks to all/mìle taing.

My parents Jim and Moira Kidd helped as ever with the history; they can always be relied on to say they know nothing about a particular subject only to ring twenty minutes later with a perfect quote from Smout answering my query. For the rest, I made great use of the National Library of Scotland's digitised maps holdings, and their wonderful 'Word on the Street' collection of broadsides, and of the Wellcome Collection's digitised copies of Smellie and other C18th/C19th medical texts. A. W. Bates *Anatomy of Robert Knox* was useful for Knox's early career (although, as noted elsewhere, I played loose with the detail).

The team at Black and White could not be kinder publishers. Thanks to Campbell and Ali for trusting in me and the book, to Rachel for kind and insightful editorial, and to Hannah and Lizzie and Thomas and Tonje for all of their contributions to design, production and shouting from the rooftops. The broader Bonnier team welcomed me so kindly, especially Kevin. Big thanks to Fiona Atherton at Stonehill Salt and to all the many bookshops, festivals, journalists and others who have supported the book so generously, and moreover who have been such great company.

Having been rather on the Dark Side historically as a publisher and then arts funding person, I have always been a bit shy of author spaces. This year I went along to my first Edinburgh meet-ups and have been made very welcome. Thanks to Mary Paulson-Ellis and Lucy Ribchester especially for that.

Last and greatest thanks as ever to Tom Morgan-Jones, for reading and comments, map-drawing far beyond the call of duty, putting up with the night terrors the subject matter occasionally caused me, and for the kindest support always, in all things.

About the Author

Mairi Kidd is the author of *We are All Witches*, *Warriors and Witches and Damn Rebel Bitches* and *Feisty and Fiery and Fierce*, as well as a number of books for children, and drama for TV, radio and stage. She has a passion for exploring untold stories, and particularly women's lives in history.

Mairi is Director of the Saltire Society and has been Head of Literature at Creative Scotland and CEO of Seven Stories the National Centre for Children's Books. She has also been a publisher working to open up the written word to children and young people with dyslexia, when she had the honour of publishing household names including Julia Donaldson, Michael Morpurgo, Michael Rosen and Quentin Blake.

Mairi is a Gaelic speaker and regularly appears on TV and radio discussing books. She lives in Portobello with her husband Tom, an illustrator, and their very handsome cat.

She did not mean to
But she has killed, and killed, and killed again.

Poor Creatures

Dundee, 1812. Isabel Baxter awaits the arrival of
Mary Godwin, a girl of precocious intellect and
grand passions, sent north to cure an ailment no one
understands. Nestled in woodland on the banks of
the Tay, the Baxter family estate seems a perfect place
for a troubled girl to recuperate. But The Cottage is
a place of secrets, memories . . . and monsters.

23 October 2025